SEVEN
BEAVER SKINS

SEVEN
BEAVER SKINS

A Story of the Dutch in New Amsterdam

Written and Illustrated

By ERICK BERRY

THE JOHN C. WINSTON COMPANY

Philadelphia
Toronto

FIRST PRINTING, MAY, 1948
SECOND PRINTING, FEBRUARY, 1950
THIRD PRINTING, JANUARY, 1952
FOURTH PRINTING, APRIL, 1954

Made in the United States of America

OTHER BOOKS BY ERICK BERRY

CONTENTS

FOREWORD

SEVEN BEAVER SKINS covers the period around 1660, before
the British took over the New Netherlands for the first time,
and while Peter Stuyvesant was still Director General of the
West India Company and governor of the colony.

As is permissible to the fiction writer, I have taken a few
slight liberties with chronological exactitude: for example,
the windmill beside Fort Amsterdam had ceased to exist a
few years before Kaspar was lodged in the lockup. But the
windmill was so typical a landmark for that Dutch town that
I granted it a little more time of life and usefulness.

Kaspar de Selle, Grita Hoorn and her family, the boslooper—these are all creatures of the author's imagination.
Not so Kiliaen van Rensselaer and his sons, Johannes and
Jeremias. Peter Stuyvesant needs no authentication; van
Cortlandt was the patroonship's agent in the Manhatens,
and his daughter, Maria, later married Jeremias van Rensselaer and became, as a widow, an important figure in the
patroonship. Andries, the Negro slave, was at least as lazy
as here depicted, if one may judge from Jeremias' corre-
spondence.

In the same letters may be found the unhappy director's
concern over the quarrels among his tenants, his troubles
with collecting the rents for Rensselaerswyck, the gradual
failure of the beaver trade and the growing importance of
wheat. Perhaps some readers will take issue with me for my
failure to conform to the present fashion of viewing the
patroonship system as a form of feudalism. But I can write
only as I see the period, and after considerable research on
this, my fourth book on the colony of New Netherlands, the
virtues of the patroonship seem greatly to outweigh its evils.
As set down by the first patroon, Kiliaen, and as adminis-
tered by Jeremias, the system was both honest and liberal.
Even in this day it would be generous; in the seventeenth
century it was revolutionary.

Kiliaen's original purpose seems to have been to found a

ix

colony that would be capable of provisioning his ships bound
for South America and the settlement at Curaçao. Ships sailing up the fresh waters of the Hudson would free themselves
of barnacles, reload with supplies in Rensselaerswyck and do
a little trading; but the primary plan was for little more than
a port of call. By the time Jeremias was director, the patroonship had grown in importance, and between ungrateful
tenants at his front door and importunate relatives and
stockholders in the homeland, Jeremias had his hands full.

As for the Indians in my story—the Maquas, so called in
all the early New Netherlands accounts, were a clan of the
Mohawks, though the Mohawks as a whole were called
Maquas by the colonists. Jeremias always referred to New
Amsterdam as "the Manhatens." By "Mahicans" or "Ma-
hikans" the colonists meant the tribe we call Mohegans. Between the Dutch and the Indians the relations were excellent,
much better than those which prevailed between Indian and
Swedish, or Quaker, or British. There were a few raids and
murders, on both sides, but it is remarkable how often in the
records the "quarrelsome" Dutch are willing to admit that
responsibility for such incidents rests upon their own coun-
trymen. The Dutch, of course, were of great value to the
Mohawks as a source of firearms with which to extend their
conquests over other Indian tribes.

When I first began research for this book I found such a
wealth of story material as to make a choice difficult. There
was a story in Kiliaen van Rensselaer, First Patroon, a pic-
turesque figure with his vast shipping interests, his diamonds
and pearls, his fine country estates, his house in Amsterdam
that must have seen a constant stream of travelers from all
over the world. But in the patroonship of his day there was
no story, for he himself never came to the little struggling
colony, and during his lifetime the settlement was so small
and frail as to be scarcely more than a cluster of houses clinging to the skirts of the West India Company fort.

There was a story, too, in the long struggle between the

West India Company and the patroonship. The W.I.C., wishing to keep the country purely as a trading post, had no sympathy for, in fact an active dislike of, the upriver colonists who were beginning to furnish them with lumber and bricks, wheat and corn. Though like New York City of today, they were glad enough to purchase such produce when needed.

Another story might have been the British occupation, but the British rule was easygoing. There was slight loss of prestige to the patroonship owing to the adjustment between the jurisdiction of Beverwyck and Rensselaerswyck, and a slight increase in trading opportunity to offset this, but no interesting conflicts of aims or personalities on which to hang a tale of the day.

Peter Stuyvesant with his violent loyalties, his strong character and silver-banded wooden leg is a tale in himself; and someday his whole story must be told, for he was certainly one of the fathers of America; but tempting though his story must be to a writer, his was not the story of the patroonship.

In the end, avoiding all these delightful temptations, I chose to write of the first patroonship itself. And for my period, used that time when the first aim of Kiliaen van Rensselaer had reached a critical moment and seemed about to fail. The function of the West India Company was that of middleman between Indians and the merchants of the Netherlands. The function of the patroonship was not buying and selling, but actual colonization and production. The two purposes might well have been complementary, for the West India Company offered a market for all that the patroonship could produce. But they were also competitive, for the rich West India Company with its thriving fur trade tempted many colonists who had come over as wards of the patroonship.

It was this clash of opposing ideas, profits versus colonization, trading versus farming, narrowing down to beavers versus wheat, that I chose for my theme in SEVEN BEAVER SKINS.

SEVEN BEAVER SKINS

Chapter One
First Night in
the New World

LISTEN, BOY!"
The man had been speaking in a conspirator's whisper ever since they entered the waterside tavern; now his voice dropped lower. But Kaspar was listening; he had to. pinned down here in a corner of the high-backed, tavern settle, the table over his knees.

It was just a repetition of what he had heard before, what the man had been saying for the past hour or so. Hoping not to seem impolite, Kaspar let his attention wander around this, the first room he had entered in the New Netherlands.

1

A little disappointing it was, so similar to any bare, water-front alehouse at home in Amsterdam, even to the dried tropical fish swaying by a cord from the rafter, the tall blue and gray pottery drinking mugs with pewter lids, the heavy wooden tables and backless stools.

Except for this Wouter Fries and himself, there were only two other occupants of the room, a thin, sour-looking individual, and a short, pot-bellied man with a red, angry face. One glance gave you as close and long acquaintance with them as anyone would desire. They weren't drinking to any purpose, for, though their beer mugs must be emptied, their thumbs still held up the lids, as a sign they did not want them replenished. Nor were the men talking; they seemed merely to be waiting and watching.

Perhaps it was the falcon that had caught their interest. Kaspar rested the bird and his gloved left wrist on the table. The peregrine shuffled her feet and set the small bells on her legs to tinkling. Then, weary with so much talk, roused and stretched her wings. Lucky for Wouter Fries, thrusting his heavy red nose across the table, that the falcon was hooded, or she might have mistaken that red nose for a gobbet of raw meat, and pounced.

"You're not harkening, boy." Wouter pressed the table against the arms of the settle. "But here's the offer again, and for the last time. Break with the patroonship of Rensselaerswyck, and we'll make it well worth your while."

'Twas no different an offer from the one made an hour ago. But as to why it should be made, an offer so suspiciously pressing, Kaspar couldn't guess. Restlessly ne moved on the settle. What a fool he had been to come here; he should have refused the invitation, back there at the foot of the gangplank, when Wouter had linked arm in arm and insisted that they celebrate their arrival with the finest shore meal in the New World. That meal had been commanded half an hour ago, but it was still in the tavern kitchen.

"Break with the patroonship? Why?" asked Kaspar again.

Wouter thrust out his big, rough-shaven chin. "Well you see, boy," he whispered hoarsely, "you tell me you're trained to the peltry trade like your uncle before you, and in the past few weeks aboard I've been able to try out your knowledge. Now what we need over here, in New Netherlands, is someone who understands the grades and the prices of furs and pelts in the old country."

As if by accident, he leaned even closer across the soiled and narrow oak table top. "So, boy, we're holding you here. Whether your answer is yes or no. And it had best not be 'no.' "

Kaspar drew a deep breath. "No," he stated firmly.

He slid his feet beneath the settle, and with what looked like a casual gesture, unhooded the falcon. If he suddenly needed two hands to fight with, the bird must be free to find her own way out.

But Wouter's threat hung fire. He sat back—a loosely fat, big-boned man with a hat of Flemish beaver felt crammed low on his bullet-round head, its two plumes much stained by sea water. Beneath his none too well-shaven chin the falling bands were soiled, the rich cloak and bucket-topped boots of good Spanish leather were shabby and unkempt. Suddenly raising his voice, so that the two men standing together on the farther side of the tavern must hear every word, he announced surprisingly:

". . . ten guilders on account and I'll let you go, if you give me your word to pay the other thirty guilders in prime beaver skins."

The alteration in tone, the change of attack was so swift that Kaspar, braced for a different kind of threat, was slow to react. But the two men moved across the room, one long and sour-looking, the other round-faced, with dull little eyes that betokened slight intelligence within, moved across so promptly as to seem in answer to a signal.

"What's this, Mynheer Fries?" demanded the taller one. "An absconding debtor?" And to Kaspar, threateningly,

"There's a small dark room in the fort, well barred, for such as seek to defraud honest traders."

Who could this man be? By the short sword at his side, one of the town constables.

"I owe no money in this town," Kaspar protested; though he was sure that the protest was valueless. Wouter had rigged this trap in advance.

"Easy to find out," said the constable. "Their Honors, the magistrates, will hold court in a week's time."

"But the skipper of the *Pigeon* starts upriver tomorrow," Kaspar objected.

"So-ho," said the constable. "You have here, Mynheer Fries, one of those plaguy people from the Patroon's Colony, who, just when it suits them, decamp and set at naught the jurisdiction of the West Indian Company! Our magistrates will teach him wisdom, I warrant."

Three to one it was, and that one hemmed in behind the table.

"Only say the word, Mynheer Fries, and we'll take this *zwok*, this slippery fellow, along with us." The shorter man raised an unpleasant-looking club. "A tap on the head with my persuader will make him come quietly enough."

Kaspar's left hand threw the falcon doorward. With a sudden swift heave he had the heavy trestle top resting on Wouter's lap. Another heave, bracing his leg against the back of the settle, and the man's stool crashed over backward, the table pinning him down. A high-pitched scream of alarm from the weedy one as the falcon, skimming beneath the low tavern ceiling, found the man's head in the way. Instinctively her talons menaced his eyes.

The other constable's club was raised, was crashing down as Kaspar dived beneath it. He butted the man on his broad silver belt buckle, sent him tottering backward.

Then out through the open door, before Wouter's shout for help could be answered by the landlord. Out into the un-paved street, where a half-dozen pigs were rooting in the trash. A goat, some chickens, but not a man in sight. Kaspar stopped, and whistled.

Down over the roof top swung the falcon, her pointed wings barely clearing the narrow gap between house front and pear tree. Delighted at her freedom she swooped, her leg bells tinkling lightly, soared up again high over the houses, circling in beautiful, triumphant flight.

After so long away from game she might even stoop on one of the stray chickens. Kaspar couldn't afford to stand here, waiting. He ran on, whistled a third time. And this time, having enjoyed her little freedom, she closed her wings and stooped as if to kill; shot like a bullet at Kaspar, wings flattened to her side. A yard from his fist she suddenly spread her wings wide again, every flight feather separate, then dropped her feet, gentle as thistledown, on his gloved fist. She folded her wings and came to rest even as he grasped the jesses, the thin leather straps that held her ankles. He broke into a run.

"Think you're clever, don't you! Pleased with yourself," he scolded her affectionately. And she was too, pleased with herself, and with good cause. It wasn't every peregrine falcon, after long weeks of sea voyage, that would come to fist like this. At the very first chance he must give her a flight, a real flight; just as soon as he could get her clear of the town and out into open country.

First Kaspar had a duty. He was two streets away from the tavern now. He glanced back; no one was following. He slowed to a walk and looked around him. This was the Manhatens, the first town of New Netherlands, head of the West Indian Company. He had heard much about it on his journey from Amsterdam on the *Golden Bear*.

To his eyes, accustomed to the fine tall houses of his own Netherlands, this town seemed not so fine a place. Only one street was paved, and that with cobbles; down the center of the others flowed an open ditch, where pigs grunted and rooted—one seemed to be eating a dead cat—and chickens scratched or sunned themselves. The narrow, two-story or two-and-half-story houses were set, gable end to the street, as at home. A few had white picket fences to keep out the animals, and perhaps later in the year their yards would be gay with flowers. He could glimpse behind them small orchards with fruit trees beginning to show a cloud of faint green. But the house roofs were mainly thatched, the door settles and the steps unpainted. Still it was marvelous what had been done in so short a time, so far away from the homeland: glass windows, some of them even stained glass, or with coats of arms painted on them; fine brass lanterns outside the wide double doors; even here and there a house of stone or brick, though mainly they were of wood.

He must, he told himself, be less critical in his judgment if he were to be happy in this country of his choice; he must throw overboard comparisons with the homeland, enjoy what was at hand and forget what he had left behind.

A woman, rug in hand, came out on a doorstep and paused between the settles to shake the dust from the carpet. Her full outer skirts were pinned back over a bright petticoat of red, no redder than the full cheeks framed by the pointed, white cap with the ear flaps of a Marken Islander. Her black eyes, beneath heavy brows, lit inquiringly on the bird on Kaspar's fist.

"For sale?" she demanded. "Can you eat it?"

What savages indeed, not to know a good falcon! He struggled for politeness.

"Not to eat, but for hunting," he told her. "Can you, Mvrouw, kindly direct me to the house of Mynheer van Cortlandt?"

She smiled then, noting the broad shoulders under the decent brown doublet, and the breeches of brown cloth, not leather such as worn by tradesmen and apprentices; noting too, no doubt, the fineness of his linen falling-collar and the rakish tilt of his new castor hat, the best beaver in Amsterdam. "Yes, indeed," she told him, and pointed with a plump

pink hand. "Go on to Marketfield Street. The brewery; you
can't miss the smell of the malt."

When he looked back before turning the corner, she was
still standing there, smiling, and half raised her hand in farewell. So, 'twas no doubt a friendly country; he should not
judge it by Wouter Fries alone.

He subdued his impatience to a respectable walk. Oloff
Stevensen van Cortlandt, agent for the patroonship of Rensselaerswyck, had been down to the *Golden Bear* this morning, checking over such stores as were to be transshipped up
river. He seemed an able Netherlander; he would listen to
Kaspar's story and tell him what to do.

The next narrow street might be Marketfield. Here on a
stoep bench a woman, scarce more than a girl, sat picking
over a basketful of hops. She was pretty, certainly no servant
girl, to judge by the pearls in the small ears beneath the
Friesland cap of fine linen and lace, the lace border to the
apron that protected her skirt of India calico.

Hops? Hops and malt went together, didn't they? Kaspar
touched his hat.

"Is Mynheer van Cortlandt within?"

When she smiled, a dimple deepened in the corner of her
mouth. Her glance rested curiously on the hawk on his fist.
"You must be Kaspar de Selle, who came this morning on the
Golden Bear from Holland. Father spoke of you. Can I be
of service?"

The sensible thing would be to tell the girl, Juffrouw van
Cortlandt, of his danger, and ask shelter in her house till the
patroonship's yawl sailed upriver; she looked clever enough
to understand. But when the girl is pretty and already seems
slightly amused, perhaps at your accent from the Patria, the
homeland, so different from the speech in this new country,
you feel a little on your dignity. You say offhand, "It is your
father whom I seek. A matter of business."

She smiles a little more, and says, "What a beautiful hawk
you carry! Father spoke of it too."

"A peregrine falcon." Less stiffly.

"She is your own?"

"Yes, but a gift for the Honorable Jeremias van Rensselaer himself. My father was falconer and farmer to his
father, Kiliaen, the First Patroon."

You might have said more. But you remembered: "My
business, I regret, is urgent. Where could I find Mynheer,
your father?"

Quick-witted she was, not wasting time in chatter, but giving clear directions. "In the Burghers' summerhouse, in the
Company's orchard. That's north of the town, under the
stockade."

And as that man who had turned the corner down there
broke into a run, you clapped on your hat and were off again,
in the long striding fenman's lope of your native province.

To the southeast, round the corner by the narrow canal
with little boats moored to its side. Round another two corners to the northwest. Up a side street, where a few phleg-
matic townsmen turned surprised gaze on one who traveled
so fast. Crossing a street unusually broad, littered with what
were perhaps the remains of last year's haystacks. An orchard ahead, in the thin spring sunlight of late afternoon,
its bare boughs showing a haze of spring green. Kaspar
leaped the low fence with the ease of one raised where high
banks and broad dykes stretch over the pasture land.

Apple trees, pears, medlars, plums and many others; the
earth already plowed between them, and now soft from the
winter's frost. A well-groomed turfed path, a well-cared-for
bowling green and a small building, mainly roof—the summerhouse. Men's voices inside were raised in heated argument. Mynheer van Cortlandt was not alone.

Kaspar hesitated. While he waited, considering what next
to do, down there where path met road a carriage stopped.
It was odd to see any carriage in this town, but even in Amsterdam this turnout would have been striking. More a coach
than a carriage it was, drawn by a fine pair of matched bays,

the sides of the coach gleaming with paint and polish. Polished to gold, likewise, the brass helmets and buckles of the two soldiers who sprang down from the perch behind, swung open the near-side door and stood, stiff as ramrods, while out stepped a man with a wooden leg. From beneath his arm he took a wide hat and clapped it on his head.

Beribboned breeches, wide, plumed beaver hat, scarlet cloak billowing in the breeze, this was a man of importance; even his wooden leg, banded with bright stripes of silver, drove forward with determination. The carriage door clapped shut, the two soldiers formed up behind him, fell into step; each swung forward the drum on his back, raised sticks, rattled out a quick roll, then settled to march beat.

His Excellency, Director General of the New Netherlands, was coming!

Kaspar glanced back toward the summerhouse. Burghers, warned by the drumming, were advancing a prescribed distance to meet their governor. No way of escape in that direction. To leap fence and ditch and take to his heels might start a fresh pursuit. Best to stand his ground, and doff his hat, as any citizen of the town would be expected to.

Sharp eyes, a little stern, seemed to take in Kaspar and the falcon; a firm, strong-tempered mouth murmured return of Kaspar's salutation. But it was the nose, long, broad and high-bridged as a hawk's, that made that face, once seen, impossible to forget. He and the drummers swept by, a small but impressive procession. The burghers at the door parted respectfully, and Peter Stuyvesant went in.

Kaspar, considering what he had just seen, was trying to reconcile that urban carriage and matched pair with the pigs rooting in the unpaved streets; the pretty daughter of van Cortlandt, pearl-earringed and aproned in lace, with that high stockade just ahead of him and all that it implied of savages and unspoken perils. No, 'twas too early to form a picture, to pass judgment on this new land. As for the town, he would return to it later; he must indeed.

Kaspar swung off to the north. No chance of getting word with Mynheer van Cortlandt, now the governor himself had joined the assembly in the summerhouse. Nor would it be wise to go down to the dock and take refuge in the *Pigeon* till she sailed upriver tomorrow morning, for of course the constables would look for him there. The thing to do was to get out of the town by the nearest exit and let the whole thing blow over. Anyway, he had as good as promised the falcon her flight. Beyond the stockade should lie open farm land and no doubt wild birds of one kind or another.

The stockade lay just ahead. Logs, made of fair-sized tree trunks, one end thrust into the ground, the other sharpened to a point, made a noble fence which would keep out bears, wolves, and even the more dangerous human enemy. As he drew nearer, Kaspar could see what heavy labor had gone into the task of making the stockade; each log was peeled, each knot or roughness carefully pared away, each fitted to its neighbors so closely that not even a fingerhold lay between. On the near side, earth had been built up into a raised walk for the defenders, and every so often the stockade thrust out in a *V*. From the river on the west, the wall seemed to stretch right across the whole island to, no doubt, the river on the east.

In spite of all this care and precaution, the narrow gateway stood open and utterly unguarded. Kaspar slipped through. So the tales of the terrible Indians with which his ears had been stuffed on shipboard could be given a discount of a few good styvvers on the guilder! That, or the settlers on this island, the Manhatens, were unusually brave. Or careless.

On either side of the rough road short green grass sprouted from black tussocks, where last year's coarse aftermath had been burned to encourage early spring grazing. How like this was to the homeland! To travel all these weeks, all these thousands of miles to find the same black and white cows, eating what seemed like the same grass, clanking the same tuneless bells on a neglected pasture burned over in just the way a shiftless farmer did it outside your own village, made you wonder if you hadn't sailed in a circle and arrived back in the Netherlands once more. Only the sky was a different blue, softer, darker, and the air bore a crisp hint of far-off ice. Nor were the birds quite the same, nor the trees. No, this was not the Netherlands, but the New World.

A boy came into sight, driving home in the late afternoon light a small herd of cows to be milked in the town; his buckskin garments gave a touch of strangeness. Nor would a boy of that age and class be trusted with a firearm in the Patria.

Kaspar gave him a dry greeting. As a falconer he scarcely approved of firearms; people too lazy, too unintelligent and impatient to train so much as a merlin hawk, could pour a fistful of powder and shot down the muzzle of a gun, and go out and call themselves hunters. Hunters, indeed! More like assassins! He loped on at an easy swing, the hawk riding lightly at his wrist, bowing and fidgeting her talons, casting a bright glance above and to every side, as a falcon will when eagerly expecting a flight.

"All right. Just a moment more," he promised her. The trees were thick here, suited for the flight of a baser round-winged hawk. But a noble peregrine, with her wide wing-stretch, needed more open country.

And such came into view: a deserted farm, cleared some years back and growing up again to patches of bramble. There must be game birds of some sort in that cover. Yes, there one went: a partridge, or something similar. But just diving from cover to cover.

Ah, here was a better patch of ground. A deep hollow lay to the left. "Now's your chance, my beauty!" He cast up the falcon, his hand releasing the jesses as he tossed her in the air.

How perfect was the wing stroke of a haggard peregrine! In the bright air, in the level rays of the late afternoon sun, her long narrow wings seemed to cut the air like sharpened blades. Could any draftsman describe more perfect circles, he wondered, as she spiraled upward into the chill thin light "making her point" and "waiting on" for the game to be flushed? It was sheer delight to watch her. Now was the time to send forward old Klaus. But the dog, gray of muzzle, was back in the Netherlands, for, at his age, he never would have stood the voyage. Kaspar would have to be dog and falconer both, and do the best he could.

He kicked his way into the dried bracken; a rabbit or small hare scurried out. But the peregrine ignored it. The bird, exulting in its freedom after so long imprisonment, rose higher and higher. Kaspar could scarcely blame her, but 'twas most unprofessional. The lass had a good eye for country; she had proved it time and again. Surely she could see that the quarry, when flushed, would glide to cover again on the other side of the gully, before the falcon could reach it.

Well, that was her business. He would give her a chance and if she went to bed hungry, 'twould be her own fault. Two hungry bellies would be company for each other.

He cut himself a stick, slashed and banged at one clump of undergrowth after another. Ah, at last a bird flushed, whirred its way a few paces, then in false sense of security, spread wings to float across the hollow. Kaspar glanced up.

Like a stone the falcon plummeted, wings flattened to her sides. A blow; he could hear the strike of the talons. Then—and that was the really skilful touch—she disengaged as her prey fell lifeless another five feet, and the moment it had struck the ground, engaged again. That was real art! Not one bird in ten, as young as this, learned the trick of saving their legs and needle-sharp talons from the shock of hawk and quarry hitting the earth together. Oh, she was a jewel!

Recklessly, for anyone but a falconer, Kaspar leaped down the slope, hurdled bushes, balanced from rock to rock and came exulting to his triumphant bird. The quarry—yes, it was some sort of a partridge—needed no coup de grâce. He let the peregrine "plume" her, even eat a few beakfuls, then took her up. If he let her gorge to the full, she would be unlikely to kill again today, and that would mean that Kaspar himself would go hungry.

In hawking, one kill leads to another. A solitary bird, by its flight a duck, winged toward them from the east across the island. Kaspar threw off the falcon for a second flight, dropped the partridge inside his shirt and raced after her in pursuit. It was clear from the outset that this would be a long chase, for the duck had espied the falcon and swung off north with a long lead and the advantage of height as well. As a ship of the line must maneuver, if it can, to windward of the enemy before pouring in the broadside, so must a falcon rise, not only level with her prey, but sufficiently above to dive and use the force of her dive to strike in her talons. Climbing and speed don't go together, and at first the solitary duck seemed almost to be drawing away, to be increasing its lead.

A falconer must run head up, eyes on the sky; his feet must have eyes of their own, must skirt rocks and tree trunks, leap fallen boughs and all lesser obstacles. His mind, with an instinct that only practice can develop to its full, must map the country as he passes, so that he may foretell by distant signs such bogs, streams and dense woods which he must skirt if he is to keep falcon and quarry in sight. And . . . he must run, really run. Run, not in the impossible hope of keeping up with the swift flight of the bird overhead, but to be near enough to mark down the strike when it comes, and arrive at the kill before the falcon has sated herself and is in danger of being lost.

As moodily as the falcon herself, Kaspar had fretted at being mewed up on shipboard. As joyfully as the falcon up there in the sky he thrilled, now, with the swift chase, drew in deep lungfuls of the clear evening air, reveled in the smooth easy stride of his long lean legs. But also he worried. Dusk was coming on; the gate of the stockade would be locked behind him. There would be no chance now, to shelter till dark near the summerhouse, then to creep through the streets and take shelter with Mynheer van Cortlandt.

Worse still, falcon and duck were now little more than
specks in the distant. If the chase went any farther, nightfall would close down; a lost eyas, trained from a fledgling,
will often return to its mews, but a lost haggard such as this
bird, caught and trained when a full adult, has no such hom-
ing instinct. Anyway, this falcon knew no home in New
Netherlands.

Kaspar put forth every jot of speed, every ounce of energy
he could draw on; at least he was holding them in sight. And
now . . . oh, wouldn't the falcon strike? Surely she now had
sufficient height.

And strike she did. The two dots merged, dropped suddenly earthward. Somewhere beyond that clump of trees
they were.

Kaspar marked down the exact treetop. Directly behind it,
too far for an exact estimate but perhaps five hundred paces,
should be duck and falcon. Heaven send, it wasn't thick
woodland, but open farm land, that he would need to search,
with nothing but the faint tinkle of falcon bells to guide him.

On . . . On . . . He lined up another tree still farther
off, plunged through dense undergrowth into the forest and
was grateful for the sparseness of the spring foliage. Came
out on the far side and all but leaped into the water. And
there was the falcon, wheeling in easy circles, skimming low
as a swallow and almost brushing the river with her wings.

He called her with his summoning whistle, threw out his
gloved left hand. Over she came, playfully teasing him once
or twice by raking off again. Then settling gently to harken
to his praises while she preened herself pridefully. The
quarry, no mistaking it, floated dead upon the water. It was
too cold, at this season, to swim out for it, especially as Kaspar would probably have to spend the night out in the open.
But the current of the wide river formed an eddy in the small
bay; and yes, the eddy was bringing the bird close to shore.

Twice, tantalizingly, it came nearly within reach. Then,
almost as darkness fell, with a dead bough he raked it ashore.

"A meal for me, my lady, as well as for you."

A meal not too easily accomplished. The last trace of after-glow had faded from the sky, and low clouds had blotted out even the starlight before Kaspar found what he sought—dry punk from the inside of a hollow tree. It might be the right kind of tree, or it might not, most of them being strange to him. He powdered the punk with the handle of his knife, made a little hollow in it, and taking from his pocket a little purse of leather, shook out a cast-off musket flint and a small strip of linen, brown with age and brittle. Tearing off a piece of the tinder no bigger than his thumbnail, he shredded it fine into the hollow of the punk, and with the back of his knife and the musket flint, struck the necessary spark. It was equal chance that even inside the leather purse the tinder would be damp; there is nothing like linen for tinder, but nothing soaks up moisture as thirstily as does the thread of the flax.

If only he had the barest pinch of gunpowder; just one grain would have done the trick. But by making the sparks fall on the same part of the tinder, and not spread them-selves around, he had it at last.

The gentlest possible blowing was all that he dared risk, as with his knife point he teased the tinder together. Now there was a thread of smoke and he could blow harder. He risked some of the wood punk. It was catching, a nice little red glow, as big as a button. A few straws of coarse grass, a handful of pine needles, and the fire was safe.

The falcon, secured by her jesses and leash to a fallen bough, had watched the proceedings with puzzled interest.

"It won't be like your comfortable mew at home," he told her, "nor even your quarters on shipboard. It's going to be cold; it may even rain or snow; but we'll do the best we can for you." The falcon bowed and shuffled at the sound of his voice, and in the firelight started to "bate" at the leash.

"Oh, no, you don't. But just to make sure, as I'm going to be too busy for a while to keep an eye on you, I'd better hood you to make safe."

On the edge of the clearing, by sheer luck and in the dark, he stumbled across a shock of cornstalks and burrowed inside. That would be reasonably dry and warm. Now the fire was going, it was easy enough to transfer a few blazing embers to the front of this improvised hut, to fix a perch for the hawk and give her her supper of raw partridge while he skinned the second catch and roasted the duck meat on a greenwood spit. A fine meal indeed, his appetite told him, for his first on dry land; and a far pleasanter feast than he might have had with Wouter Fries in the tavern.

A few more fallen boughs to drag in to the embers, some slight precautions to prevent his shelter catching fire; he spread wider his burrowed entrance so the heat could penetrate as long as the ashes glowed outside. Then naught to do but crawl inside with the falcon, and with his cloak around him get a good night's sleep.

This land of New Netherlands was better than he could have hoped for. Where else in the world could you have your hawk, your lodgings, your meal and this wonderful sense of freedom?

Those terrifying Indians couldn't be so dangerous, since the gate of the stockade was left open all day, and numbers of them seemed even to live among the white folk in the town. Perhaps they were really no worse than dogs, or bulls; some of them dangerous enough at times, but not all of them and not always to be feared, if you treated them aright.

The fire dropped to a dim glow. He reached a leg out of the shelter and hooked another bough across the ashes. Then snuggling deeper into his cloak, and with a smile of satisfaction on his mouth, fell instantly asleep. His first night in the New World.

Chapter Two
Kiliaen van Rensselaer,
First Patroon

AT THE FIRST TRACE of dawn Kaspar stretched his cold and stiffened limbs and sat up, yawning. The glumly brooding falcon, her feathers ruffled a little against the damp chill, favored him with a malignant stare. Naturally the fire had died out while he slept. What else did the bird expect? And the damp of the river hanging in a clammy fog, dripping from the trees and hiding all around him, was scarcely Kaspar's fault.

Sleepily, half-heartedly he raked through the fire, and found a living coal. A few bits of wood lay near enough to the ashes to remain dry. He added these, and soon had a

17

small comforting glow; but the addition of dew-soaked sticks
gave no more heat, only a harsh smoke which hung in the
fog as in a low-ceilinged room, and started him coughing.
No matter, for the sun was rising and the usual dawn breeze
began to fan the fog and dissipate it.

"Back now to Mynheer van Cortlandt, my lady." He set
the bird on his gloved hand. "We must get through the gate
as soon as the herds come out and before all the burghers are
awake."

It was a good, sound purpose. But not more than a mile
had he gone, stretching to a long fast lope, warming and sup-
pling his body, when a heron flapped slowly overhead.

Herons, over here in the new world? They must be wild
birds, then, and not the private property of some gentleman
who owned a heronry.

Up went the falcon before Kaspar even gave himself time
to consider. Not in straight flight this time, but rising as if
climbing an invisible winding staircase; spiraling upward, as
a pigeon or a bee. The heron above had checked his course
and was climbing too. No need this time for a wild, cross-
country race. All Kaspar had to do was wait where he stood.

When the falcon struck, the two birds were high overhead. Together, almost to treetop level, they fell. Then that
same neat and beautiful disengagement; and, as the heron
thudded to the ground at Kaspar's feet, the falcon had already checked her descent with outstretched wing feathers,
and binding lightly but firmly to her prey began to "plume"
it of its feathers.

He picked her up, and she offered no objection, for few
falcons will eat either heron or rook. Then collecting the
heron, he set off again without further delay.

There might be, there probably was, a straighter road
inland, but he dare not waste time in seeking it. Here, following the curves of the shore, the trail dropped down to
mud flats, climbed steeply over rocks. Perhaps only a cattle
path, but good enough for a boy who had learned to run as

early as he had learned to walk; who, like all boys of his village, claimed that he could just about skim over water, if the water was muddy enough! Mostly it was a trick of course, this marsh running. If one tussock in three would bear your weight, on the others your leg went limp as soon as it felt the ground give way; you reached that third tussock almost on your knees, lifted yourself by just that one stride, and went on again. Like a flat stone skimmed over water, you sank if you slowed down. And the faster you skimmed, the safer. You could learn it only as a child, for your bare feet had to do it of themselves, and the first time you put on shoes you were as helpless and clumsy as a man from the eastern hill provinces.

How different this was, from pounding bored feet along the cobbled, city ways of Old Amsterdam! Or standing for untold hours passing fur pelts along a greasy counter, grading them for size, for color, quality and condition. Or sitting for hours, cross-legged, cutting fine strips with a razor and stitching, stitching like an aged woman. Well, a boy must learn a trade to earn a living. If only the fur trade and falconry could go hand in hand! He set the thought aside, as too daring, too much to hope.

Another few minutes and he should come in sight of the stockade. Pasture land, but as yet no cows at graze. What lazy folks these townsmen were. Why in his homeland village the beasts would all be milked and out a good half-hour ago, for that extra half-hour would mean a lot to the milk yield. And . . . the stockade gate was still closed.

What now? Try to scale the wall? And perhaps be shot, if there were any guards inside! A just about impossible feat anyway, with one hand encumbered by a hawk. No time to waste though. He swung back toward the river. Perhaps there was some way around. If need be, he'd have to risk the chill of the ice-cold water and, fastening the falcon to his head by tying her leash under his chin, turn the obstacle by swimming out and around.

Ah, what a stroke of luck!—a boy, sculling a small boat from the stern, keeping close under the bank to avoid the current. And the boy had marked him too, for the boat turned in closer.

"Seen any Injuns?" the fellow piped up in squeaky tones. He was thin and hard and freckled, and a good head shorter than Kaspar.

"What Indians?" asked Kaspar and measured the distance that separated him from the boat. A few yards wading would be better than a fifty-yard swim, with unknown currents.

The boat glided in a little farther, then stopped. "You blind?" piped the boy. "Or don't you know an Injun signal fire?" He jerked his head to the north.

Kaspar turned to look. Faint above the trees drifted the thinnest line of blue. He suppressed a laugh. It wouldn't do to offend this youngster if he wanted to ask a favor of him, but that smoke came from his own fire, from those sodden sulky sticks that had at last deigned to catch. He should of course have put the fire out before he came away, but on bare ground with everything soaked around it, there had been no danger of its spreading, and he had not thought of any other risk.

"M-m-m." He twisted his face into an expression of concern. "Then that's an Indian signal?"

"What else?" said the boy scornfully. "And likely enough a huntin' or raidin' party, seeing there's no villages hereabouts." Then curiosity caught him, as Kaspar had hoped it would. "That a young eagle you've got there?"

Kaspar suppressed his horror at such ignorance. "A tame hawk." Maybe the boy would understand that better than "haggard peregrine falcon." "I use him for killing game." He held up the dangling heron to prove it. "Want to look at the hawk?" Time was racing away, but he dare not risk losing this heaven-sent opportunity.

As the boat edged in cautiously he measured the distance

again. Now he could get aboard whether the freckled urchin wanted him to or not; and, if only the boy would agree, perhaps he could cut out the difficult visit to Mynheer van Cortlandt, drop down on the current to the tip of the island and come safely, and unsuspected by Wouter, to the small river yacht, the *Pigeon*.

One step and he was in the rowboat.

"Hey, I didn't say you was to come aboard!" protested the boy at the oar. "Who are you anyway, and what you doin' outside the stockade this hour of the morning?"

"I told you already. Flying my falcon. You don't catch herons on the public streets. And anyway, dawn and evening's the best time for hawking." Then he had a sudden idea. "Look, would you like the heron? There's far too much on it for me alone, and we've eaten a partridge and a duck already."

The boy clamped the oar under his arm and leaned forward to examine the heron. The talon marks were unmistakable.

"That little bird of yours kill this big 'un?"

"Little bird!" Kaspar had to swallow again. Except for one of those Norwegian falcons or an eagle, there wasn't a hawk to compare with the peregrine, in size or strength or courage. But this wasn't the time to set the stupid fellow aright.

"You going anywhere with your boat?" he asked casually.

The boy set down the heron and sculled a safe distance from the bank before replying. "I was headin' upstream while there's tide to help. But if there's Injuns round . . ."

"Oh," said Kaspar, "they'd see you out here on the open water before you could catch a glimpse of them ashore."

"Likely." The boy headed the boat downstream. "Then I'd best go home and tell about the smoke."

"If you'll take me down around the point, and set me on the van Rensselaer's yawl, the *Pigeon*, you can have the heron," offered Kaspar.

"Set you aboard the *Pigeon*?" The boy seemed to be amused.

"That's it," said Kaspar.

"Well, I might, at that." As he stood sculling in the stern, he was glancing over Kaspar's shoulder. The joke, whatever it was, looked as if it was beginning to hurt him.

"I don't see anything so funny about that. It's a fair enough price for a short row."

"Shorter'n you think, maybe. Turn your head, if your neck ain't froze stiff with pride."

As Kaspar turned to look, an angry voice hailed them: "Gek! Idioot! You, Jan Lansing, get out of my way!"

The small, broad-beamed sailing vessel, drawing sluggishly upriver, close in to shore, was almost upon them. "Wat dunder! Don't you know, fools, that downstream you keep to the middle river?"

"Mynheer Strycker." The boy stopped sculling. "I bring you your passenger. Fifty paces I've rowed him for the price of one heron. Ha, ha, ha!"

So broad in the beam and blunt in stem and stern, the *Pigeon* looked much like an outsized barrel, sawn through from top to bottom. Made on this side of the water, of course, and without the carving, the scrollwork and finish that it would have back in the Netherlands. The captain brought her up into the wind and held her there, sail flapping. She was so low in the water that when the sides of the rowboat and the river boat came together Kaspar had only to step over the gunwales and find a footing among the boxes and barrels and bales.

The captain, scowling, let the yawl's head fall off; the heavy boom swung over as Kaspar ducked to dodge it; and they were on their way upriver. Then he turned to wave back at young Jan, and the boy raised a hand in a derisive and vulgar farewell salute. Kaspar grinned. Let the lad have his triumph. More than likely they'd meet again someday; then he would tell Jan who it was that started that Injun fire!

He found a perch for the falcon on a coil of mooring rope, made fast her leash, took her hood from his pocket and put it on her till she should become accustomed to her new quarters. Then he rubbed the stiffness out of his left arm. An adult falcon is a good weight to carry around on outstretched fist, hour after hour, particularly when long weeks, pent up on shipboard, have softened the muscles.

Next to make sure that the patroonship goods were all aboard. True enough that Mynheer van Cortlandt had taken charge of them on the *Golden Bear* and had seen to their transfer to the river yawl. But there was no sense in counting them all in Amsterdam, checking them aboard the barge that carried them up the Zuider Zee to the Texel, checking them again aboard the *Golden Bear,* if you didn't see them safely to the end of the long journey and into the hands of Mynheer Jeremias van Rensselaer, only a few days upriver.

The goods were here, with their initials *JvR* to identify them, including his own small cowhide traveling trunk that he had scarcely hoped to see again. With a pleasant sense of a duty nearly discharged, a responsibility almost at an end, he dodged the short clumsy boom as it swung over, climbed back over the cargo to a place beside the falcon, and began wishing for some breakfast.

How did people live on board these little river boats? Did they tie up at riverside villages and buy their meals? Nobody else seemed to be interested. The captain was busy knitting a long red woolen stocking, steering on one tack with his knee hooked over the wooden tiller bar, on the other with a heavy wooden clog thrusting against it.

The only other passenger, a large big-boned man, with a rough black beard, lay stretched out beside a musket smoking a short wooden pipe, his head pillowed on a bale, and a shaggy fur cap over his eyes. A puzzle, from his fringed garments that seemed neither of cloth nor tanned leather, to his hands which were neither gnarled and calloused like a workman's, nor as clean as a gentleman's.

With a feeling of envy, Kaspar averted his eyes. No one, surely, could be so comfortable and relaxed if he hadn't breakfasted.

Up in the bows was the dull-looking boy who must be the captain's son. Hidden by the sail and the stumpy foremast he seemed to be busy over something. Kaspar, stretching out in imitation of the other passenger, sat up with a jerk. He hoped his nose wasn't lying to him.

Yes, up there in the bows was a cast-iron kettle, hung from a stick that stretched from gunwale to gunwale. Under the kettle the boy was feeding short lengths of twigs into a small fire on a rough clay hearth. Kaspar had noticed the odor of smoke before, but now, as the iron pot began to simmer, came a wonderful aroma of meat and vegetables. Warmed-over stew!

It might be included in the price of his passage. If not, he still had enough styvvers to buy his meal. Now there was nothing to do but wait. Kaspar lay back and closed his eyes. The sun was delightfully warm after the chilly dawn, and the movement of the boat was soothing.

But not soothing enough to bring sleep when everything around was new and strange, and demanding attention. How many days would it take up to Rensselaerswyck? Was it a town like the Manhatens? Was this river as long as the Rhine? There went four Indians in one of those eggshell boats that were said to be made of the bark of trees, rowing, without rowlocks, the short oars held in both hands. Close ashore some other Indians in a semicircle were standing in the shallows as they hauled in a net, just as folk did in the home country. But what big fish they were taking! If those fish were fit to eat, there would be a fortune in fishing this river. Also the timber which could be sawn from just one of those trees that lined the banks looked enough to build a whole house. And the farms that were now astern did not join field to field, but left wide stretches of uncleared land in between.

Mynheer Kiliaen van Rensselaer, First Patroon, had been right, though few had believed him in the homeland. He hadn't exaggerated, he hadn't even told the full truth about this new land. Forests that had to be seen to be believed, each tree of which would be worth a small fortune if it grew in the Netherlands. A big river so full of fish that the Indians had to keep lightening their net as they pulled it in, by throwing fish ashore. So much land that farmers could not use it all, even right under the stockade of the town.

"Homelander?" asked a voice beside him.

So he had been gaping like a yokel come to town, had he? Well, there was enough to make a man gape. Casually he said "Amsterdam." Which was true enough. No point in saying he was born at Cralo, for the man with the musket would never have heard of the village.

"Amsterdam? Honest?" The man sat up eagerly. "I'm from there myself!"

"Been over here some time?" The big man didn't fit any trade or class that Amsterdam had ever known. At close glance the material of his shirt and trousers was a soft-worked skin, deerskin no doubt; and his footwear must be the moccasins that it was said the Indians wore instead of the wooden clogs and the stout leather shoes and boots of the homeland.

"Quite awhile," the man admitted.

His eyes were blue even for a Netherlands fisherman; he wore his uncombed black hair as long as an old-time nobleman; and though his hands showed no sign of heavy toil there was nothing about his heavily muscled frame to suggest he had ever sat at a craftsman's bench or perched on a stool in a merchant's counting house. Though he didn't fit into any class that Kaspar knew, he was friendly and here was a chance to get some news of the place that was to be Kaspar's future home.

"Then you must have been to Rensselaerswyck, and seen the patroonship? What's it like? I mean how many people

are there now? Is it a town, or just farms?" The pent-up
questions jostled out.

The man seemed to lose interest. Lazily he removed his
pipe. "Oh, there's a few folks; don't know as I've ever
thought to count them. And you might call Beverwyck a
town, or you might not. And there again Beverwyck isn't
Rensselaerswyck." He laid his pipe down beside him, pulled
the coonskin cap—yes, the rings on the tail showed it was
coonskin—farther over his eyes and again settled himself to
sleep. Friendly he might be, but clearly disinclined for further talk. Kaspar took the hint.

Judging by the land, the wide shallow-draft yawl was
making more headway. The captain had set course in the
middle of the river, which showed that the tide had now
turned and was setting upstream. The very last farm had
dropped behind, and they were long past the cove where
overnight the falcon had killed her duck. And that reminded
Kaspar. He unhooded the bird, and from his pocket produced one of the two raw legs of the partridge that he had
saved for her. As he put on his glove she bated off her rope
perch and leaped eagerly to his fist and began to eat.

His mouth watered, for a change in course brought another gust of cooking from the bows; that combined with
the falcon's voracious tearing at the partridge leg . . . he
swallowed his spittle and swung his thoughts far away. To
Amsterdam. To Mynheer Kiliaen van Rensselaer.

What a long way he had come. And all because Mynheer Kiliaen, the First Patroon, that wealthy and respected
shipper, pearl and diamond trader of Amsterdam, had been
dead these many years. But while he had lived he had had a
finger in many pies, as even Kaspar knew: South American
shipping, to Curaçao, to Brazil, importing spices and pearls
from the East Indies, importing furs from the New World,
exporting furs to Russia, and interests in land, in crops, in
horses, in sports, in falconry—but most of all an interest in
human beings that had remained with him all his life. It was

this concern for all his fellow men, and for his Netherlanders more than others, that had led him to establish the patroonship of Rensselaerswyck in the New World. Now his son, Johannes, was patron, "patroon," in his stead; and Jeremias, a younger son, director of the colony.

Kaspar recalled him now as he had first seen him; as he had stood that day in June, back in Amsterdam. A slight, frail old man in a white tie-back wig, and a modish, brocaded full-skirted coat. Under the lace ruffles his thin hand rested on the newel post at the top of the wide flight of steps that led to his office. He was saying, in that pleasant voice that grated a little with his years, "So this is Kaspar de Selle? Well, Jacobus, he looks to be a good stout lad. I am glad to see you Jacobus . . . and your son. Before you go I will call Elsa, and ask her to bring the boy a cup of chocolate."

And, turning away, his voice had continued, "Now about your journey to Valkenswaard. Come up and we will discuss it." And Kaspar was left alone, to wait in the hall below.

He had sat there, he remembered, for over an hour; his feet dangling from the high, straight-backed chair, his fingers playing with the teeth of the snarling lions that terminated the arms. The hour had not seemed long as he watched the dancing shadows of plane trees on the high, leaded windows, and harkened to the occasional rumble of a dog-drawn cart over the narrow, cobbled streets outside. Harkened, too, to the adult conversation that went on in the room a half-story above him; and though at the time the talk had meant little, it had remained with him all the years between.

At first it concerned the falcon market, soon to be held at Valkenswaard; and the young Kaspar's ears stretched wide. If only by some miracle he and his father could go to that; a good ten day's journey it was, to the country south of the Rhine. What stories he would have to tell, once he got home again to Cralo!

But there seemed little hope of that. Father was a home lover, not one who ever wished to roam. Nor did he wish his son to wander. Why, it was only by the greatest of good fortune that little Kaspar had come as far as Amsterdam; and only at his mother's insistence.

"Take the boy out of the fens and bogs, Jacobus," she had urged his reluctant father, "before his feet strike root and he turns into a willow tree. Perhaps," she had added sharply, "if Mynheer van Rensselaer sees the lad in some place other than Cralo he will do something for this only son of his old farmer and falconer. 'Twould be only right and proper. As it is, Kaspar is to Mynheer just another tree or bush on the Cralo estate; no more to be noticed than one of the fowls or pigs."

But listen as he might, in that big, high-backed carved chair at the foot of the stairs, he could catch no sound of his own name. The talk went on: of the Spaniards, still holding those provinces in the south; of whether the hawk market would, after all, be held this autumn; and if it were held whether it would amount to much, almost under the shadow of the Spanish guns. Then for a time the talk wandered to other matters, and Kaspar sat back, kicking his heels and wishing for that promised cup of chocolate; that too would be an event.

There seemed to be argument, something about a printed paper which Mynheer Kiliaen wished to have circularized among the Netherlanders. Another voice chimed in, now and then, a younger voice, which said at last, "Well, here's a good man to try it on; he's just the type of fellow we need in the patroonship. Hand him the prospectus; see if it attracts him."

Then Kiliaen's voice again, reading this time. Kaspar could recall that reading, every word. Or perhaps he had memorized the phrases later from the printed slip that his father brought home, which lay, even now, among the folds of Kaspar's other garments in the cowhide traveling trunk.

"Opposite Fort Orange," the grating, pleasant voice had read, "on the south point of De Laet's Island, are many

birds to be shot: geese, swans and cranes. Turkeys frequent
the woods. Deer and other game are also there, also wolves
but not larger than dogs. On De Laet's Island are many tall
and straight trees suitable for making oars. Fat and excellent
venison can be obtained in large quantities from the Maquas,
principally in the winter; three, four or five hands of wampum for a deer . . . at the fourth kill are pike and all kinds
of fish. Here the sturgeon are smaller than at the Manhatens. One can be bought from the Wilden with a knife."

The gentlemen had pressed Father for an opinion. Father
said, cautiously, that indeed it was a wonderful country of
which the writer spoke. Not satisfied, the gentlemen insisted
that he speak out, and say whether he himself would be
tempted by the description to go to the New World.

Reluctantly came Father's answer. "If I were fool enough
to believe such printed romances, Mynheer, you would not
judge me fit to manage your farm, your horses, and your
falcons at Cralo."

The gentlemen had burst out laughing. So pleased were
they with themselves when they came downstairs that Mynheer Kiliaen had presented little Kaspar with a golden coin,
a whole guilder, which he came near to losing a dozen times
before his father took it from him for safe-keeping.

Then back they had gone to Cralo; his father taciturn as
ever; but Kaspar willing enough to dream his dreams: of
Valkenswaard, and of the island, or whatever it was, beyond
the sea, so full of game and fish—and wonderful, no doubt,
for hawking. Each night, at first, his father talked of the long
sea voyage and the marvels to be seen at the end of it—but
remembering to add that only an idiot would believe such
stories. Mother, understanding what lay in his mind, bent
over her mending to hide a smile, pursed her lips and answered, "If it be God's will!"

Yes, Kiliaen van Rensselaer wanted settlers for his new
patroonship. Settlers?—whole families in fact, and the more
the better. He was even willing to pay their passage to the

strange New World out of his own pocket. And so real had
the dream become to young Kaspar, it seemed almost as if
they had said farewell to Cralo, had embarked already for
the long weeks of voyage. But Kiliaen wanted also to keep
his farmer and his falconer; and wanted more his farmer
than his falconer. So that Kaspar, as soon as he was old
enough to run the long distances with the hawk on his fist,
from dawn till nightfall if need be, was set to exercise the
neglected birds. A right good life it was, at that.

Until, on another day, his mother had looked him up and
down and said, "Jacobus, it is feathers, now, and no longer
willow roots that the boy is growing. That is no future for
him. For in these days who goes hawking any longer, when
'tis the fashion for every noble and rich merchant's son to
carry a fowling piece?"

"I suppose," said Father dryly, "you would prefer fur to
feathers!"

And, as it happened, fur it had been. He had been apprenticed to his mother's brother in the peltry trade. This by the
advice of Kiliaen himself. Then followed those long dragging years, pent up between high brick walls in the city shop,
an apprenticeship only to end when his father had died suddenly, a year after his mother. And then the patroon had
sent for him. Not Kiliaen, of course, for the old patroon had
died. But his eldest son, Johannes, the new patroon.

"You know something of the fur trade," he said bluntly.
"Sort and price me these beaver skins."

There, strangely out of place in that fine, wainscoted office,
with the beautiful turkey carpet on the heavy, carved table,
was a newly imported bundle of skins. Kaspar unfastened
the bundle, flicked through them as swiftly as a scholar impatiently turning the leaves of a book; grading by sight, by
touch, blowing the fur here, parting it with a thumbnail
there, sorting them into four neat piles.

Confidently he told the price of each pile, even to the half
styvver's worth; pointed out those that would serve best, un-

plucked, for stoles and collars, and such as would be most profitably turned into castor, for "beaver" hats. An easy task, after so much training; he could have done it blindfold, or at least viewing only the backs of the pelts.

Then Johannes had said, just as bluntly, "There is no future in the fur trade in Amsterdam, where buyers and furriers are three for a styvver. Your father planned to cross the seas, but left it till too late. Do you wish to go?"

Five months of waiting, till his passage could be secured. Those five months were spent at Cralo, and with his father's falcons. All were to be sold, or given away, for the new farmer scarcely knew the difference between a goshawk and a barnyard fowl. It was even more true now than it had been ten years before that hawking was a dying art, except among the very rich who still made pretense to cleave to the ancient ways. Five months of hawking, skating during the frosts, till his legs, long cramped by the years of apprenticeship, could again carry him easily, tirelessly, as legs should. Then the doubts and fears of the voyage, even some talk of "Turkish" pirates. But the passage, save for sight of an occasional blowing monster of the deep, had been smooth, almost uneventful.

Now here he was, incredible as it seemed, with the best of the Cralo falcons eating a leg of New Netherland partridge on his fist. And a debt of seven beaver skins for his passage, to be repaid someday soon to the patroon in Amsterdam.

Chapter Three
They All Know
Gideon Dolph

A SHOUT from the boy in the bow: "Maquas!"
As the other passenger sat up, Kaspar looked to see
what had caught the man's interest. Down-river
came an eggshell of a boat: an Indian boat, made of bark
apparently, which curled gracefully to a point in bow and
stern. It was loaded down almost to the gunwales. Two
women squatted amidst bundles on the bottom of the boat;
two men, one at the bow, one at the stern knelt to their
paddles.

His fellow passenger let out a curious howl, or that's what
it sounded like. He was answered by the Indians, and spoke

again in an odd, chanting sort of speech unlike any language Kaspar had ever heard before. The canoe closed in on them, and the fellow passenger, after another weird song, turned to Kaspar with obvious pride.

"Ha! Even down here the Indians know Gideon Dolph, the boslooper."

The canoe, which had been paddling downstream, swung about, and in a moment two brown braceleted arms reached out to grasp at the gunwale of the *Pigeon*. A nervous protest from the yawl's owner was met by Gideon's reassurance that the Indians would not come aboard.

Then started a strange conference, or argument; Kaspar couldn't tell which. Gideon Dolph's hands seemed to do as much talking as his tongue, and the Indians, too, flashed outstretched fingers, thumped palms, put hands to head, made chopping, crisscross, pointing, circling signs, in an unceasing accompaniment to their talk.

The subject of the talk was a bundle, wrapped in deerskins and raised from the damp bottom of the canoe by a dunnage of twigs. In the course of the argument the bundle was untied, to display pelts, mostly beaver skins.

Gideon kept pointing downstream, back toward the Manhatens, and using a word that sounded like "Susskooks." At length the two men nodded, repeated the word, cast off, and paddled on down-river.

Gideon Dolph blew out his chest, and big enough it was even before that. . . .

"The Maquas, the Mahicans, the Oneidas, and even the Algonquins of the north, they all know Gideon Dolph. He is not one to cower inside a stockaded fort, but goes freely to their towns, their camps, their hunting parties. And the scalp of the boslooper still grows on his own head!"

Kaspar considered the man with amusement, but a shade of doubt. It was hard to imagine that heavy body running swiftly, lightly, through the forests, as the name, boslooper, woods-runner, suggested. Why the man was built like an ox.

Perhaps his fine proportions would appeal to the Indians, or perhaps his simplicity, his obvious honesty. If he were a trader of some sort, as the argument over the bundle of pelts suggested, he didn't look as if he would try to trick them in a deal and so arouse their indignation, as others in this country were said to do.

Then, oh most welcome, most wonderful, a call to food. The stew of meat, probably venison, was ladled out, steaming, into wooden bowls, and served with a strange kind of coarse yellow bread that crumbled in the fingers but was good for sopping up the juice. Kaspar set the falcon back on her rope perch, and with the aid of his knife finished off two helpings.

Rinsing his bowl and fingers over the side of the boat in the chilly water, Kaspar hoped that his first cooked meal in the New Netherlands was a fair sample of what was to come. This was a good country, where, like a Mynheer, you could eat your belly full of meat even at breakfast. With such victualing, even a commoner, a tradesman or laborer could surely afford to keep a hawk or two.

Strange it seemed, that half the people in the Netherlands did not come over and settle here; mile after mile of shore line all forested with noble trees, which showed how good the soil must be. Unlimited water; and if, by any chance, the river banks were ague-ridden, there to the west huge cliffs mighty as the walls of a giant's castle, carried on their summits higher and healthier land. From their tops, once a man had cleared land below, he would be able to see his cattle anywhere within five or ten miles, and mark every passing boat.

What a pity that Kiliaen van Rensselaer had never set foot upon this land of his. Yet with the eye of his imagination he had seen it, had seen it all, and with his wealth gained as a pearl and diamond merchant, had made it possible for a man, or even a whole family, no matter how penniless, to cross the wide ocean and enjoy these riches. He would even supply farms, cattle, seed, corn, house and barn, and at a rental far less than would be asked for the same acreage in the Netherlands. And, if a man wished, the farm could be his and his son's, forever, without danger of the rental price increasing, or of his being thrown out for any cause except nonpayment of the rent. How lucky to be born in these modern days, how fortunate to be born in the Netherlands where such an opportunity was offered and—Kaspar grinned to himself—to lie at ease in the warm spring sun with falcon beside him, and enough food to last a whole day comfortably stowed inside.

The dull-faced boy had moved down to the stern to relieve his father at the tiller. Now he baited a hook, threw out a line, and hauled in a fish almost as soon as the line was in the water. His second bite was a far smaller fish. Kaspar expected to see him throw it back; but instead he settled the big hook more firmly in the small jaw, and paid out the line again. It wasn't five minutes before something struck. It hauled the line violently to one side, then to the other, raced up level with the boat, and before the boy could haul in the slack, had shot downstream again. Dull-witted the boy might be, but he did seem to know about fishing; as the line raced through his hands he ran it around a tholepin to ease the strain. But the last yard was almost gone before Kaspar could scramble to his side and help him check the fish and begin to haul slowly in.

Getting the fish aboard was a puzzling task for it was too big, too heavy just to be jerked up on the slender line. But Gideon Dolph solved that problem. Knife in hand, he leaned overboard. A flash of the blade, a frantic swift struggle of the fish, and with a lift of his massive muscle he swung the monster over the gunwale and shook it off his knife.

"Boslooper and bear, that is the way *they* fish!" he boasted genially. "Not with a silly line and hooks. They go to the edge of the water; they watch. Along comes a fish, to which this one," he stirred it with his toe, "would be but bait. Then

in with the paw, or in with the knife. And out with the fish.
Ha!" A smile flashed through his black beard.

Kaspar chuckled. You couldn't help liking this big fellow,
rather like a bear himself. And if his stories held ten styvvers
to the guilder of truth, what a feat it would be to go with him
someday on one of his distant journeys!

That afternoon, just as a squall of rain blew up, they
struck on a sandbar. Not hard enough to shear the mast or
start a leak. As soon as the sails were dropped and the four
of them leaped overboard into the icy shallows, the current
of the river floated the *Pigeon* off again, almost without hauling. The captain resumed the tiller and his knitting, and
ordered the boy to drop his fishing and go up into the bows
again, where he could keep an eye on the channel. The rain
continued to come down, and, rather belatedly, Kaspar
thought, the captain sourly left his tiller to the boy, to haul
out some torn pieces of tarred canvas and spread them over
the already dripping merchandise. Passengers, less valuable
than cargo from the homeland, received no attention.

Just before sunset the skies cleared again, long enough to
give a touch of warmth, though not to dry Gideon's deerskins, nor Kaspar's good thick Netherland cloth. The falcon,
released from the shelter Kaspar had contrived for her
among the cargo, hopped back to his fist, and fussed and
fretted at the endless stream of birds; duck, pigeon, heron,
even a few geese, and others new and strange, that seemed
to fill the evening air. Some, the smaller ones, were going
back to roost; others were seeking new and safer feeding
grounds or waters for the night hours. As tantalizing to falconer as to falcon; but when at last the captain put in to shore
it was too dark for a flight. Too dark to see more than the
dim outlines of the barren island in midstream.

Gideon the boslooper protested. Now was the time, if they
had tied up to the mainland bank, when he could shoot a deer
coming down to water, and so provide tomorrow's meat.

"Indians!" explained the captain gruffly.

Gideon roared out a laugh. "Hark to him, boy," he told Kaspar. "The good captain says 'Indians!' And ties onto a useless mud flat in mid-river! On the Manhatens they say 'Indians!' and live like pigs, all in one sty. At Beverwyck they sit close under the fort like children holding to a mother's skirts. And what do they say? 'Indians!' But where would the furs come from for these folk to trade; where the Indian corn and the wheat, the barley and oats to keep them alive, if we all said 'Indians!' and stuck our frightened heads into a mud bank?"

"Only six months ago . . ." the captain muttered.

". . . the Indians killed a white man. I know. And perhaps the white man had killed an Indian. It is all folly. There are forests enough and streams enough for all."

He raised his nose and sniffed. "Fish! Whew! When good red meat lies ready for the taking; red meat that would put courage in your veins, Mynheer Skipper!"

But the fish stew was good, even the more tasty, Kaspar thought, for being cooked with the remains of the meat. And so was more of that new strange yellow bread. Though the falcon had to make do with the second partridge leg, she seemed content. And the sheltered cranny between two bales of merchandise, with a tarred canvas drawn over, made snug sleeping quarters compared with those of the previous night.

So passed the days. The wide river stretched endlessly in front and behind. Surely it must be bigger even than the Rhine! A following breeze set the water gurgling against the *Pigeon's* blunt bows. Then for two days came almost a calm, while the captain knitted, knitted, knitted. More, incredibly more, of unbroken forest and wide majestic river, often without a single Indian canoe in sight for hours together.

Early each morning and sometimes in the evening, Gideon persuaded the captain to set him and Kaspar ashore, to hunt or fly the falcon, and rejoin the boat a mile or two upriver. Since the boslooper found and killed his deer as easily as a farmer's wife catches and kills a rooster, the *Pigeon* had more meat than was needed. Since there was no need of extra meat, the falcon, as always happens, provided yet more, killing as many as three ducks in the hour or so ashore. Since there was a surplus of meat, the captain's son baited with it, and added fish to the glut. The boslooper hailed passing canoes, seemed to talk business with them, and handed out venison. The kettle simmered from dawn to dusk, and never in his life had Kaspar so gorged himself on meat.

On one day an increase in the number of canoes, and a yawl like their own drawing out from the bank and hailing them as it passed on downstream, suggested that some settlement was near by. If there was, it was hidden by the trees. The next day they had to tie up at a small wooden jetty while merchandise was unloaded. Gideon and Kaspar were invited ashore for a meal at one of six lonely farmhouses. Kaspar, hoping to offer sport in return for hospitality, cast off his falcon over the farm land.

But the cover was too close. Twice the peregrine made her point too high in the heavens, and when she stooped all but impaled herself on the berry bushes where her quarry had sought refuge. Kaspar swung his "lure," a bundle of feathers on a cord, and brought the peregrine back to fist. Then, when another partridge was put up, he hurled the falcon at it, as some ostringers hurl their lowly goshawks.

The peregrine bound to the quarry and killed it, to the surprise and satisfaction of the onlookers. But both falcon and falconer went back to the *Pigeon,* ruffled and a little ashamed at so ignoble a feat.

Later in the week they arrived at a real settlement, in fact a village, Esopus, on the west bank of the river. First a gap in the forest where farm land had been cleared right down to the water's edge. Then canoes appeared, some drawn up on dry land, others still loaded and in the water. A wide creek opened out; the skipper considered running up it, then, uncertain of the force of the current, nosed the *Pigeon* into a rough wharf of stone-filled cribbing, and dropped sail.

Falcon on wrist, Kaspar leaped to the jetty, made fast the mooring line; and thought best to make himself scarce before the captain called on him to help in unloading. He was growing tired of the man and his everlasting knitting and surliness. A little toil might improve his disposition. A muddy path zigzagged up the bank. It must lead somewhere; probably a short cut to wherever the broader wagon trail came out.

As he climbed to higher ground he could see more and more canoes, and a few white man's boats, square boxlike affairs of sawn planking, farther up the creek. Farm boats, just as he had known them back home; only here it was a river, not a canal, down which would float haystacks, cattle, and bundled corn in season. A high stockade, like the one at the Manhatens, with a narrow gateway just wide enough for an oxcart. A few Indians, even a woman with her child, squatted or lounged in the spring sunlight against the log walls; and from inside came a buzz of voices, merchants calling their wares, the high yapping of a dog turning to a snarl, even the grunting of pigs. If this wasn't a main market day, at least a market was in progress, and a busy one at that. But first, to give the falcon her much-needed flight.

Around the corner of the palisaded defenses, and yes, there was a fine stretch of open ground. Garden land nearto, bare fields with only the stubble of last year's corn showing above the snow-bleached earth, and beyond, divided by fences of torn-up tree roots, but stretching right out a halfmile or so to the dark rim of the forest, was grazing land. There'd be game of some kind sheltering under those fences.

But—and it was a big but—what to do about the straying livestock? The cattle would be safe enough, and so would the few small pigs rooting around in the stubble; and even the squawking, high-stepping geese. But could even the best trained falcon, puzzled by the many strange birds in a strange land, be trusted within sight of that hen, clucking along with her half-grown brood?

Reluctantly he turned back. Well, at least he could walk his bird through the market. A haggard in particular, not being reared in captivity, needed constant association with humans if she wasn't to revert to her wild ways and go manshy.

An ox sled lurching out of the gate, bound no doubt for the waterside to pick up the *Pigeon's* goods, suggested that Kaspar still had plenty of time to look around. The market place was worth a visit; quite unlike anything he had seen before. No stalls of sweetmeats and trinkets, of cooked goods and butter and cheeses; in fact almost no stalls at all. Indians, almost bare except for a breechclout and sometimes a tattered blanket thrown over one shoulder, sat or stood on the muddy ground before bundles of skins. With seeming reluctance they untied the bark ropes and let a white man, squatting on his heels, examine the pelts. Duffel, a coarse Netherland cloth woven for this trade and dyed a gay red and blue, seemed the main article of exchange for the beavers; blankets, small ax heads, knives, iron cooking pots of a shape outmoded in Amsterdam, stood in little piles to be bargained for. Dogs, pigs and children wove in and out of the dense and odorous throng.

Sometimes it was an Indian who gravely retied his bundle and sought another settler who might give better prices; sometimes, and more often, it was the white man who moved on to appraise another set of pelts. But what a strange mixture of "prime blanket," the best and biggest beavers, and small pelts that could scarcely be called "halves," and to judge by the dark marks on shoulder and rump, must have been trapped or killed early last autumn, before the beasts had their full winter coat.

Some, and of those a few that might have been the best and most valuable skins, had been smoke-dried and almost ruined. Kaspar bent down to examine more closely, and an Indian, his dark eyes on the strange bird on the white man's wrist, offered no objection.

Yes, there were pelts caught so early that there were little more than guard hairs on the underside; the soft undercoat grown to keep the beast warm in the winter had scarce begun to thicken. He ran a fingernail along another one; that was better, perhaps a December trapping. But heavens above, caught in proper season and reasonably well prepared, just this one bundle would be worth five times what it would fetch in its present state. Sheer wanton waste. It was to check on this, perhaps, and get better value for the patroonship money, that the patroon had wanted him to come to the new country.

Moving on, from group to group, Kaspar began to get a better understanding of this local trade. Hard it was to believe, but he saw with his own eyes, a white trader holding a musket upright on the ground while the Indian piled beavers up beside it. Neither seemed concerned for the quality of the skins, or perhaps even the size. As soon as the height of the piled pelts reached the muzzle of the musket—and it was an extra long-barreled musket—the white man placed one hand on the pile of skins, the Indian one hand on the musket, and the white man's two hands steadied the pile of skins. Someone had been cheated, but which one it was hard to say.

Beaver and otter and marten and even fox pelts were there. A pity he couldn't understand the language. For often, when he squatted to judge a pelt, the Indian would grunt out a few words. Here, for instance, was a magnificent marten, really unusual in size, silkiness and color. If only he could explain to its owner its real value, and how even more valuable it would have been if caught a month later.

Then a large hand slapped him on the back. He would know that hand anywhere! Gideon Dolph exclaimed, "The Indian asks, 'How many skins for your bird?' "

"Tell him it's not for sale," said Kaspar.

Gideon said something, then added in Netherlands speech, "They'll buy just anything, if it strikes their fancy, from a shining pewter button to a hat buckle. Like to see some fun?"

The joke wasn't obvious at first. All the boslooper did was to stand behind a white trader and, unseen by him, make signs with his hand. The trader, who spoke the Indian tongue, was, quite obviously and as all traders do, disparaging the wares he wanted to purchase. Then Kaspar saw the Indian look up, and a flicker of interest pass across his old and wrinkled countenance.

Gideon leaned his firearm against his chest, and now both his hands began to talk as they had to the Maquas in their canoe. In flying signs that seemed to flow rapidly one into the next, as words flow into a sentence, the boslooper was telling the Indian something.

The red man dropped his eyes to the trader, muttered a few words through barely opened lips. The trader's voice rose angrily; the Indian must have demanded more.

The trader untied a roll of duffel, tugged it this way and that to show its strength and made to cut off a length. The Indian tied up his skins, shrugged and stalked away.

Gideon, grinning, had moved away first, still unseen by the trader.

Five times that happened. Each time, just as the bargain was being closed, Gideon's sign language seemed to break up the deal. Each time too, in a most casual way possible, he chanced upon the Indian a moment later, talked with him a few sentences in ordinary speech, and brought in that word "Susskooks" and "Manhatens."

Then he was caught at his game. A man he had already thwarted spotted him spoiling the sale of another trader. Kaspar saw trouble coming and decided to keep out of it after all it was Gideon's joke, not his. He made for the gate, leaned casually against the stockade, and taking a goose feather from his pocket, began to stroke the falcon.

Gideon was still grinning broadly when a knot of angry citizens, too awed by his proportions and knife and hunting ax to manhandle him, hustled him to the gate and warned him in good strong Netherland speech never to come back.

"But what was it you told the Indians?" Kaspar asked when he had caught up with him on the path down to the creek.

"Oh, different things. Like praising up their pelts. And saying that the 'white man's skins,' that duffel stuff, had been made out of season, and wasn't a prime pelt, nor likely to last. And of course advising them where they'd get a better bargain down-river."

It was with a feeling of relief that Kaspar, falcon still safe on fist, dropped aboard the *Pigeon*. The boslooper's joke then had purpose as well as humor to it. This new country seemed to breed new ways, and new notions of right and wrong. If Gideon had played that trick in Amsterdam, or anything like it, he would have been hauled before the city magistrates and fined for spoiling other merchants' trade.

The incident was as puzzling to a newcomer as the trick of Wouter Fries's. Had Wouter's claim of debt been no more than a clumsy sort of joke to amuse his two friends at the expense of a simple homelander? At the time it had seemed more serious than that. But after all it was the only possible explanation, humiliating as it was to think of how he had fallen for the trick, and bolted out of the town to escape the law, while Wouter and his friends ate the good dinner promised to Kaspar, and laughed themselves sick at his expense.

Well, if a newcomer had to learn new ideas of what was funny, as well as all the other new ways, he'd best start in early, and save himself a lot of trouble. This very evening he would find out more about the boslooper's joke.

After the evening meal he had his curiosity satisfied, though not in the way he had expected.

"Here in this land a man must fight for himself," explained the boslooper, looking anything but pugnacious: belt unbuckled, weapons laid aside, his short wooden pipe stuck in the middle of his large, amiable face.

"Settlers complain that I spoil their trade, because I go out into the woods where they are afraid to go. Every few

years they pass more laws; laws to stop me and people like
me from earning a living. And always when I bring my skins
to the Manhatens they make trouble. So-o, two can play at
that game. When the Indians bring in their furs to the settlers, I too can make trouble, praising the skins to the Indians, setting a higher value on them, and advising the
Indians to take them elsewhere, where they will not be
cheated. Ho, ho, ho! When it comes to Indians, Gideon
Dolph is no man's fool."

So that was it? It did seem to make it rather fairer.

More days passed. But still the magic of the river grew,
even though the river itself shrank to half its width and its
banks became flatter and less imposing. The sea could be
frightening with its fury that tore down sea walls and flooded
pasture land, that tossed sailors from the rigging, swept
crates and livestock overboard and sometimes sent the ship
down after them, but the slow purposeful flow of this giant
fresh-water tide was to Kaspar more impressive. It was the
difference between a maniac wasting his strength in pointless
destruction, and a giant concentrating his force to a steady
endeavor; the difference between the fierce bears of which
Gideon spoke, and a friendly team of oxen steadily drawing
a plow for the benefit of mankind.

"Where did it come from?" Kaspar asked the captain. Unwillingly as a man whose words were coined gold he spared
few. "From Beverwyck. Beyond, maybe. How should I
know?" The boslooper more willingly told what he knew, but
it wasn't much. Somewhere just north of Beverwyck, which
seemed to be the West India Company's settlement close to
Rensselaerswyck, which belonged to the patroonship, the
river divided into two. One branch came from the west, the
other north. But no white man, unless it was the French from
the St. Lawrence River to the north, had seen where this
southern river had its source.

Bog-running, skimming the river's muddy shores, in pursuit of the falcon and her quarry, and floating over its smooth

expanse the rest of the day, Kaspar began to accept the river as his friend. A friend which, if need be, could support whole communities along its banks on no more than what its waters and the air above it offered in food. If a man wanted grain, so Gideon said, there was wild rice to be harvested in season by beating the stalks over a canoe with paddles. And greenstuffs and roots for people who liked such truck, and couldn't be content with fish flesh and fowl.

But later he was to see the same river as a destructive enemy.

The nights were colder; it would have been clear, even without sun or stars. They were traveling north, almost due north. No longer were the banks fringed with green and with early spring flowers. Snow still lingered in the hollows, and here and there along the edge of the river, ice crusted the pools. Now Kaspar found himself growing impatient to reach his goal, and was not sorry when the captain announced one evening:

"Tomorrow, unless the wind fails, we reach Beverwyck."

Nosing his craft around in the semidarkness, standing upright beside the tiller the better to search for an island safe from his haunting dread of Indians, the captain gave a sudden exclamation.

Gideon and Kaspar, sitting low down among the cargo talking furs while Kaspar stroked the falcon, had noticed nothing. Nor had the dull-witted boy bending over his evening kitchen.

"A fire!" The captain pointed to the right bank. "It is Wolfert's farm ablaze. Those murdering Maquas!" And as he spoke, the blaze increased.

Gideon jumped to his feet, buckling his belt, slinging on powderhorn and bullet bag. "Wolfert's farm ought to be farther upstream, but we'd best go see. Might be someone in trouble. Hi, what're you doing there? Set the boat closer inshore!"

But the captain had no such intention. "Yes, of course you are right Mynheer! Wolfert's place must be many leagues

from here." Too dark to see the captain's face, but his
quavering voice betrayed his fear. "Yes, of course; and Wolfert, the good man, has by now eaten his supper and stretched
his feet before his own hearth. No need to go closer and perhaps run aground."

Gideon wasted no words. A push from his big hand and
the captain fell forward among the cargo. The tiller swung
over and the *Pigeon* headed for shore. Good for the boslooper! He might play tricks on fellow traders, and even
help the Indians against them, but if a white man was in
danger, no fear of Indians would make Gideon Dolph cower
in safety in midstream.

The captain was protesting, that Wolfert was already
killed; that Wolfert's farm lay far upstream; that they
would all be killed too, and tortured . . .

Kaspar scarce heard the craven appeal. He felt for his
knife. That would be his only weapon; the falcon would have
to stay aboard. He bent down and made sure that she was
secure, and hooded her for greater safety. A shiver of fear
crept down his backbone. The captain couldn't be more
scared than he was himself. Terrible tales of Indian cruelties
had been carried to the homeland; perhaps even now they
had this lonely settler tied to a tree and were burning him
inch by inch by the light of his blazing homestead.

He could imagine the dark shore swarming with stealthy
cruel shadows, perhaps waiting for this white man's boat and
its plunder to be attracted by the blaze, like moths to candlelight. But fear didn't matter, unless you let it stop you. Fear
was as natural as hunger and thirst. If Gideon Dolph should
go ashore, he would not go alone.

Suspense grew as the stretch of invisible water narrowed.
Neatly the big man headed the *Pigeon* up into the wind, just
as the murmur under the keel told that the boat was about
to ground. Then overboard, sinking nearly waist-deep and
gasping with the cold. Then onto a rock. Then leaping lightly
across a quivering flat of mud and last year's reeds.

Then fumbling for handhold up a steep bank, Kaspar felt the hackles on his neck smooth out a little. So far no Indian tomahawk had cloven through his skull; no yell of fury had rent the night air. Gideon Dolph, a strange silhouette with the powderhorn still held between his teeth, was running with bent-kneed, woodsman's lope beside him. No hope of help from the captain, of course.

"There isn't a clearing here, or any building." Gideon had dropped the powderhorn from his teeth, now they were clear of the water. "But there's the fire." His voice became less cautious.

They slowed to a walk. Stopped. Then had to retreat before the blaze.

"Just burning undergrowth and last year's leaves," came the boslooper's disgusted tones. "Look, there was another fire farther up the hillside."

A few minutes cautious circling; and it was not too comfortable outlined like this against the blaze, an easy target for a twanging arrow. From upwind they could look across to the far side of the fire. But there was no trace of any farm; only the tall trunks of the forest reaching out of the smoking ground to their bare wintry boughs far overhead.

"Who could have started the fires?" It seemed safe now for Kaspar to speak in natural tones.

"Mahicans, likely enough; though up here the Maquas too claim hunting rights. They do their spring burning so as to have no underbrush to hide the game, or crackle beneath their feet. The Indian isn't as improvident and hand-to-mouth as white folk will try to tell you."

Well, that all seemed a little flat after being keyed up to meet certain danger and possible death. Nothing to do but retrace your way to the *Pigeon*; with a slight shakiness of the knees, now the excitement and danger allowed you to feel it. And a dryness of the mouth too, though that might be from the heat of the fire.

Down to the shore line again, to peer across, and bending

low, try to outline the yawl's sails against the lighter sky. It began to look as if white people could be improvident too, and in their haste to rescue an imaginary settler forget to provide a safe retreat for themselves. Not a sign of the *Pigeon* anywhere. Kaspar ran out on the mud flats, covering a wide circle, not daring to stop lest he sink and be swallowed up. Covered another circle. But no *Pigeon* in sight.

Gideon hailed. "Hi there!"

No answering sound floated back over the dark waters. Only the croak of a frog, and the rustle of some night bird in the swamp. A fog was rising, beginning to blur out lines of river and sky.

The two joined up again. "That skipper may be over to the far bank by now, or lickin' downstream to spread an alarm of an Indian raid," came Gideon's disgusted tones. "I'll try a shot though, just in case he's waiting offshore for us."

The flash of the gun and the roar of its heavy charge, then the sweet, brimstoney smell of the gunpowder. The echoes died, and the same damp, heavy darkness and silence reigned —except for the crackles and occasional explosion of the fire behind them, and the red glare reflected upon smoke and fog above the treetops.

"If the shot calls up the Indians who started the brush fire, what then?" asked Kaspar. In this strange new life it was best to be prepared beforehand, so as to avoid what might prove to be a deadly mistake.

"Ask 'em if they've got a canoe hidden hereabouts. Then take a pine torch and go looking for Mynheer Skipper! And nigh to scare the breeches off him."

It didn't quite work out that way. For the shot fired on the flats probably went unheard, masked by the high bank and imitated by the roar and poppings in the fire. Anyway no Indians came.

Kaspar found the *Pigeon* at last, a good quarter-mile downstream, aground, stern on. The skipper, candle lantern in hand, was cursing in a low, frightened whisper and fran-

tically splashing around, trying to find a channel through
which to float off. Without letting himself be seen Kaspar
went back and summoned Gideon.

"Minded I am to pound the skipper's head on his own
wooden shoes," said Gideon furiously.

And the captain would deserve it, and more! First the
surly coward had been willing to abandon, as he thought,
this Wolfert to his fate. And when Gideon had prevented
him, he had again put his own safety first. If there had been
Indians, as he must have thought there were, his running
away with the *Pigeon* would have cut off the boslooper and
Kaspar's one hope of escape. If the boslooper pounded a little
decency into him, Kaspar would not object!

But as he led the way downstream he had a better idea.
When they got nearly opposite the boat, he whispered.
"There she is. There's the light. Wait here, or I won't find
my boots and breeches again."

He peeled them off, sodden wet, set them under a stone on
the bank, and slid off into the darkness.

Yes, he had guessed right. Downstream of the *Pigeon* the
water shoaled. If you kept moving so as not to sink into
the icy mud, you could swing out, far beyond the *Pigeon*. At
the farthest extremity, he let out a wailing sound, faint as if
it came from a long way off. It was all guesswork; an Indian
call might sound like that in the distance, or it might not. But
anyway, the chances were that the captain wouldn't know.

Back almost to where he had started on the bank, to make
the call again. Then back and forth, through mud and shallow water, drawing closer to the *Pigeon,* and giving the
grunting sounds with which the Mahicans in the market place
had seemed to converse.

The captain's candlelight suddenly vanished, as if blown
out in a panic. Kaspar swung in a shorter semicircle, drawing
closer and closer to the boat. The splash of his feet might
easily be mistaken for the approach of canoe paddles.

Then back to Gideon, to haul on his breeches and boots.

Gideon smote him delightedly on the back. " 'Twas you, I reckoned. But if I hadn't guessed it, I might have been worried. What next, boy?"

"We just get off by the skin of our teeth. And there's a whole Mahican war party behind!"

Gideon started to laugh, then turned the guffaw into an eerie falsetto scream that set Kaspar's teeth on edge. "Well, this bank is colder than an ice cake. Let's get started."

There was no longer need for silence, in fact the more they splashed, the more frightened they would seem. They waded and ran, stumbling to the dark outlines of the *Pigeon*.

"It's us, Captain," quavered Gideon Dolph. "Don't shoot. Keep your powder and ball for them red devils."

"Cast off, or we'll all be killed!" said Kaspar, choking down his laughter and producing a good effect of tremulous fear. "There's not a moment to lose."

"If we're going to save our scalps," Gideon supplemented.

"I can't shove off. We're aground," squawked the captain.

Gideon sounded resigned to the worst. "Then all we can do is wait for the end."

"Or try to swim downstream?" suggested Kaspar.

"No, no. They're all around there. Fifty. A hundred," the captain cautioned him. "I hear their voices, I hear their canoes. Stay here with me; don't leave me. And the good Wolfert, is he dead?"

Kaspar was prepared for that, had been holding his already chilly hand overboard, in the ice cold waters. He could just see the captain's outlines as he drew in his hand. "Here's all I could bring away." With his left hand he spread out the captain's fingers and stiffening the chilly fingers of his right hand dropped them into the reluctant palm.

He withdrew it again, at the captain's gasp, and bent as if to pick it up from the deck.

"We'd best keep watch," Gideon suggested. "Not that it'll do any good. They may attack now, or hold off till dawn. No telling."

But in the darkness Kaspar noted that the boslooper was crawling under the tarred canvas; he himself was just about frozen. Chuckling, he saw to the needs of the falcon and made himself comfortable; chuckled still more pleasurably when his outstretched legs encountered the warmth of the dry but cowering boy; and five minutes later hoped, with a grin, that when he fell asleep he wouldn't snore so loudly as Gideon, for fear the captain, straining his terrified eyes into the darkness, might hear.

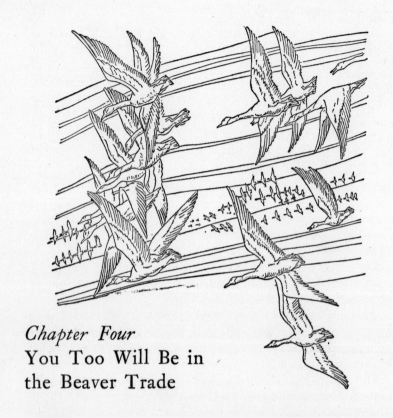

Chapter Four
You Too Will Be in
the Beaver Trade

WITH GRAY DAYLIGHT, Kaspar, rubbing his eyes to improve their vision, found it was fog and not his eyes that were at fault. Fog which hid the near-by bank and the top of the stubby mainmast forward. It turned the water into a steaming cauldron whose contact seemed to burn the flesh, till the mind corrected the false impression and decided that it was chill, not heat, that caused the brief shock of pain.

The fog could have concealed a multitude of murderous redskins, but the captain's resentful glance raked Kaspar and the boslooper, as they emerged from their crannies un-

der the tarred canvas. A red-eyed, weary and resentful captain, after his night's vigil, who seemed disposed to blame
his passengers for everything from his running aground last
night to this morning's fog.

Gideon wasted no pity on the man. "Next time, skipper,
you may be willing to help a fellow white man, even if he
needs no help. You may need help yourself someday. Now
how about getting on to Beverwyck?"

Sulkily the two sails creaked up, as if they shared the
captain's discontent. They hung dripping and powerless for
lack of breeze. The captain's son hauled in the killick, the
stone weight, which served as anchor. Still the boat hung
there, between invisible shores and upon all but invisible
water.

The captain dropped sail. "We wait," he announced.

"No need to," Kaspar suggested. "There's three feet of
water just astern, I found it last night."

Stripping stark naked he slid overboard and gasped with
the chill. The boslooper followed. Rocking the sloop, one at
each gunwale, they broke her out, let the current help push
her astern until she floated once more.

The dawn breeze rose; they scrambled aboard again,
washed clinging mud from feet and legs, and to warm themselves hoisted sail. Then demanded and got some breakfast
to still the chattering of their teeth.

Back into his still damp but comforting clothes, Kaspar
eyed the clammy river fog with impatient disgust. Somewhere behind that dank curtain lay Fort Orange and Beverwyck; he could hear the faint distant crowing of cocks. So
near to the end of his long journey and all the new sights he
was aching to see; to be brought in, as it were blindfolded,
seemed unfair, unreasonable. But food at least was warming,
and with the freshening of the morning breeze the mist
lifted at last. There, gleaming in the sun, were thatched roofs
of the village of Beverwyck behind the pointed logs of the
stockade; and high on the hill behind the wall, the timbered

fort itself. Blue smoke curled cheerfully from many chim-
neys, the windmill's sails turned slowly, a cow lowed, there
echoed the homely tinkle of cattle bells, and from the less
inhabited east bank, over in Greenbos, came the intermittent
growling of a water-driven saw.

Gideon straightened up and tapped out his pipe. "Well,
boy, I'll be leaving you. Skipper, put me ashore in Greenbos."

The captain, rumpled and depressed after his night's false
alarm, seemed, now he knew himself to be safe, almost to
resent that his scalp hadn't been lifted. He was more than
willing to be rid of the boslooper. Obediently he put the
tiller over. The *Pigeon* came up beside the steep mud bank.
The boslooper clapped Kaspar a resounding slap on the back,
slung a deerskin bundle over his musket, leaped, clutched
ground, and started off up the trail. The *Pigeon* had gone
only a few yards from the shore before he vanished into
the darkness of the trees.

The boat seemed empty with Gideon gone. It wasn't just
his great bulk, but his cheerful puzzling character that Kaspar missed. Puzzling because, though he spoke of Amsterdam as his home town, he seemed strangely ignorant of it.
Puzzling in his simple contempt for the rich comfortable
burghers who lived safely behind stockades. He sounded
sorry for them, at times, as if the town defenses were their
prison bars. He seemed to have no wife, no family, no house,
no money, no debts, and no desire for most of the things for
which people lived and toiled. His was a sort of freedom
unknown in the homeland. Yes, quite a puzzle.

On the Beverwyck water front a number of men, with
ropes and a team of oxen to lift a heavy wooden pile driver,
were making good the winter's damage to the stockade. The
jetty, the twin of the one at Esopus, had also been damaged,
either by ice or flood, the end twisted off and the rest badly
out of alignment. But men came running down it, unmoored
a sailing scow and eased her downstream to make room for
the *Pigeon*. If the skipper's fear of Indians last night had run

him on the mudbank, at least, Kaspar noted, he showed sufficient skill this morning. It could have been no easy matter, with the river so high and its current so strong, to come up under the lee of the stone-packed wooden cribbing, drop sail and glide gently up, so that scarcely an egg would have been cracked between bow and jetty.

They had a hand-winch here, overhanging the water; but no one bothered to use it, since the gunwales of the *Pigeon* stood nearly level with the decking of the jetty. Goods were handed overboard; someone signed a receipt. The captain bargained for a return load in a day's time, and in half an hour they were off again.

Kaspar felt a curious sense of excitement, coupled with a twinge of apprehension. For now they were on the last mile of the long, long voyage, and the roof of the director's house, which had been pointed out to him from the jetty, was clearly in sight. When you have torn up your roots, when you have left every friend and familiar sight behind you, and come to a new world, utterly strange and almost unbelievable, it seems only reasonable to worry a little.

So much depended upon the director of the patroonship. Supposing after all, Jeremias van Rensselaer should feel that he had no need for a fur expert? Supposing he should choose to resent and ignore the letter of the patroon, his brother, back there in Amsterdam? Kaspar cast back in his mind, not for the first time, and tried to remember Jeremias as he used to be at home in Cralo. Was he like Johannes, the present patroon? Probably not, since they had had different mothers. More like Jan Baptiste, who had been director over here a few years ago. But all Kaspar could recall of Mynheer Jeremias, were three brief pictures. A young man amusing himself with an ancient and outmoded crossbow. Another, of that same young man recklessly galloping a black stallion across new-sown fields. Kaspar's father had complained to Mynheer Kiliaen of the damage to the future crops, and Kiliaen had prohibited his son for six months from any rid-

ing whatsoever. Later a brief glimpse of him passing the
furrier's booth where Kaspar was apprenticed. But none of
these pictures told anything.

The three-story building came into view; disappointingly
small it was, and unpretentious. The first floor was of stone,
half below ground level. The second was of good brick, with
an entrance onto a side hill; but its three heavily shuttered,
deep-set windows that faced south, and the four that faced
east, gave it pleasant proportions and an air of dignity. From
the gable-end just above the mooring place dangled the usual
pulley, in order that heavy goods might be hoisted for
storage in the attic.

As the *Pigeon* drew closer, a long lean black man saun-
tered out from the lower floor, then strolled back inside. A
moment later he returned at a smarter pace, this time followed by a white man. The white man hailed the *Pigeon* by
name—near enough now so Kaspar could appraise him.

So this was Jeremias van Rensselaer, this short, rather
plump, softish man, his full baggy breeches and slashed
doublet a little shabby and outmoded, a crease of worry between his brows. But when he spoke it was as if Kiliaen
spoke again; for a moment Kaspar felt a return of that awe
and admiration he had had.

"Cast your line, Skipper! Andries, make the *Pigeon* fast
to that bollard. Quick, man, before she drifts downstream
away from you!"

Kaspar threw his own goods ashore, a little apart from
the rest, perched the falcon atop them, and lent a willing
hand with the remainder of the cargo. Mynheer Jeremias,
checking the goods as they were passed from the yawl against
a list that the captain had given him, paid Kaspar no attention. Then a middle-aged man, blond, sturdy, square and a
farmer to judge by his boots, rode up on an unsaddled horse,
with a coil of rope over his shoulder. He dismounted, hitched
the horse, entered the house and a moment later flung open
the third-story door in the gable.

He rove the line through a pulley and dropped the two ends, then tossed down a square of rope netting. Andries, the Negro, hitched one end of the rope to the horse and stood waiting. Kaspar grinned to himself; Andries looked as if he would be good at just waiting.

Kaspar spread out the net, laid a few bundles on it, brought up the corners and tied them to the rope and lifted his hand as signal to hoist away. Deftly, the man inside the attic swung the load inward; a pause while he unloaded and Andries led back the horse to slack the rope. Then a simple repetition of the same three simple actions went on for the next half-hour. It then reversed itself, and bundles of beaver were swung from the attic window and loaded into the *Pigeon*.

But the loading of the *Pigeon* did not take place until Jeremias himself had taken the skipper to task for the dampness of the loads he had brought upstream, had set the captain's boy to bailing and wiping out, and strictly bidden the skipper to put into shore at some convenient place and cut himself some fresh dunnage to lay under the skins and protect them from the wet floor boards. Kaspar approved of that; damp skins would never survive the long sea voyage, especially with summer coming on.

Van Rensselaer handed over a package of letters, saying, "See that these are put directly into the hands of Mynheer van Cortlandt." And the *Pigeon* cast off.

Kaspar stooped to rub some dirt from his hands on a tussock of last year's brown grass. All this way, from Cralo to Amsterdam, from Amsterdam to the Texel, from the Texel to the Manhatens, and now from the Manhatens to Rensselaerswyck. It seemed almost impossible to believe that the long voyage was ended and that at last he was here.

"Well, boy?" Jeremias voice startled him back to the present and the jetty. "I thank you for your help; but do you intend to swim to the boat?"

Now was the moment. Kaspar opened his bundle and took out his letter from the patroon.

"M-hah." Jeremias read it, the crease of worry deepening between his eyebrows. He gave Kaspar a keen, shortsighted stare. "So you are the son of old Adam de Selle? Welcome on that account. At Cralo I should have recognized you. Out here I scarce expected you, so you must condone my mistake. But what we want with a furrier here in Rensselaerswyck, Heaven only knows!" He went on reading the letter.

When he refolded it he stood for a moment in thought. "If my good brother would condescend to ship to us what is needed, and not what he thinks is needed, the colony would better thrive," he remarked with some bitterness. "Well, 'tis no fault of yours, boy. The contract is made, I see, and we will abide by it the best we may. Here, Andries . . ."

The Negro seemed to wake from a deep sleep and approached at a dragging pace. "Help Kaspar de Selle with his bundles and show him where he may wash. He will dine with me this noon."

"Come," said Andries, and with a neat turn of speed possessed himself of the lighter of the two bundles.

Down in the stone kitchen the Negro set out a bowl of water and a gourd of soft soap, his eyes never leaving the falcon. "What for, the bird? He talk?" he asked.

Kaspar, luxuriating in the warm water and soap, and a real towel, grinned amiably. "No, it doesn't talk. And it's a she, anyway."

"Lay eggs. Leetle, leetle eggs?"

Kaspar sluiced down his arms and tossed the water out the back door. "She catches ducks, herons, pigeons, rabbits. Maybe she'll even be able to kill a wild goose."

The Negro seemed to appreciate that. "And fly with them right home?"

"Well, no. You have to run after her, and pick up the bird where she's killed it."

Slowly Andries shook his head and completely lost interest. Perhaps it was the thought of running that was so discouraging.

As Kaspar climbed the steep stairs to the second story he wondered at the roughness of the bachelor home of the director of the patroonship. Compared to the elegance and style in which his brother, the patroon, lived in Amsterdam, this place was even crude. The kitchen below had a damp mud floor, three smoke-grimed windows almost level with the ground outside, and a hollow in the lowest corner, with a gourd and a bucket for bailing it out like a boat. Arranged round the stone walls were less than half the gleaming copper utensils that a housewife would consider necessary.

The second floor was almost as disappointing when Kaspar set foot in it. The large room, which occupied all the second floor, except for a small room partitioned off for a bedroom at the back, held a few comforts, but little luxury. A fireplace of brick decorated with tiles from the homeland, several finely carved chairs that had suffered from too much voyaging, and, on the clean polished floor, two good carpets. Kaspar recognized the huge mirror at the end of the room as being of Italian make; but it was strange to see, scattered among these, several backless benches of raw lumber and a long trestle table of local craftsmanship without carving or embellishment. But there was no need of oil paintings on the walls when through the eight volkosynen windows one was always conscious of the sweep of the mighty river and of the blue mountains to the east.

The meal, when it came, was as simple and as ample as that of any farmhouse; a beef stew, followed by partridge roasted on a spit and served with the good Beverwyck beer of which Kaspar had heard even Gideon speak with enthusiasm. The director, while he chatted of the home country and demanded news of Cralo, drank from glassware, cut up his meat on a shining blue plate of Delftware, and settled his digestion with a thimbleful of imported cordial.

Dinner was barely over when a thin, querulous-faced man, garbed in black as somber as a pastor's, limped hurriedly up the steep stairs, made his bow to the director, and, waiting only to be bidden, helped himself generously to the now cooling meal. His clever, restless, light eyes flicked a glance at Kaspar and returned again as if to reconsider or amplify his first opinion.

"Well, Nicholas," Mynheer Jeremias spoke impatiently, "if you have brought skins, they are too tardy to be shipped. The *Pigeon* has already sailed. What news of Schenectade?"

Deferentially Nicholas set down his knife before replying.

"With your permission, Mynheer Director, not good, not good. There are more buyers than beavers; even now, at the most favorable time of the year. And the prices . . ." He turned his eyes to heaven. "Terrible, terrible!"

Jeremias frowned unhappily. "Each year the trade seems to grow worse. The Company can overbid us, since each one of our skins must pay its five per cent duty to the Company."

". . . and the fur smugglers, Mynheer Director, they grow ever more brazen; not even the Company can restrain them. They scour the country, making their deals deep in Indian country where no honest man would dare to penetrate. Under cover of night they run their goods down the river, doubtless piloted past the shoals and other dangers by the Devil himself."

This was interesting. Fur smugglers? . . . it was the first Kaspar had heard of them. The West India Company was of course the government of the whole of New Netherlands, and under orders from the States General at home; and the patroon was more like a large estate owner of the olden times, with power to make certain minor laws for his tenants and hold courts of law for small debts and petty offenses. But the fur trade belonged to the Company, and it seemed they had the right to tax all trade, even from the patroonship.

"And from where do they ship these illegal skins? Have you discovered that, Nicholas?"

"Who can say!" Nicholas' light eyes again rolled ceilingward. "Perhaps from somewhere down the river they carry them overland to the wicked English."

"M-h-n." Jeremias van Rensselaer sounded doubtful. Even to Kaspar it seemed that a long overland journey, over rough and dangerous country, might eat badly into the profits.

Then followed some talk of farm buildings needing repair, of overdue rents owing to the patroonship which had too long gone unpaid, of the tenants pleading that they had no means to pay and, if pressed, would be forced entirely to abandon their farms. That sounded strange to Kaspar's ears. In the old country a landlord often threatened to eject a tenant, but a tenant would scarcely threaten to desert his land, refuse to pay his debts and go elsewhere. The law would have something to say to him! Over here debtor and creditor seemed somehow to have swapped places.

Nicholas, the clerk or agent or whatever he was, had brought pelts back with him. The director bade him bring them up and list them.

"Kaspar de Selle here, the son of our farm manager at Cralo, will help you," he said. Then, as if he had never heard of Kaspar's training as an expert in furs, he went on to explain that the beavers must be sorted into three sizes, halves, kilderkins and wholes. And if there were any of extra size, these must be set apart.

Kaspar's first indignation melted into puzzlement; but if for some reason the director wanted him to appear unskilled, unskilled he would show himself.

So for the next half-hour, slowly and with a show of hesitation, he sorted, while Nicholas checked the list. Curious, how at first sight, and before there was any reason to, you liked the boslooper. And how, with no more reason, you found yourself disliking this pickle-faced clerk. Perhaps people's characters had a way of writing themselves on the lines of people's faces. But distrusting the man you worked with was no sort of way to start a new job. At least you could keep your attention on the job itself, and forget the clerk.

It was good to have your hands on pelts again, and silently, in your own mind, to grade them as they should be graded: by quality and season and how they had been cured. Twice, and only just in time, Kaspar stopped himself from professionally parting the fur with a thumbnail; most reluctantly he laid with the others, one that was beginning to smell and would certainly breed worms on the damp, warm, sea voyage.

The director, writing letters at a stand-up desk under the window, looked back occasionally at the work in progress and his eyes seemed to narrow a little, in calculation or amusement.

All very puzzling, and Kaspar was relieved when the ordeal ended.

Here was the time to make his present to the director. It was difficult to think of parting with the falcon. But later and if he kept her longer, it would grow so difficult as to seem impossible.

"Mynheer," he said, "I have brought with me the last bird from the Cralo mews." Fortunately he had his short speech all worked out, and so oft repeated, that after the first word the rest followed of themselves. "A haggard peregrine, she is, as beautiful in flight, as skilled and obedient, as any in the Netherlands. By the grace of your brother the patroon I was permitted to buy her. I have the bird below." He gulped. "She is yours, Mynheer, in slight return for the favors that my father's family have enjoyed from the family of Mynheer Kiliaen van Rensselaer." He drew a sigh of relief that he had got it out, all straight.

Jeremias set down his goose quill. "A noble present—and quite undeserved." The smile made his tired face look younger. "But a falcon is no barnyard fowl. She is the half of a team of falcon and falconer. One such peregrine I have already flown here, who for her brief life reigned queen of the New Netherland's skies. But she pined away, by my own fault, since with my many affairs I had too little time to fly her. No, the hawk is yours—and see that you do better by her than I was able."

So unexpected was this refusal, that it took Kaspar a moment to believe that he had heard aright, and that the peregrine was still his. His gift had been, not rejected, but graciously returned to him, and for the best of all possible reasons, for the sake of the falcon herself. He stood a moment, dumbly fumbling for words, for the proper show of gratitude, when Jeremias waved an impatient hand.

"A lady, even a falcon, should not be kept waiting. Get you down to the Flatts, boy, and find her a heron or a plover."

Kaspar almost fell down the steep stairs to where the falcon waited.

On with the heavy glove, and as he loosed the jesses the unhooded falcon leaped eagerly to his wrist and began to "bate," to bow and crouch in happy anticipation of the hunt to come. Then out past the astonished Andries in his kitchen, a quick glance at the lay of the land, and Kaspar broke into his easy, long-striding lope.

If from early childhood you have trained yourself to running, there comes the feeling of freedom as of a bird in flight as the legs swing into their stride, and the lungs, stretching under deep, easy breathing, send blood coursing through the veins. Without need of words or even conscious thought, Kaspar's mind considered the long flat western banks of the river, the bare pasture and sere plowland stretching south to the stockades of Beverwyck village, and the more rolling country inland, where small farm clearings ate into the deep pine woods and a few dejected cattle searched for browse or grazing. The sky was lowering, which as a rule meant that quarry would fly low.

The riverside was tempting, with its multitude of ducks and here and there a heron wading in a still backwater.

Almost at his feet a snipe got up from a marshy patch, threw itself into swift, tumbling zigzag flight, and was gone. No loss, for a bird so small was unworthy of a peregrine. As well fly her at a bumblebee.

Two plovers swung up, in flapping, round-winged haste.
The falcon marked them eagerly, but Kaspar reserved her
for a more certain kill. A plover is an acrobat whose turning
and tumbling can spoil the hardest stoop of any falcon. Mynheer van Rensselaer, who must have hawked this countryside
before his bird died, had counseled "heron." But the birds
either continued to wade solemnly in the shallows or, when
stirred to flight by a well-aimed stone, fanned their way with
disproportionately large wings almost touching the water,
across to drop their long legs into the marshes on the east
bank. Kaspar cast inland in a wide semicircle.

The forest land was of course too dangerous, for if the
falcon killed somewhere over the dense woods he would
never be able to follow her flight from below, or find the
quarry; which would mean that in a new place like this she
would not know where home lay. A curious humming noise,
like a swarm of bees, made him glance up. This, whatever it
was, had just cleared the hills on the east bank and looked
more like a cloud. Only no cloud could travel so fast, and
against the wind.

Birds of some sort, in incredible, stupendous numbers,
swift in flight as pigeons. By hemel they were pigeons!—
though like no pigeons he had ever seen. Not migrating, for
they were traveling from east to west. Just a flock, it seemed,
changing feeding grounds. But what a flock!

Low over the cannon of Fort Orange they swooped—they
must literally have darkened the place—then, changing their
mind, swung off again, to the southwest. Someone at the fort
let off a firearm and Kaspar saw a few bodies tumble to the
earth; there would be pigeon pie there for supper.

A glance from the falcon reminded him that he had been
too astounded to loose her. A partridge got up ahead of
him; the falcon's eye was on it even as she took the air. She
flew it down, struck prettily without towering or diving, all
within a couple of hundred paces. Without halting his run,
Kaspar scooped up the quarry, called the falcon to his wrist

and swung on. Two more partridges, killed in just the same
fashion, were tucked inside his shirt.

"This, my lady," he told the peregrine, "is more like rat-
catching than falconry. Let's get something really to stretch
your wings."

The chance didn't come at once. A few little birds bobbed
out of the dry grass; some larger ones, like the blackbird at
home, took clamorous refuge in thickets. A plunge down into
a deep gully and up the other side under the guns of the fort;
here was a deep-rutted trail which headed west and must go
to an outlying settlement, perhaps Schenectade that the boslooper spoke of. Swinging round on the far side of the stockaded village, he headed down toward the river where he
could still hear the pile driver striking its occasional thudding
blow.

Here were the usual plowland and grazing ground, the
usual clumps of still, leafless trees left perhaps for future
fuel supply, the usual domestic animals free to wander at
will until the first sowing, and of course a few ducks and
chickens. No hawking to be found here, that was obvious.
But the peregrine had cocked her head and was looking
brightly upward. Kaspar followed her pointing, but could see
nothing.

The first warning that reached his ears was a faint honk.
Then, far off and high, almost to the low clouds, he distin-
guished a long *V* coming from the south. With all these farm
birds fussing around, it was a risky gamble, but the peregrine's attention was on that distant and growing wedge of
gray, and once a good falcon "marked" she seldom changed
her purpose. 'Twas now or never, for the birds were coming
fast, and the falcon would need as much time as possible for
her climb.

He cast her up in a well-judged swing, then stood and
waited.

Nine hawks out of ten would have flown straight for that
flight of geese and given them warning. But not this one. Like

a bee leaving a hive, like a pigeon rising to take its bearings, she climbed the air in wide steep spirals. The approaching phalanx was darker; from the commander at the tip to the birds on each far flank it must have measured a quarter-mile, and the number of birds was beyond count, thousands, seemingly.

On, on it came—and now the falcon herself seemed to have disappeared. A sharp cry, surely an alarm signal. A speck had hurtled down from above; it shot through that approaching wedge as a musket ball through a sheet of paper.

Then the dot swung up again, by the force of its own dive, and struck once more.

That was puzzling. Seldom before had he seen her miss her first strike. Perhaps some system of defense within the phalanx had defeated her purpose. Straggling a little, as they shifted their line of flight, the geese edged off across the wide river. Kaspar almost danced on his feet in anxiety. Had these birds, each heavier and stronger by far than the falcon, learned some trick which they used against the eagles of their own country? Had they learned somehow to combine their forces? But if so, surely they wouldn't have been headed off.

No, there was the falcon again. And there, ahead of her, and a little above, since the falcon had lost height in her last dive, was the quarry she had cut out from the flock—heading north. Kaspar broke into a run, a real run this time, not a lazy swinging lope.

A split-rail fence, a root fence, a little wall of stone, a narrow stream—he took them lightly in his stride. Then the stockade, too high, loomed up ahead of him. But the southern gate was near at hand and open wide. Kaspar, his eyes still following the falcon, wove a swift way through four pipe-smoking arguing burghers, leaped a goat, took an ox sled blocking the gateway as he would take a bank or a fence, ducked to avoid a low limb of a tree, and shot like a scalded cat up one of the two main roads of the settlement.

At sight of the wildly flying figure, a group of children stopped their play. A dog took up the chase behind him, was joined by another; hens squawked and fluttered away in panic. A goat, bolting from the dogs, overturned a child in a doorway, whose frightened squalls added to the clamor. Kaspar scarce heard them. A road that seems empty enough to an idle stroller is a whole series of obstructions to one whose eyes are on two faint spots in the skies and whose speed allows little time for livestock or humans to part and let him through.

A mere touch of Kaspar's elbow spun a startled Netherlander twice around and all but caused him to collapse on his coattails in a puddle of mud. A woman flung open a window, possibly to empty slops into the street, took fright at what she saw beneath her, and began to scream, "Stop thief! Stop thief!"

Fortunately the northern wall of the stockade was now close at hand. Kaspar swung up the inside earthworks, grasped the top of a pointed post, and dropped over—a blind drop, and a long one at this point. But he slackened his knees, pitched forward, tucked his head under, rolled twice head-over-heels and picked himself up, none the worse.

Down into the deep ravine again, splashing across the kill at the bottom; up the other side. The small speck had caught up with the larger speck; was even with it, but high above. Now of a sudden the top speck flashed down. The two merged, and plunged on downward, growing larger, clearer, the falcon riding the goose down toward earth.

Now they whirled in the air, spinning over and over. The falcon drew clear; the big gander regained his balance, made a desperate effort to flap onward on his course—till the falcon struck again. This time Kaspar could even see a tuft of pale feathers float back and seem to hang in the air. He dodged a house that swung up in his path; paid so little heed to it, his attention on the birds, that he noted neither building nor Negro wide-eyed, with gaping mouth. It was undoubtedly Andries.

The gander and falcon were falling again; now more floating feathers were behind him. A good falconer uses the fall of feathers, with allowance for wind drift, to align his pursuit on where the quarry will fall. He distinctly heard a thud, somewhere ahead of him, but out of sight.

Kaspar's mind, without his telling it to, plotted the distance as if on a map. His legs crossed the map, measuring, not in numbers of paces but by the more subtle process of long practice, the distance he had gone on it. Now, but for obstacles, he could almost close his eyes, run to the exact spot, open his eyes, reach down and pick up the bird.

He was nearing the farmhouse now, and the closer to the house the higher grew the fences of stone or root. This one ahead was a combination; big rotted roots hauled up to top a piled stone wall. He dived for it, flung himself over—and pulled up with a jerk face to face, almost touching, a remarkably angry girl.

Not that he noticed her at the time, except as an obstruction. He dodged past her, picked up the falcon, praised her, made much of her. Then bent to examine the dead gander.

The girl stood watching him, her hands on her hips, her large, very black eyes snapping furiously. "The skies rain unpleasant things today," she remarked caustically. "First the corpse of a big noble goose—"

"Gander," corrected Kaspar.

"Goose," snapped the girl firmly. "Who should be soaring on her way—"

"Not soaring," said Kaspar, weighing the great bird pridefully in his hand. "Geese don't soar."

"—soaring on her peaceful way. And then a murderous hawk drops out of the skies—"

"She's really a falcon, a haggard peregrine."

"—hawk, and just like all the other hawks that try to catch our young chickens. And then from the same sky drops a long-legged oaf of an idle boy with nothing better to do than to kill poor harmless geese."

She was very pretty standing there, her capless black head held angrily high, her great long braids blowing out in the wind, and her skirts tugging like a sail.

"Just one gander—and Mynheer the director will enjoy the meat," said Kaspar and grinned at her. "Is this the Hoorn farm?"

"It is," she admitted, though reluctantly. "I'm Grita Hoorn. Oh, and you, I suppose, are Kaspar de Selle. And you're coming to live with us. I was afraid you might be." She looked him coolly up and down. "And I suppose you too will be in the beaver trade." She spoke as if 'twere something one should be ashamed of.

"I suppose so. After all, the beaver trade is the lifeblood of the patroonship. And even of all New Netherlands."

Chapter Five
Danger of
the Deep Forest

BEAVER TRAPPER INDEED! We've got enough trappers. Beavers will be the ruination of this country. Not the poor little defenseless creatures themselves, but the trade in their pelts. There, Isaak, finish your milk," Grita snapped at the small boy, "or you cannot hope to be a brave beaver trapper when you are a man grown!" And, immediately her quick smile begged forgiveness. Only—oh dear, it was going to be a pesky, vexing thing if Isaak got himself a spell of hero worship for this Kaspar de Selle!

The big kitchen, with its floor fresh-sanded over, its wide puncheon planks, its glow of well-polished pewter ranged on the dresser that Mathias had brought from the homeland, its plants blooming along the deep window sill, was warm with the breakfast fire, though outside the wind was rising and last night's rain had commenced again. Grita gave the fire a vigorous poke and shifted the crane impatiently.

Perhaps, she told herself, she was misjudging the stranger, newly arrived from the homeland, simply because she was wearied of this rain, rain, rain. Venting her ire upon him because she was tired of the lagging spring and the sodden, unworkable fields. Pleasant in his ways, he was, and in his appearance. He had helped Father with his chores, was good with the young ones, courteous to Mother. And now, instead of idling about the warm, dry kitchen had gone straight off to his duties at the director's house. Gone running too; not that that counted for much, as he seemed always to run instead of walk.

Nelle Hoorn, picking up the empty elm bowl and horn spoon from Kaspar's place, remarked: "I do not think that boy ate enough. And rushing off like that, right after his meal, because he thought the director would need him."

Grita snorted and snapped a long black pigtail briskly over her shoulder. "Maybe he thinks Mynheer Jeremias cannot purchase a beaver skin without his help!" 'Twas one thing to try to be fair to the boy, but quite another to find cause to pity him.

Catalina raised a milky mouth from the last dregs of pease porridge in the bowl. "Can we go visit the falcon and stroke her with a feather, the way Kaspar does?"

"Lift your sister down from her high chair, Lijntje. No, we can't stroke the falcon; Kaspar's taken her with him."

"I'm going to catch me a falcon when I grow up. And be a falconer." Isaak, plaiting a leather halter for the new calf, glanced up from where he sat by the hearth and nodded his dark head to confirm his decision. "And wear a horsehide glove. And carry the bird on my fist wherever I go." Touching with words of longing the things he wished to do.

"No, son, you will do nothing of the sort," Nelle came to Grita's aid; and, to Grita's way of thinking, none too soon. "There's no sense in such rushing about the country, such tearing of the clothes to ribbons and wearing out good shoe leather. You'll be a good honest Netherlander farmer, like your father and your grandfather before you. Yes, Mathias, what is it?"

The wooden klompen and heavy tread of Mathias Hoorn could be heard on the stones of the back entry. As soon as she saw his large, good-humored face set in those stern lines, Grita knew that something was wrong; something serious. Not once in half a year did the kindly father of the household allow himself to show anger.

"Isaak, my son, when you drove the cows into the barn last night did you count them over?"

Isaak's first expression was one of surprise, then his face crumpled in worry and concern. For a moment Grita feared he was going to burst into tears.

"Oh, Father, didn't I tell you, after I stopped to help Kaspar put up the perch for his bird?"

"So." Mathias looked less stern.

That falcon again; without the falcon poor Isaak would have run straight in to tell his father. Of course he would.

"Then, since yesterday, Rosey is missing. No, I do not think a bear; it is still early for bears. Nor that she has fallen into the river. Simply that she has calved. And now because of the carelessness of my son I must spend the morning searching for her. And the plow to be repaired, and a hundred other tasks which must be left unfinished."

Well, that was over. Father Mathias would say no more, not even if the cow was never found again. Isaak, though he had been careless, must not take it too much to heart, must not be left to brood and exaggerate his thoughtlessness into a gloomy sin.

"Can't we others go search for her, Father—Isaak and Catalina and I, instead of you? If Rosey has gone to the woods, the three of us can spread out and cover more ground." Grita offered the suggestion. If Isaak found the cow, he would feel that it atoned a little for his wrongdoing.

"So," said Mathias, and as usual left the decision to his wife.

Nelle pursed her lips doubtfully and paused, turning in the center of the kitchen, and Grita, always a little impatient, watched while she ceased her tasks to set her mind in motion for a slow, cautious consideration. One could even imagine what her serious plodding Dutch mind was telling her: There is Isaak's osier basket for the broody hen not yet ready. And children must be taught to complete the work to which they set their hands. And Catalina was to finish that last yard of wool cloth on the loom today. And Grita, a dozen things she should do, or they will not be done. Still, Mathias has the plow to repair, and without plowing is no corn, without corn we cannot eat.

"Yes," she decided, "you may go. But not my little Joan. As for the rest of you, hurry back, for absent hands finish no tasks. And a hands-turn left undone today grows to thrice the task upon the morrow."

Almost before the sentence was finished Grita had slipped her wool cloak from the peg, had tied on its hood, and paused to straighten the hood of Catalina's scarlet cape. She herded the two ahead of her through the short entry, and closed the heavy door behind her. In the act of closing the door, a whimper, which in a moment would grow to a lusty howl, told that Joan, aged four, wanted as usual to tag along.

Grita darted back. "You're going to be another lost calf, dumpling. And of course you don't make a sound, or we'd find you before you were ready. We'll be back soon, and we won't know where to look—under the table—or on the bed." She dropped a kiss on the snub nose, so absurdly a miniature of Nelle's, and was gone again. No howls this time, but a pleasant memory of Nelle's grateful slow smile. The children were easy to manage, if you knew their language.

Grita slipped into her wooden klompen, to set a good example to the younger ones, who, ever since the snow had left the ground, had been clamoring to go barefoot. She met Isaak's excited "Maqua hunting party?" with a nod of agreement.

"Till we get to the woods," she promised. "Then we'll have to start calling, so Rosey may answer." Rosey might, but more probably wouldn't.

The fields were nearest, and had best be covered first. The wind blew her cloak out in swirling folds and tore at her long black braids. The two Indian braves accompanying her took stealthy cover behind fences, raced eagerly across the barely greening pasture land, plodded valiantly ankle-deep through plowland. Not that Catalina particularly cared to be a Maqua, but it was always easier for her to follow Isaak's play than to make up one of her own. And more fun too.

Down to the riverbank, where the swirling brown flood seemed to have risen a little overnight, but no cattle tracks led down to the summer watering place, for at this time of the year a small stream still ran beside the barn. The other four cattle, their winter coats still shaggy and unkempt, were standing together disconsolately, occasionally dropping their heads to see if a brown tuft of last year's grass tasted as uninteresting as it looked. All the other fields were empty; from the higher ground above the barn you could scan every corner of them. Well, then it must be the forest.

A quick spatter of rain fell on Grita's face as she hurried along behind the two children. If the rain were as heavy upriver as it was here, there was every risk of a bad freshet; not that it mattered so much, early in the year as it would later, when the corn was sown on the rich tempting flatts that bordered the river. But it would silt over some of the grazing ground and wash away the good topsoil where land had been bared by the plow. Each spring, each summer even, there were these floods. And surely they were growing worse. Oh, if only people would see that each beaver they trapped on each stream that led down to the river was adding to the danger of floods. But even the director laughed at her for the idea.

It stood to reason, didn't it? Surely, no matter how fool-ish the English were, good Netherlanders should have more sense. Yet Netherlanders, born and raised in the old country, under the shadow of dams and dikes which alone saved their farms from the hungry seas, seemed unable to understand that a thousand, perhaps ten thousand, perhaps more, of beaver dams, spread all the way up the river and among the hills, were just as important a safeguard as a man-made dike. They would pen back sudden rushes of water due to thunderstorms and cloud-bursts, and feed out that same water in trickles, slowly, slowly and safely. Yet the same men who, in the old country, would leave family and home and hearthside and risk their very lives grappling desperately to strengthen a threatened dike, had no more sense over here than to kill off the beavers who controlled the floods of the river. You'd have thought they'd have more fellow feeling for fellow dike builders, if nothing else. Not a stream around in all these hills but showed the melancholy testimony of man's senseless greed. Broken beaver dams, the water gone, the poor beasts' lodges no more than piles of moldering sticks on which the vegetation was already creeping back. Oh, it was shameful! She hated every murdering hunter of them, and every grasping trader.

But thoughts such as these did no good; they had no place in a busy life, and the Hoorns had no dealings with beaver.

They came now to the edge of the woods, thick pine it was, and spread themselves out. All three began to call, "Rosey. Rosey!" And listened.

A scuffling in the thick undergrowth, which grew up to meet the sun on the edge of the forest, aroused false hopes. No more than a clumsy porcupine. Isaak threw a stick at it and it shuffled away, making noise enough for a bear.

The boy began to call, away off on the right. Catalina from

the left, echoed it in her clear treble. A scramble and they
had fought their way through the sumac, scrub oak and fallen
boughs to easier walking under the taller trees. Grita stopped
often to listen. An occasional glimpse of Catalina's red cloak,
as she closed in, gave a little human reassurance among these
majestic, overawing trees. Isaak's call coming at slower in-
tervals. Cattle droppings, but from last year when the small
herd had come here to shelter from heat and flies. Signs of
deer aplenty; a faint musky odor of skunk or fox hung in a
hollow, and here a coon had passed only last night. You
didn't have to be a Maqua to read some of the forest signs.
Skunk cabbage in lush growth, a few hepaticas already in
modest bloom, a wake robin, though the robins had not come
as yet.

A faint hail from Isaak: "Turk . . . ies!" He must be
wishing that he already had the crossbow that Kaspar, last
night, had promised to show him how to fashion.

Grita continued to call, and listen. It was very still among
the trees, unstirred by the wind outside. A little awesome too.

Then she stood stock-still, her heart thumping. How long
was it since she had seen that red cloak, or heard the little
Catalina?

Grita changed her call, from "Rosey!" to "Cata—li—
na!" And stirred by growing anxiety, to the more affection-
ate, "Lijntje! . . . Oh, Lijntje!" Then to tones grown
sharp with apprehension: "Catalina? Where are you? Answer me at once!"

Only the solemn stillness of the forest broken by the far-
off sound of Isaak's continued call. No sound from the little
girl, no flash of her red coat. Grita took a deep breath.

"Isaak! Come in!" she shouted. "Catalina's gone!"

He came, for he was a good, obedient boy; she heard his
hasty footsteps snapping the rotted twigs among the fallen
leaves.

He was full of his story of how close he had crept to
the gobblers. Moreover, his young scorn was reassuring.

"Catalina's just being silly. She's watching a woodpecker or something, and won't answer 'cause she's afraid of scaring it!" But when he was set to the manly task of backtracking Grita's own trail, so Grita could swing off to about the course taken by the little girl, he plunged willingly into the fresh search.

Again Grita called. "Catalina! Catalina!" From her left came the long drawn "Ros . . . ey! Ros . . . ey!" Well, if Isaak thought it was silly to call his younger sister, the call to the cow would serve just as well. Impossible, Grita tried to assure herself, that Catalina could be lost, so near to home, and in these woods where she had safely played a hundred times. Yet every settlement, English as well as Netherlander, had its tragic story of a child who disappeared and was never seen again. Lost gathering berries, stolen by Indians, killed by some animal, or just, it seemed, spirited away. Rosey no longer mattered. If the cow sought a sequestered spot to have her calf, that was her own responsibility, and what were the life of cow and calf together, compared with the safety of Catalina?

Here, just ahead and back almost at the fringe of the woods, was the sort of place that Rosey would chose. Fire, or perhaps the ax of an early hunter or settler, had cleared a patch among the big trees, which had since grown up to a tangle of second-growth pine. Grita gave another call. "Catalina . . . Catalina!"

And heard, or imagined, a deep soft note, almost too low for human ears to catch. Certainly it wasn't the voice of a child. Was there some fierce predatory beast that made a noise like that? Surely not.

Guarding her face with a crooked elbow, stooping under some branches, dodging others, thrusting some aside, snapping others, Grita fought her way to the center of the tangle. A bed of pine needles, deep and springy, lay beneath her feet. Something big had been lying just ahead, had flattened the earth beneath with some great weight. Then cow tracks,

fresh ones. And yes, signs of calving. So Rosey had had her
baby. Again that low deep note, like a soft wind blowing over
a chimney.

And there stood Rosey. She was standing facing to one
side, the calf lying behind her.

And on the far side of the cow, only her arms showing
clasped around Rosey's neck, was Catalina.

"Lijntje! What are you doing? Why didn't you call?"
Grita spoke sharply.

The little girl dodged under Rosey's head, took one wide-
eyed glance at her older sister. Then pointed in the direction
in which Rosey was staring.

"You mustn't frighten us this way, Lijntje. It's very
naught—"

Then something, its outline blurred by the tangle of twigs,
moved. And came into focus. A wolf.

A big old wolf, graying at the muzzle, half crouching,
seeming ready to spring. But more probably just patiently
waiting, knowing that his patience could outwear the vigi-
lance of both child and cow; and then would come his opportunity.

Isaak's call, "Ros . . . ey!" went unheard, unheeded, so
far as the anxious cow was concerned. Grita answered,
"We're here, we're all here. And there's a wolf."

Isaak came crashing in to join them, gave a shout at what
he saw, and was answered by a doglike snarl of disappointment or of warning from the beast.

"Run!" Grita commanded. "Run Isaak. Tell Father we
found the calf and to bring his firearm." Yes, that was the
best plan. Isaak could be trusted to find his way out safely.
She, Grita, was duty bound to stay behind to protect Catalina,
and even the calf.

As the boy crashed off through the brush she put her arms
around the little girl's shoulders, felt her give a shiver of
relief. She spoke a few calm words of reassurance to the
troubled mother cow.

Then the wolf began to circle, hoping to get behind the three defenders and spring upon the calf. It was a trick as old, no doubt, as the earliest wolf. And Rosey's instinct, to keep strong body and sharp horns between child and would-be murderer, was just as sure, just as ancient. As the wolf circled she shifted her big body, and not for the first time by many hundred, as the trampled ground so clearly testified. Perhaps all night this slow, unrelenting duel had been in progress. Well, it would soon be over now. Soon the tired mother would be back in the barn, her calf tied up beside her.

Grita began talking in a low, reassuring tone to the little girl. "Why didn't you answer when I called?" she asked.

"The wolf," whispered Catalina. "He bared his teeth and warned me not to. He was going to spring if I shouted to you. He told me so. So I didn't dare."

"You're brave enough now, aren't you, Lijntje? Helping Rosey and me to hold the brute off."

Although it was Rosey really who was defending the whole party. Without weapons, without so much as a heavy stick, even a full-grown man or woman would come off badly if attacked. A lone wolf, left behind at this time of year, when the main wolf packs had already moved northward, would be hungry and desperate. A wolf bite in summer was known to cause madness; the poor victim slavering, and even howling just like a wild beast, when the last paroxysms came on. Oh, why didn't Father hurry!

The wolf, as if recognizing that help was at hand, and that the war of waiting was over, made a sudden swift feint to one side, and charged in. Grita and Catalina were nearly bowled over as the cow pivoted, and head down, eyes rolling, swung in to meet him, and hooked sideways with her strong horns. But the wolf had stopped, jerked off sideways, and then tried again.

Another hook of the horns, missing only by inches. Grita dragged Catalina back, to stand beside the calf. Only there would the child be safe from those plunging hoofs and sweeping horns. Round again. This time the wolf was nearly past the defenses. In open ground Rosey might have had the advantage, but here, with trees, their close-set trunks offering no obstacle to the wolf, but hindering her at every turn, the situation was desperate.

Strangely enough, Grita never considered retreat. She hoisted Catalina to safety in a tree. So long had Rosey defended the child, along with her own young one, that it was unthinkable to desert her now. Grita stood her ground beside the calf, following in a smaller circle the fight that raged around her. If the wolf broke through the outer defenses—Rosey's defenses—perhaps a hard kick from heavy wooden klompen would hold him off the calf, till the mother could turn again and renew the fight.

Then the wolf retreated. Rosey charged after it, and dangerously far from her calf, Grita felt. Perhaps Rosey did too, for slowly, cautiously she backed again, still with her head lowered menacingly.

A sudden explosion, deafening to Grita's taut nerves; a curl of smoke from a musket barrel; and there stood Father Hoorn, stopping with reassuring calmness to reload.

Isaak, brandishing the big kitchen knife, bounded forward; but the wolf, bowled over by a heavy musket ball, struggled to his feet, snarling so viciously that the boy wisely pulled up short. A few paces only the wolf ran. Then sank down again, kicked, and when Isaak stirred him with a daring toe, lay without moving. Mathias came striding up.

The danger was over.

"You can come down now, Lijntje," Grita reassured the little girl.

Catalina threw her arms tight around Grita's neck, buried her face in the heavy folds of her cape and began to sob. Tears of relief and reaction.

"The little one's not hurt?" asked Mathias anxiously.

"No. No. She'll be all right. I'll put her to bed as soon as we're home. She was a brave girl. When I first came she was helping Rosey fend off the wolf."

Mathias unslung his bullet bag and powderhorn. "Take these and the musket, daughter. And with Catalina's help, drive the cow."

He stooped, set the calf across his shoulders and started for home. Isaak, behind them, was already starting to skin the wolf.

Chapter Six
Strange Boy from
the Homelands

SINCE YOUR FATHER says 'yes,' children, I cannot say
'no,' " agreed Mother Hoorn. "A family cannot have
two heads," and she began to scoop the hot ashes from
the stone oven, while the raised loaves waited on the table,
ready to be shoved in on the long-handled oven peel.

Mathias gravely nodded his head. Grita smiled. Not in
twenty years of marriage had he come to guess that it was
really Mother who made the decisions, even when they came
in Father's voice. How wonderful marriage must be when
two people became so much one that they honestly didn't
know, never even stopped to think, which of them it was who
had given permission for the children to repair the boat.

"And Kaspar?" Grita asked. "Can he help too? The boat is too heavy for us to turn over."

Father puffed slowly at his after-breakfast pipe and looked at Mother. Mother said nothing but went on working, perhaps some wordless message passed between them.

"If the director does not need him today," Father decided.

Good. It was time, Grita realized, that she got a chance to learn more about this stranger who had come to live under their thatching. Like any well-brought-up Netherlander he spoke little at meals, no matter how much the women folk and children chattered. He took his turn in the daily reading of the Scriptures, removing his hat and reading in a firm clear voice before the meal began. But between meals he was out of the house, either working at the director's office or helping Father with the seasonal fence repairing and the wheat planting.

It really was necessary to know more about him. Already the little ones were beginning to imitate him; Isaak now wore his Sunday fur cap with just the rakish tilt of Kaspar's handsome wide-brimmed, silver buckled beaver; and Catalina, not very successfully, was clearly attempting to speak in the boy's shy deep tones. An elder brother might be just what the young family needed, somebody a little more approachable and nearer their own age than dear Father; but that depended on what sort of elder brother.

Grita, leading her small work gang down to the riverbank, was determined to find out. It was a glorious spring morning, the clouds high and windy; in the sunlight the two girls raced on ahead. Isaak had lingered a moment to see how the wolfskin was curing on the wooden stretcher Kaspar had made for it. He came along now with Kaspar, his shorter legs imitating the other's long, loping stride. It was good of the stranger to cut down his pace to Isaak's shorter one.

Yes, he was considerate, even kindly, Grita admitted with reluctance; kindly, that is, for one engaged in the cruel beaver trade. But she must put thought of the poor beavers behind her, for to start the morning with a disagreement would be no way to find out what she wanted to learn.

"I've left the falcon in the barn; she's rather moody. I hope it doesn't mean the sea voyage and the change are going to make her molt," he explained. "She shouldn't at this time of year."

One lead was as good as another. Grita switched a long braid over her shoulder. "Were you a falconer in the homeland?" she asked.

"My father was. And a farmer too. For Mynheer Kiliaen, the first patroon." And by the time they had covered the short distance to the boat he was telling her of Cralo, the Cralo in the home country, for which the one over at Greenbos had been named.

It sounded a happy life; and not so very different, when you came to consider it, from the life here, on the Hoorn farm. Perhaps that was why Kaspar seemed to fit in so easily, to do the little tasks that Mother expected of her menfolk, to bring in wood and water without being bidden, to wipe his feet at the door, or leave his wooden klompen outside.

His story and her inquiries had to cease awhile, as they considered the morning's work. The square-built, boxlike boat lay upturned on high ground where Father and the team had drawn it last autumn, to be safe from the winter's floods. First it would have to be scraped, to rid it of the caking of moss and mud which hid the seams.

Isaak was sent to the barn for ax and adz, Catalina to see if she could borrow the kitchen knife from her mother; Joan raced back with them just to be on the move.

"If you were happy at Cralo," Grita asked, sitting down on a warm stone in the sunlight while they waited, "what brought you over here?"

Cralo was one thing, Kaspar explained. But being apprenticed to a furrier in Amsterdam was altogether different. No one should be made to sit cross-legged ten hours a day, cutting and sewing, brushing and polishing. Restlessly he took off his wide hat and threw it down beside her, while the wind blew his yellow hair around his face. His eyes, very blue, gazed out over the free and open river. "Back there, there was only a wall to look at in the daytime, and the same counter to sleep under at night. Can you blame me for disliking it?"

"So you escaped?" and in spite of herself there was sympathy in her voice. It was difficult always to remember those beavers.

"Not escaped exactly. My father died. Mother had died two years before. And the patroon sent for me; not Mynheer Kiliaen of course, for he too was dead, but his eldest son, Mynheer Johannes."

Funny how his voice changed whenever he mentioned old Mynheer Kiliaen; someday when she knew him better she must find out why he felt like that about the first patroon.

She twisted and twirled the long curl at the end of her black braid around one finger and maintained an inquiring silence.

"Oh, it's a long story. My father wanted to come across, years and years ago, only they needed him at Cralo. I think Mynheer Johannes thought it fair to give me the chance in his place."

"So you've got no family either," Grita heard herself saying. Strange; she hadn't meant to say that.

"No family." He shook his head. He didn't even seem to mind not having one. "But you, you've got a big family." And his glance swung back to the Hoorn house which sheltered them all.

"They aren't mine you see. I'm adopted," she admitted.

"Well, isn't that just as good?" he asked. "I mean there's no difference between you and the others."

"Oh, but there *is!*" She couldn't explain now, for the children were racing back. Anyway, it wasn't something you could talk about easily. He wouldn't understand that if you had never known your parents you had no clue to your future, you didn't know what you ought to be like, when you grew up. You couldn't guess even whether you would be tall or short, fat or thin! You daren't set your heart on becoming anything. You were like a duckling hatched by a hen, who might never think of learning to swim!

Kaspar and Isaak started work at once. Isaak, holding the ax head between his hands, resting the blade flat upon the upturned boat bottom and pushing it away from himself, plane fashion, soon had a plank stripped of its mold. Kaspar, using the more ungainly adz, kept pace with him along another plank. Grita, with knife point and fingernail, probed the uncovered wood for signs of rot. Then at Catalina's clamant demand, handed her the kitchen knife so that she too might scrape. Joan was no problem; she sat serenely content wherever she was put down; and if nothing was given her to play with, seemed able to make up an amusing game out of her own ten small fingers.

A slow task it was, and scarcely a woman's; but pleasantly satisfying to have the four of them all working together, all lending hands and minds to the same purpose. This was how a family should work; as a family had to work on a farm where so many tasks were too heavy for one pair of hands, or too long and dull and needing to be shortened and livened by companionship. But it was odd that already in these few weeks this strange boy from the homeland should have become so much one of the Hoorns, that unthinkingly you called on his help to scrape the old boat before putting her in the water; odd too that he and Isaak, busied with their scraping, should be chatting of hawking and falconry, though a month back Isaak had never heard of either sport.

She felt a twinge, perhaps of envy, at the easy friendship these two males had struck up. Was it just because they were menfolk, young as Isaak was, that they had developed this common interest and left her outside? Or was it her own fault, really, because from the beginning she had resented

the falcon as well as her master? She had accepted Kaspar,
more or less, but she couldn't help feeling that falconry was
a silly sort of pastime for a grown man. She said so now,
though she put it as mildly as she could.

"If you need to earn your living, isn't it a dreadful nuisance having to carry a falcon around on your fist and having
to spend time exercising her every day? I mean, there're only
twenty-four hours to earn a living."

Perhaps she had been too tactful, for Kaspar missed her
point entirely. "Oh, no. Isaak and I have just agreed that the
more you're with your falcon the better she knows you, and
the better she'll obey. You see, a peregrine isn't an eyas; she
was wild and full-grown when she was caught." And he and
Isaak again were back to their theme.

When they rolled the boat over on one side, Grita, with an
impatient jerk of her head, and a little more bite in her
remark, tried again.

"But if the falcon takes up so much time, why own one at
all? And anyway, what's the use of falconry?"

Kaspar nearly let slip the short log he was using to prop
up the boat. He stood there, staring at her a moment, as if
he wanted to be sure whether she were joking or not. Grita
felt her cheeks flush hotly.

"What's the *use* of falconry?" as if to make sure he had
heard aright. "Oh, well, what's the use of anything? Of food,
for instance? Of course, if you don't eat you die. But you're
going to die anyway. No, I don't suppose falconry's any
practical use any longer." Frowning, he puzzled out his
thoughts. "But . . . but there's no better sport in the whole
world. You learn to be gentle and patient, because you have
to, whether you like it or not. And it trains your eye, and
your lungs and your whole body. Before guns were invented
there wasn't a man in all the Netherlands but was a falconer
or would sell his soul to be one. And not in the Netherlands
only. Time was when not a king or a prince or a noble would
stir from his castle in peacetime without hounds at his horse's

feet and a falcon on his fist. And, of course, the hounds were
just for putting up the game, and the horse was just to let the
king or knight keep up with the flight that went on overhead."

"And I suppose," said Grita tartly, irritated at the way
Isaak's eyes were getting bigger and bigger with excitement,
"they just provided kings as perches for falcons."

"Oh, no, the king was a lot more than a perch. He had to
train himself to the sport just like any other falconer." Kaspar's direct enthusiasm should have been disarming. "No
matter how many falconers he had, to keep his mews, the
king needed to learn . . ."

"Well, I don't need to, thank goodness!" Grita tossed
back a braid. "And even in those days the women had too
much sense and too much work to do to play with silly birds."

Kaspar kept his temper and grinned. "There's an old jingle
about that. It tells what kind of hawk a lady should have.

"An eagle for an emperor,
A gerfalcon for a king,
A peregrine for an earl,
A merlin for a lady,
A goshawk for a yeoman,
A sparhawk for a priest,
A muskyte for a holiwater clerk."

A merlin for a lady? In spite of herself she was dying to
ask what a merlin was. She asked it.

"Oh, you wouldn't want a merlin. It's just used for small
birds, larks and things like that. And it's delicate too. But,"
he offered with a rush of generosity, "someday you must fly
my peregrine."

"Someday," she accepted the peace offer, "when we're
caught up with the farm and housework, we'll all go hawking with you." And it wasn't just politeness. Hawking, as
Kaspar's enthusiasm depicted it, didn't sound so foolish now,
and certainly not harmful. Not even, like some kinds of fish-

ing, an excuse for idleness. Just—she decided with a little
amused tenderness—just a masculine way of wasting time
and strength which could be better used at a task.

The boat, now they had it stripped, was in worse condition
than Grita had expected. The planking itself was sturdy
enough, as it had to be, since on occasion it had to ferry a
full grown pig, or even a horse or a cow, across to Cralo or
down to Beverwyck, but between the planks were gaps
through which you could see daylight. Each one of those
cracks had to be scraped out clean with the back of a knife,
for calking wouldn't cling to rotten wood. Isaak was sent off
to the forest's edge to gather soft resin from the stumps of
pine trees felled last year.

"And Catalina," Grita ordered, "see what feathers you
can pick up in the barn. We'll need a lot of them, I'm afraid."
That would take some time, but Grita was still busy scraping
out the last of the cracks.

Kaspar picked up Isaak's ax and split one of the oak logs
on which the boat had rested through the winter, dividing it
thinner and thinner into long flat slivers in the way shingles
are made. Then, laying them on the upturned boat, he planed
them down with his knife to fit them in the gaping seams.

"We can drive them in," he suggested, "and when the
boat's in the water and they swell, they ought to hold tightly
enough. A boslooper I met on the *Pigeon* told me that he was
the one who first taught the Maquas to sew their boats with
elm bark."

Grita's eyes were twinkling; she couldn't help it.

Kaspar looked puzzled and started to explain further.
"He seems to have been everywhere and done everything,
right up and down this river. Of course, he must have been
out here a long time because he can't remember much of
Amsterdam where he was born, though he pretends to."

Grita began to laugh. "Amsterdam! He's never been
nearer to the Patria than the point of the Manhatens. 'So
much boasting,' Mother tells him, 'would drive a windmill

on a still day.' And the Maquas certainly stitched their bark
boats long before they saw Gideon Dolph."

Kaspar had to join her amusement. He hadn't really believed Gideon, but it was a good enough story. "So you know
the boslooper do you? He told me a still better tale of how
he had to build a birch bark canoe between dusk and daylight, so as to escape in it from the Hurons. I forget if he
had a knife or whether he had to do it all with his teeth!"

"He told Isaak that one too. But his best is where his
musket misfired and he had to club his enemy. And the musket went off as he did it, and killed another enemy creeping
silently up behind him. Whenever Gideon stops with us,
Isaak goes around telling the most awful stories for days
afterwards—and half believing them too. But that's not
nearly so serious as the way the boslooper's stories make
Isaak want to be a fur trapper too. Beavers and such."

"What's wrong with beaver-trapping? It's a good living,
isn't it? And not too difficult by Gideon's account," challenged Kaspar, fitting another sliver of wood into the boat's
cracks, tapping it firmly home with the back of the ax, and
shaving it off flush with his knife.

"I've got to learn all sides of the beaver business if I'm to
be of any use. I'm hoping the director will send me out next
winter, as soon as the pelts are prime, so I can learn how to
trap and spear."

"Trap and spear? Even Isaak could teach you that."
Scorn had crept into Grita's voice. "You make a hole in the
dam and when the poor little unsuspecting beaver goes to
repair it he steps in your trap. Or you drive a barbed spear
through the top of their lodges. Or a whole big whooping
Indian village goes out when the colony is frozen over and
marks down each refuge hole in the bank, frightens the poor
little creatures out of their homes and catches them as they
swim under the ice to the holes in the bank." Her black eyes
flashed furiously. "Oh, I wish the beaver could fight back
and kill a few men in return!"

"*Heere, mijn tijd.* Well, well!" said Kaspar, and whistled. "So that's the way you feel. But the farmer kills his tame hens and cows and pigs, doesn't he? At least the beavers haven't been tamed first." He was growing hot in return. "If it weren't for the beaver trade, neither of us would be here, and there'd be no West India Company and no patroonship."

"M-m-n, you might just as well say there'd be no West India Company if it weren't for the Spanish treasure ships they used to seize and rob in the old days," Grita countered indignantly. "But people don't prey on the Spanish ships any longer, and there's no reason why they need to prey on the beaver. And anyway, people are just harming themselves in the end; for someday beaver hats are going to go out of fashion and then where'll your old beaver trade be? And the trappers and traders and all the rest of them? And it will serve them right!"

"If that happened, we'd have to find another trade; or our great-grandsons would," he parried.

"And in the meantime, of course, you don't care if you ruin this country; you don't care if you destroy all the beaver dams and so increase the floods. Nor if your fur trade tempts men from honest farm work for the sake of your quick profits . . ." Long stored up, her indignation poured out. "And perhaps have us driven out of the country by the Indians."

"Lieve hemel! The Indians need the fur trade more than we do. If it weren't for the beaver, they'd have no iron, no blankets or duffel cloth, no awls or needles or thread . . ."

"And no guns to murder each other!" Grita reminded him. "Just why do you think the Maquas from the West are driving the Mahicans from our part of the country, and raiding up north into Huron country? They don't need all that land for their farms, and wouldn't in a thousand years. They don't even need it to hunt for meat and deerskins. But when the Maquas can buy muskets with their beaver skins, with those muskets they can drive out other tribes and get

more beaver skins. To buy more muskets of course and make
still more wars.

"Oh," she went on, almost desperately, "I wish I could
make you understand what's happening. You, or Gideon
Dolph, or the director. Or just anybody outside the family.
Father agrees with me, but then Father doesn't talk much."

Painstakingly Kaspar kept on working. It was additional
exasperation that he never once looked up from his tasks,
though Grita was too indignant to keep on with hers. He
fitted another long thin wedge and drove it home, as far as
it would go. "Gideon says the beaver are getting scarcer,
even since he first started to hunt and trade," he remarked
disarmingly. "And the director says there are less of the big
ones, blankets and wholes, each year; which is a sign that
most of the old beasts have been killed off."

The scraping, it seemed, was finished. Grita drove the
point of the knife into the boat with a force that boded ill for
beaver traders. "If they begin to lose their profits, *some* of
them may see sense."

An awkward silence followed, which lasted a good ten minutes, and was broken only by Catalina's arrival with an apron
full of feathers.

Then the stiff quills had to be cut off, and the plumes split
down the midriff. As Grita and the little girl prepared the
feathers, Kaspar finished his plugging and fashioned a
wooden calking tool. Isaak, remembering last year's methods, had delayed to melt up the resin with tallow in one of
Nelle's small iron kettles. By the time he arrived, the work
was going smoothly again.

Grita, with the back of the kitchen knife, was pressing the
feathers into such cracks as were too small to take a wooden
plug. Kaspar, following after her, tamping the feathers in,
switched the subject by asking her about farming, and why
people farmed so dangerously close to the river. Isaak,
smearing sticky compound down the seams of the boat, completed the family work party.

Grita's indignation had already smoothed out. After all, this boy, newly arrived from the homeland, had scarcely had time to judge for himself and was simply repeating what others had told him. It was natural enough that he should believe what an experienced boslooper and even the director himself believed. No matter, she added to herself, how utterly wrong they were. And now with a modesty which was surely rare in menfolk, he was actually asking for information.

"The Flatts are good rich soil, and Father says they were clear of trees even before the white man came here. The yield is so heavy that if a farmer can get in two harvests out of three, he can well afford to lose the third from flood. Only the floods really do seem to be getting worse."

Just in time she edged off the dangerous topic again. Kaspar's tap-tap-tap, with the improvised calking iron, went smoothly on.

"I grant you," he said, "that farming is a surer trade than beavers, for eating is never likely to go out of fashion. But why do the farmers over here fail so often? Why do so many desert their land and start to trade, or brew, or try their hand as sawyers or millers or charcoal burners? The director says there are more deserted farms in the patroonship than there are farms still occupied."

"The soil wears out, they say." This was a subject near to her heart. "And then the tares and the weeds come in. And even if there's enough value still left in the land to give a fair crop of wheat, there's no way of separating it from the tares after threshing. So they grow the Indian corn instead, for a year or two, and finally ruin the soil. Then they clear more woodland and in a few more years that is as bad as the first. And then they just give up, in disgust."

"But why?" Kaspar was heaving the boat back on its side, so they could get at their work more easily. "That doesn't happen in the homeland. My father's grandfather was farming Cralo, and perhaps his father before him. I can see that

the Indian farms might wear out quickly, because they keep
no livestock. But why should ours?"

"If it were cooking now, or weaving . . . But what does
a girl know of farming methods? But I've wondered sometimes if, over here, our people haven't too much land. Just as
a woman can have a house too big for her needs, and too big
to keep really clean." She felt her resentment over the beavers fading away, for the time anyway. Kaspar was paying her
the compliment of close attention. Perhaps, if he were interested, he could give her an answer as to why the patroonship
farmer wasn't so successful in the new land.

"Supposing," she suggested slowly, "a man took a smaller
piece of land, so he could keep it really clean, tilling and
grazing and mowing right up to the fence corners; wouldn't
that help keep down the tares? And though wheat is more
trouble than Indian corn, it sells far better in Beverwyck and
the Manhatens; we Netherlanders like our wheaten loaf.
Cleaner wheat, without tares in it, might even be worth sending to the homeland instead of beavers."

Kaspar nodded cautious agreement. "Yes, the director
sends wheat over each year, he says. But for the ordinary
farmer . . . Could it be done?"

Grita cast him a challenging smile. "That's for a man to
work out." She finished her last inch of calking. The tedious
part of the task was finished and the children had kept at it
manfully, but there were still final touches to be put on the
boat.

Catalina dumped the last of the feathers from her apron
into the river and watched them float swiftly away on the
bright dancing current, and skipped back, ready for the next
task. Isaak stood up and stretched. Grita recognized the signs
of restlessness.

Her hands began to flicker swiftly. Forefingers described
marks across her face, then hands gave a milking action, a
finger pointed toward the house, made the gesture for
"bring."

Silently Isaak, giggling, gestured "Where?" But he surely must have known, for he had brought the resin mixture from there.

But to satisfy him her hands signed "Fire." Then off the two went.

As she turned around, Kaspar was staring. "Hey, what's all that mean?"

"Just sign language," she laughed. "I told him to fetch the paint we're going to use on the boat. It's red ochre that the Indians paint their faces with." She made the gesture again. "And milk. And Isaak asked where, and I told him 'By the fire.' "

"Are those the Indian signs that I saw the traders use down-river? Where did you get to know them?"

"Yes. Gideon taught us when he was here last fall." She smiled at a recollection, for that was a time when everything at the table had to be asked for in dumb show, and even little Joan had waved and fluttered her hands in imitation of the others. How patient Mother and Father had been! And how silent the household had seemed while the craze lasted!

"They say the same signs do for all the tribes. Is that true?" Kaspar asked.

Grita's hands began to gesture. "That means 'Yes,' " she told him. "Everywhere . . . Same, or equal.

"It doesn't matter what language a tribe speaks, as the signs are usually pictures drawn in the air, or imitations of something being done. They haven't anything to do with words. Here's another example. Guess what it means." One of Grita's hands slapped down on the other with a sharp report.

"Explosion—shooting, door slamming, falling flat on the ice?" Kaspar grinned. "I give up."

"Beaver smacking the water with his flat tail as a warning signal to his family. So the sign stands for beaver, our 'bone of contention.' "

It was pleasant to have reached the easy stage of friendship when you could admit your differences of opinion and not let them stand as a barrier between you. Working here together this morning had been something more than a pleasant companionship of the hands at their tasks. Grita felt that she and Kaspar had arrived at an understanding of some sort. He refused to be battered into submission to her views about the evils of the beaver trade—no matter how right she was!—but he didn't reject them as silly. That was fair enough.

When Isaak came with the milk-and-ochre paint, she found herself more interested in Kaspar de Selle than in the painting. Most men, just because they were men, would have felt they must offer suggestions and instructions about the painting, or would even have taken over the task themselves, feeling they could do it so much better. Kaspar did neither. He watched Isaak daubing on the stuff with genuine interest. And when Catalina took a bundle of feathers for a brush, it was Kaspar who made himself useful by holding her gourd of paint so she should not spill it. How long would the paint last in the water, he wanted to know, and did it save the wood from rotting? How many days would it be before it was dry enough so the inside of the boat could be painted?

Yes, Kaspar de Selle was willing to work, and also willing to learn, at an age when most boys thought they knew everything. It would be fun to help him, and teach him sign language or anything she could. And learn something in return, for a good learner like Kaspar would be a good teacher. As Mother said, "To teach on Tuesday, learn on Monday."

And how handsome the boat was beginning to look with its new coat of paint!

Chapter Seven
The River Takes
Its Toll

AND AGAIN it rained.

It was only two days ago that Mathias Hoorn had moved the cattle down to a far field beside the river to prevent their churning the ground around the barn into a quagmire; now he announced that he dare not leave them there, in their new pasture.

"The field is low. And back of the field where once, I think, ran a kill, the land is lower still. If the river rises yet, that pasture becomes an island, but that a cow cannot know. So if the water rises higher, the cattle will be caught and drowned."

Nelle nodded understanding. "Each year that happens to some farmer; to you it should not happen. To us the big river has always been a friend, giving us good land and water for ourselves and our beasts. That is what the good God wishes. If by our carelessness our cows are swept away and drowned, the sin would be ours." Her big freckled hands went on capably packing fresh eggs into a basket, one of the baskets that Isaak made so well. "Before the current is too swift, I will beg from the director his boat, and Andries to row it."

Grita, sweeping back the ashes on the hearth with a turkey wing, glanced up and tossed a braid over her shoulder and wished that Mother wouldn't go. But the brown hen wanted to set, and it was no use putting these eggs under her; for, since the old cock had been killed by the fox in wintertime, the eggs would certainly not hatch. Mvrouw van Ostram over at Greenbos on the east bank had good hens, none better in the whole patroonship. So Mother would give her these eggs for eating, in exchange for a clutch for hatching. Anyone else would have waited a day, or a week if necessary, till the river went down again, but Mother ordered her life by her many proverbs, and one of her favorites was "The light task of the day is the heavy task of the morrow."

Mother said it now, almost to herself. "The task postponed is the task never done."

"The task ne'er done broke no man's back," thought Grita, a little rebelliously. But she did not say it.

"And see, Grita, that the children are busied. For 'Satan sees each idle maid and marks her for his own.' " Mother sounded like a regular slave driver, but the only slave that she drove was herself. She tied on her hooded cape, kissed small Joan, again admonished the other children not to neglect their tasks, and went out into the rain. You could see her, through the wavery bluish glass of the window, plodding along toward the little dock where the director's rowboat was tied. And a half-hour later, after Mathias had gone too, Joan had to be lifted to the window to wave to her mother out in the boat. Of course, Mother couldn't see her, but would know her little one was watching. Yes, Mother waved back. Then seemed to say something to Andries, standing in the stern and sculling with his single oar.

Grita wished somehow that Mother hadn't had to go to, day. Not just today. And that she hadn't said that about the river being a friend. You could scarcely live beside it, year after year, without knowing how moody it was. Friendly and smiling one day, black and angry another, and most dangerous of all at the times when it was fickle. Like a farmer's bull, perhaps, to be loved like all his other stock, for without love no beasts would thrive. But never to be taken for granted, never wholly to be trusted.

Yes, the river was like the Hoorn's old bull that Father had killed last year when without warning it had set on Isaak, who had been the bull's best friend; so close a friend that Isaak had often ridden him down to water. It was not treachery, but just your own inability to know what the bull— or for that matter the river—was brooding over.

What nonsense! A river could not brood! Grita thrust her absurd imaginings out of mind and buckled down to her tasks. Even with the household empty of the grown-ups there was plenty to do. Or would have been if it hadn't been for something pricking at the back of Grita's memory. What had started it? Something Father had said about the cattle and the island. Oh, of course. If the cattle were in danger, what of the twenty-three hens, which only last week she and the youngsters had ferried over in the flat-bottomed boat to Willow Island? Scarce even an island it was, just a low bank in the river with a few half-drowned willows and some sparse vegetation clinging to its sides. There hadn't been room for the whole flock in the barn, only for the laying hens, and when Isaak had noted the clear mark of fox tracks one afternoon and had even seen the fox himself, it had seemed a really good idea to take the hens to the island where they would be safe, and leave a small supply of corn to eke out their foraging.

Well, if she and the children could take the hens there,

surely they could rescue them and bring them back here to
safety.

"We're going to go and fetch the chickens," she announced in mid-morning. "Before they wet their feet. We'll
take the farm boat and your new willow chicken coop, Isaak.
And we'll all of us have to row or paddle. And if we go barefoot, it'll be easier to catch the hens."

The river was high and swift from the heavy rains, and as
she led her crew, carrying their oars and paddles, down to
the riverbank and unmoored the square, flat-bottomed old
tub, she had a faint qualm of doubt. But it was one thing for
Mother to risk herself in the full current going across to
Greenbos, and quite another to pole and paddle upriver a
short way in the slack water under the lee of the bank, and to
an island scarcely fifty paces from the shore. Besides, the
rain had let up and that was a good sign. There was even a
gleam of sunshine; only to the north brooded black storm
clouds.

But even with Isaak and herself each pulling an oar, Catalina plying a paddle and little Joan trying to help by splashing the rain water that lay inside the boat, it was a hard pull.
In places the river was already over the bank, and throwing
long curling arms into the low-lying pasture land. Well, it
would be a lot easier coming back again, down current.

Not till they had passed upstream of the island did Grita
steer out from the protecting bank, and, still rowing hard,
allow the boat to drive down upon its north end. Isaak was
the first one out of the boat; he made fast to a secure-looking
root. She passed him first the osier basket, then little Joan,
gave Catalina a balancing hand, made sure that oars and
paddle were safely inside the boat, and splashed ashore.

The mud was warm and squelched pleasantly around her
ankles. The chickens, now that the rain had stopped, had left
their rough wooden shelter and were scattered along the
whole hundred yards of the narrow island, scratching and
pecking for insects. Three unexpected eggs; she gave them to

Catalina to carry back to the boat. Then the round-up commenced.

It was easier than she had thought. For it was only necessary to drive the flock onto the bare narrow strip at the north end where the water fenced them in, and scoop them up and stuff them hastily into the basket till it was full. Only ten hens would it hold, however, and that weight was all that she and Isaak together could carry to the boat. So that first voyage was successful. It was tiresome that she would have to come back again for the remainder. If only she had thought to bring sacks, but that couldn't be helped now.

The voyage downstream was easy compared with the struggle against the current; deceptively easy as it turned out. Before they could come close enough to the shore they were swept past the farm moorings. Not that it mattered seriously, for the van Rensselaer tie-up was almost as convenient. They made it without difficulty.

Mynheer, the director himself, came out from the house. "It is no day to play upon the river, children," he admonished them. "And now it begins to rain again."

"We had to rescue the hens that were on Willow Island, Mynheer," Grita explained. "And we must go back for the others. But may I leave with you the youngest? And can we borrow a basket or a box with a cover?"

It seemed that the director had no box and no basket. But he took Joan indoors and a moment later came out with a length of cord. "Tie the hens' legs; that will serve. And if you must go back to the island, hasten. I do not like the river today." As the boat pulled upstream, he still stood there, looking anxiously at that coal-black cloud in the north.

Rowing alone, Grita now discovered, would never take them back to the island; they would be worn out first. In the past half-hour the water had strangely risen. The force of the stream increased. While Isaak held the boat in the shelter of a small bluff, Grita lengthened the painter by tying to it a rope which Father Hoorn had used for fastening down a load of hay and had left under one of the seats. It wasn't very strong perhaps, but the risk would have to be taken.

She jumped ashore on the mainland and, while Isaak fended off, started to tow upstream. Hard work it was, and slow, hauling around every bend not only of the banks but of the newly flooded pasture land. Splashing through water knee-deep, even waist-deep, to try to cut these detours, if only by a little. Soon she was soaked to her skin, her skirts heavy and sodden against her legs. The mooring posts of the Hoorn's landing place were now hidden beneath the roily waters, which meant that the river had risen a foot, and was probably still rising.

There were times when the current caught full on the boat and the most Grita could do was to stand stock still, straining every muscle, her feet sinking deeper into the boggy ground, till, inch by inch, the towrope cutting into her shoulder, she could lean far enough forward to take another plunging stride. Again, for yards at a time, she could walk straight forward as if hauling nothing heavier than the small hand-sled through a winter snow. Isaak, standing upright with his oar over the stern of the boat, both sculled and steered; Catalina, possessed now of a grown-up oar, helped to keep the boat's square bow from running ashore as she crouched against the rising wind, her short hair whipped about her rosy face. The sky had darkened but still the rain held off.

Willow Island, when Grita came abreast of it, seemed to be farther from the shore; quite likely the channel was no wider, but the island itself had shrunk, and added to the seeming distance.

Here came a desperate struggle. Twice Grita was hauled back bodily by the force of the stream upon the square-ended boat; but from there on it was easier. And the rain held off. Not that a little more wet mattered now. Yet over the north still hung that heavy pall of black; it seemed to have come nearer in the last few minutes. Somewhere upstream it must be raining almost solid water, and the flood, as soon as the waters reached down here, would certainly sweep over the island and drown those poor chickens. It would seem like treachery if you let those creatures be swept away, since it was you who had taken them out to the island. And the loss of the hens, though it wouldn't mean ruin to the Hoorn household, would greatly cut down the supply of eggs this summer.

Grita came opposite the point from which, last time, they had left the shore line and pulled for the island. A stone cut on one of her bare feet, and general weariness tempted her to jump aboard the boat. But that might mean missing the island, and common sense told her not to throw away all this effort on so very uncertain a gamble. One of Mother's sayings came to mind. "A house is not built till the roof is thatched." She smiled through her fatigue, as she towed on another hundred paces, adding, as Mother would say, the thatch to her house.

Then at last came the time. She hauled up the boat, shortening the towrope. Just a moment of hesitation. Should she set Catalina ashore? But there was a risk there too; danger, if the little girl didn't keep her head, of her being caught as Father was afraid the cattle would be, between encroaching arms of the flooded river. No, best keep her safe in the boat. A big square tub like this was in no danger of upsetting.

"Ship your oar over the far side, Isaak. And Lijntje, the moment I jump aboard, leave me the oar and put out your paddle on Isaak's side."

Then a leap, a haul on her oar to draw clear of the bank, and the struggle began. A short one, but difficult. Swept helplessly past the top of the island, by bare good fortune they pulled up under the lee end. A slight delay in mooring, for no solid-looking roots showed above the water line, and Catalina's paddle had to be driven in instead.

Most of the chickens were already huddled disconsolately in the little shelter. They were quickly caught and tied and

dumped unceremoniously into the boat. Two of the three
remaining were captured with the same ease, but the third
flew squawking out over the river and was swept away; she
had always been a silly old soul, poor thing. They were ready
to go when a slight argument arose with Isaak; having helped
to build that shelter he wanted to knock it apart and take it
into the boat; and rescue it from the flood, just as they had
the hens.

Reluctantly Grita said, "No."

Isaak was about to argue further, when his mouth dropped
open. His eyes stared.

At the same moment Grita noticed the menace. The black
pall from the north now covered the hills upriver, and from
beneath it emerged a thin, white streak, from bank to bank
of the wide flood.

Thin; but even in that instant growing taller, nearer.

"Into the boat, children, hurry! No, leave the paddle,
Catalina." For the child was tugging at it. She just about
threw Lijntje in, ripped out the mooring rope and as it happened the paddle too, pushed the boat hard, and jumped in
quickly.

"We've got to race that freshet, children," she called, as
cheerily as she could above the strange, growing roar. "Or
we'll get soaked." No sense in frightening them and perhaps
making them lose an oar or paddle. But Isaak must have
guessed the danger, his face white, his mouth set.

Faster than any boat she had ever seen they shot down
with the current. Faster than anything perhaps but a horse-
drawn racing sleigh skimming over the ice. But compared
with the speed of that growing wall of tumbling white water
they seemed to stand still. Now they were almost opposite
the farm landing place, rowing square across the current with
every ounce of effort, but utterly unable to close that narrow
gap between boat and shore.

Grita's last clear impression was, strangely, of the odor of
deep woods after heavy rain on a hot day. A brief glimpse

of tree trunks, whole trees, churning over in that white wall
of water.

Then the wave struck.

Moments of choking panic, deep under the water. Then
she was gasping, swimming, in the boiling tossing flood. Isaak
was clinging to the upturned boat. Catalina splashing valiantly, still supported a little by the air in her clothes, needed
only an extra push from Grita to join him. One hen, her legs
still tied, had managed by a miracle to find a perch on the
slippery bottom of the boat. The tub had no keel, and all
Grita and the others could do was to dig fingernails into
cracks and irregularities in the planking and hold on. For
how long? The water was smoother now, but gaspingly
cold.

"I told you we'd get soaked if we lost that race," she
forced herself to shout cheerfully. And saw Isaak's white
face relax its tenseness into a wavery grin.

She raised her voice above the noisy waters. "Well, now
we're wet all over we can't get any wetter, that's one comfort. Don't try to lift yourself too far out of the water, children, that will only tire your arms." She was grateful that
for the last three years, during the hot summer months, she
had taken the children swimming so often, though Mother
had thought it was all foolishness. "When we come near the
director's wharf we'll all shout together. If Andries hasn't
come back yet with Mother and the boat, we'll have to shout
again when we get near Beverwyck."

Yes, that would be the best plan; better than trying to
swim ashore, hampered with sodden garments. The only serious danger was from the coldness of the water, she told herself. But knew that wasn't true. She watched with a sick
feeling in her heart the last futile struggles of three brown-
feathered bodies, away off to one side, and hoped the children wouldn't notice. Catalina's mouth was a thin line of
dogged determination as she clung on tightly; how like
Mother she looked now. Isaak was grinning wanly, telling

himself no doubt that this was an adventure and he'd better enjoy it to the full.

The body of a deer, head down, rolling a little from side to side, drifted towards them, then away. An uplifted bough of hickory with, strangely enough, a living squirrel on it, came toward them, retreated farther out into the full current, and was swept headlong downstream. Then, and without any warning this time, another freshet struck. Smaller this one, for there had been no preliminary roar, or perhaps that was drowned in the steady boom of the swollen river.

The river had charged them once, like a bull, but had failed to kill them outright. Now it was charging again, trying to kill them for certain. With a crash it hit, trying to kneel on them and squeeze the last breath out of their bodies.

The same choking panic. Then the same gasping and anxious search for Isaak and Catalina. They were here, but striking out desperately for the boat! The boat, now a good thirty yards away and caught by some swirl of water, heading out towards midstream.

"No! No!" she shouted to them. "This way! To shore!"

Isaak heard, and turned. Good boy! But the little girl, perhaps too panic-stricken to think or reason, was struggling onward and away from the others.

"Head for the shore, Isaak," she told him. And catching Catalina, turned her bodily around. The little one clung to her, as was only natural, and, in trying to lift herself safely above the water, pushed Grita under.

Not overgently, for the need was urgent, Grita tore off the clinging fingers. Then, with what amounted to inspiration, set one of her pigtails within their grasp. The fingers clutched and held.

"Hang on, and I'll tow you, just as I towed the boat. And kick out with your legs, just as you helped with your paddle," she ordered sharply. This was no time to risk disobedience.

Slowly, for haste would only exhaust her strength, she swam towards Isaak and the shore line. The first bouyancy of air had gone from her clothing and now 'twas no more than a heavy clinging handicap. Isaak, when she reached him, was having trouble, trying to swim with head and shoulders above the stream, and already exhausted by the wasteful, frightened effort. If he would only swim as he had been taught, he could have outdistanced Grita with the encumbering Catalina, but fear would not let him. Well, he couldn't be blamed, he must simply be added to the tow.

"Hang on to my other braid!"

He seemed not to understand, so she had to put the end in his hand. "Now swim with your feet, just as Catalina's doing." Mechanically, without thinking, he obeyed her words.

And that was all, except for a growing exhaustion, and the awful despair which comes with it. Well-known landmarks drifted by: the place from which Father Hoorn had to drive his cattle, the director's house. She remembered shouting, but not loud enough, for no one heard. Perhaps in her growing weakness she only whispered.

Between there and Beverwyck she was almost ashore, for a moment touched bottom. Only to be swept away again. Anger, at what seemed so mean a trick for the river to play, gave her a brief renewal of strength.

There was the time when she had choked, no longer able to keep her head above the water. There was the time when she heard voices and felt rough hands almost tear her arms from their sockets, as though lifting. She had the impression that the two children were safe, though perhaps that was only hope.

Then her thoughts grew quite unreliable, for here she was imagining herself back in her own bed, with the two children beside her. And hot stones, wrapped in cloth, warming them up under a deep feather comforter. Which was all quite impossible, because no one stepped straight from a cold river into a warm bed. And she certainly hadn't walked here.

Her body was cold too, which must mean she was dead. Dead? Yes, somebody was dead; she had heard the word.

Somebody was drowned. And tears were streaming down Father Hoorn's face as he put more cloth-wrapped, hot stones into the bed.

For it was Mother who was drowned. Mother who had trusted the river once too often. Grita knew she should be sorry. But she couldn't be. Because if she and Mother were both drowned, that would mean they'd be together again. Perhaps with the children too. Though how selfish of her.

She moved a hand feebly to wipe off a tear, and drifted into darkness and deep sleep.

Chapter Eight
Kaspar Keeps His
Mouth Shut

FOR WHAT must have been a full hour Kaspar waited in
Beverwyck; waited outside in the rain, holding onto
the halter of the pack horse, while through the open
window could be seen Mynheer Nicholas, hobnobbing over
a tiny glass of cordial. Well, an apprentice or a newcomer at
any trade had to expect that sort of treatment. But also he
had to stand up for himself.

In fact, he might have waited for another hour, or longer,
still in the chilling spring rain if he hadn't finally bethought
himself to lead on. He turned up a narrow passage, between
two houses, that seemed to head for a cow byre. Just as com-

109

fortless here; but to be out of sight might make the clerk grow anxious lest he lose not only his provisions for the journey, but the load of sewant intrusted for the purchase of skins. Only a few minutes of waiting, when Kaspar had the pleasant satisfaction of seeing the clerk hurrying past the end of the passage, carrying his musket. So intent was the man that one could even note, without being seen, the anxiety on his shriveled face. Kaspar grinned, the ruse had worked. He uprooted his feet from the deep mud and followed after.

At the Schenectade gate in the north side of the palisade and a little east of the fort, there was Nicholas waiting, his shoulders hunched almost to his hat against the downpour. And, as Kaspar and the pack horse came in sight, the citizen to whom Mynheer Nicholas was talking pointed.

So-ho. Mynheer had grown anxious enough to make inquiries had he? "My lady will please to note," he addressed the falcon on his wrist, "that two can play at this game of teasing. Remember that, next time you rake away in your wide circles and pretend you cannot hear my call!"

Nicholas, of course, was raging. "Is it thus that we start on a journey; by showing disobedience?" he demanded, and his long, thin nose was red with anger and two spots of color burned just below his pale, light eyes. "What would the director say!"

"Return and ask him then," was Kaspar's sensible suggestion. "The trail to Schenectade," he inquired of the man at the gate, "is it hard to find?"

"Straight as your nose and wide as your breeches," said the man, chuckling.

"Good." Kaspar led out through the stockade, along what, to start with at least, was a deep-rutted wagon road. Nicholas, he noted, salved his dignity by exchanging a few more sentences with the citizen before he followed. Honors were even so far; if Nicholas would learn to treat him decently, they might have a pleasant journey together in spite of the weather. And there was one thing to be said for this con-

tinual downpour, it seemed to keep the domestic poultry off
the greening pastures. If any game appeared, he could fly the
falcon without risk.

A rabbit broke from a clump of weeds, and bolted ahead
up the road. Kaspar threw off the peregrine. Without climbing for height to swoop, she chased her quarry, bound to him
with a tinkle of her bell and killed with one needlelike talon
pressed through the brain. Kaspar raced up to her, gathered
her on his glove, gave her the proper meed of praise, and
returned, to sling the rabbit into one of the pack horse panniers. He shouldn't have flown her at rabbit of course, nor
let her kill almost off his fist, for, if she got accustomed to
such lowly game and goshawk ways of killing, the falcon
might turn into a mere "ratter" like a short-winged hawk,
and grow too lazy to match her wings against more noble
birds, birds which flew high and fast. But Nicholas' obvious
displeasure tempted him again; this time it was one of those
swift and low-flying partridges the peregrine brought to
earth. Thence onward he let her circle in a joy flight, wider
and wider, higher and higher, whistling her delight, 'till at
the end of the clearing, before the road plunged into a tunnel
of woodland, he was forced to call her in.

Dark it was, under the overarching trees, and the rain,
curiously enough, seemed the heavier for their protection.
Not that it really was, but the downpour gathering on leaves
and twigs came down in larger drops or let fall a small
stream as from a roof gutter as they passed. Here there was
naught to do save just plod on, leading the horse, and sheltering the falcon as best he could by taking off his coat and
wearing it cloakwise. Rain never hurt anyone and he had
never minded it before; yet now he found himself growing
irritated. Puzzling it was, till he discovered the cause. And
the cause wasn't the rain at all.

Nicholas, of course.

Quite a simple trick, and nothing one could really openly
resent. The clerk had gone ahead while Kaspar flew the fal-

con. Now what the man was doing was to set a pace a little too fast for the slow walk of the pack horse, and much too slow for a horse's trot. To maintain this awkward speed Kaspar discovered that, for the last half-league, he had been hauling the horse along almost bodily. He slacked off the lead rope and dropped back to a more normal pace. Nicholas went on.

It was hard to see why the clerk should harbor such a lasting grudge. For that was just how it seemed. An apprentice or a newcomer expects to be tested and baited and annoyed, and gets what he expects till he learns to stand up for himself. Kaspar, during his first few weeks as a furrier's helper in Amsterdam, had been made to eat six square inches of a rotten skin, which he had carelessly passed as good; his two knives, honed to razor sharpness as they had to be, became unaccountably dulled the moment he took his eyes off them; his needles were constantly developing roughnesses, nicked of course with his pair of scissors. And the first trip with Nicholas, east across the river among the Mahicans, had included at first what seemed a similar kind of baiting. Naturally it was Kaspar who had had to carry the pack, with food, with trade goods and with sewant or wampum. For Nicholas had the pretext that he must be free to use the musket at any moment. And, naturally enough, the man had so overloaded the pack, that Kaspar had had to carry back a good half of the trade goods, in addition to the full weight of the beaver skins. It was only to be expected that Nicholas should pretend there was a hostile Indian behind every tree and rock; Kaspar would have tried to plague a newcomer in just that same way. And he had insisted that Kaspar should tread close on his heels for the entire journey.

Not that Kaspar had. The boslooper had told him enough about the Mahicans and the Maquas to make him feel free to set his own pace and not keep his head under Nicholas' hat. And more out of brag than anything, to show that the heavy load meant nothing to him, he had loped on ahead, had flown the hawk at the first Indian clearing he came to, waited for the director's clerk, and repeated the same process later on.

Instead of taking the failure of his baiting in good part, as any decent fellow would, Mynheer Nicholas had seemed to be soured by it. Not at any time a pleasant companion, he had refused point-blank to teach Kaspar any of the Indian speech, or even the sign language that he used to supplement it. Though surely that would have been in the interest of the director. In return, Kaspar amused himself by showing an appalling ignorance of anything to do with pelts and of concealing what Indian sign language he had already learned from Grita.

Perhaps Mynheer Jeremias had guessed something of what had gone on, for on their return he said nothing of Kaspar's training in furs, had seemed purposely to conceal it, to Kaspar's mild chagrin. He had looked forward to seeing the expression on Nicholas' face when he learned that his raw, new help was really an expert. It was Jeremias himself who suggested they take a horse when going to the Maqua country.

"But the boy is strong. There is no need . . ." Nicholas started to say. Then his lips twisted into what might pass for a smile. "But certainly Mynheer; that would be better. You are quite right." Almost too anxious to agree.

Kaspar could guess now what had passed in that devious mind; that, tied as it were to the horse's lead rope, this newcomer would have no chance for falconry, or anything else; would just have to plod at Nicholas' heels, when he wasn't loading or unloading or watering or feeding or safeguarding the horse.

Schenectade was a full day's journey, so there was no need for hurry. For a league or more he could let the pack horse take its natural slow walking pace, then by a league or so of easy trotting he could catch up with the clerk, long before nightfall and their destination. He threw the lead rope back over the panniers and wandered casually along, trying to name the trees by what Grita had told him, and comparing them with those in the homeland; considering too how long it would be before he could afford to buy himself a firearm. In this country one was scarce deemed a man if one walked unarmed. By the deer tracks crossing the trail one could see that the forests were alive with game.

Not a fowling piece such as the gentlemen now carried in the homeland; he detested them as much as Grita did the beaver trade. What he wanted was a gun with a good long barrel, perhaps as much as five feet, an Utrecht lock, firing a good heavy ball, as Gideon recommended. But it would cost as much as twenty guilders, even in the homeland.

There was a question of course, and a difficult question; how hunting could be combined with falconry. A man couldn't shoot with a hawk on his wrist; it would ruin the bird anyway. And the more time spent on hunting the less there would be for hawking.

He had passed two clearings of abandoned farms or small deserted villages, and each time welcomed the glimpse of sky again, as he came out of the dark tunnel of the forest. But the clearings were too small, too overgrown with aspen, which they called poplar over here, and that quick-growing stuff which Grita said the Indians called sumac. They were of no value for hawking.

Again the woodland thinned ahead; another clearing, bigger and this time not abandoned. Half a dozen houses of one story, with about one glassless window apiece, built of unsawn timber, and showing more mud and moss calking between the logs than actual logs. Not to be compared with the real houses of Beverwyck. Just a cluster of hunters' or traders' cabins, and not a real farm settlement, or there would have been more cleared land and more sign of livestock. Just a hole in the woods. But of course the inevitable chickens; whatever people might say against Indians, they didn't spoil a man's hawking with domestic poultry! Disappointed, he was leading by, was almost in the leafy tunnel again, when he chanced to look back.

Peering cautiously around the corner of a house was a head he recognized. Nicholas.

Kaspar led on a pace or two, with the tempting notion of pretending that he had not seen, perhaps of circling round through the woods, coming in behind and watching Nicholas hurry on toward Schenectade to catch him. He would have done it too, if the clerk had been more of a human being; but a jest should be shared between friends, not wasted on a sour-visaged pest like this one. Reluctantly Kaspar turned around, led back to the settlement and called loudly:

"Mynheer Nicholas!"

"Oh, it's you, is it?" The clerk pretended surprise. "You have taken so long that now we'll have to spend the night here."

Kaspar looked expressively at the sun, appearing pale and watery through the clouds, but still high in the heavens, and shrugged his shoulders. Three or four children had gathered, a woman looked out of a doorway, and two men appeared.

"There's an open shed at the back where you can put up the horse, and spread out the things that have got wet," Nicholas directed sourly. "You'd best stay close by the horse too, and sleep there yourself to save it being stolen by Indians."

One of the men muttered something to the clerk; Nicholas nodded. And all three looked at Kaspar as if he had the little plague. It was only long afterwards, when he traveled the same road again, that he learned that this, or something very like it, was what Nicholas had told the settlers.

There seemed nothing to do but lead around and put the beast under cover. Not much of a shelter to spend the night: just a bark roof, leaking in places, with a back and two sides. Kaspar made a perch for the falcon by driving a stick into the side of the stall, well away from the horse, lifted off the

deerskin-covered panniers and the saddle, scrubbed down the
animal's back with a handful of hay and examined him for
galls. Partly because he liked animals and believed that a
good tool, animate or inanimate, needed good care, partly
so Mynheer Nicholas would have no honest grounds for complaint. Then, through the still drizzling rain, he led the horse
down to the edge of a kill which seemed to be the village
watering place.

A sudden breath of suspicion, with nothing to justify it,
but so strong that he left the horse hitched to an alder and
hastened back, under cover of a convenient building, to the
shed. And there was Nicholas, the deerskin cover to the
pannier unfastened, and one hand drawing out a string of
sewant.

Well, he was entitled to, of course. But there was just the
chance that if he hadn't been caught he would have counted
over the goods at the next halt and blamed Kaspar for the
shortage.

Kaspar coughed. "Allow me to help you. The food is in
the other bag."

Mynheer Nicholas was startled enough to justify Kaspar's
doubts of his good intentions. But he recovered quickly.

"I must pay for my night's board, and this is a fair charge
upon the patroonship."

It might be or it might not, and it was none of Kaspar's
business at the moment. But a boy brought up in Amsterdam
is a plain fool if he doesn't learn to safeguard himself.

"Since you will sleep behind bolts and bars, it is better that
you take charge of the sewant and trading knives and duffel."
That was just a tactful way of putting it. What he meant
was that he refused to accept responsibility for the sewant,
the shell currency of the country, if Mynheer Nicholas
dipped into it for his own use and in attempted secrecy.

And the clerk was smart enough to understand. Surprisingly he made no objections when Kaspar lifted the pannier
and set it across the man's thin shoulders.

By the time Kaspar had fixed the shelter to his satisfaction, the light rain had ceased. Just outside, over a little wood fire, the rabbit and part of the partridge were grilling on a green stock; the rest of the partridge, raw, was already fed to the now drowsy falcon. And the horse, eating his evening ration of grain spread out on a deerskin before him, seemed contented enough. Kaspar alone was troubled. His wet clothes didn't bother him. As soon as he was ready to sleep, he would pull down some of the hay, stacked upon poles just overhead, and spread it over him; in the morning he'd be as dry as toast.

It was Nicholas that troubled him. There was more, a heap more to the clerk's tricks than plain apprentice-baiting. But what was behind it all? What was the reason for it? The simplest guess was that the director's clerk resented Jeremias' orders to take Kaspar along and teach him the country and the people, and was trying to sicken Kaspar of the arrangement. Since no one had ever before taken such a hearty dislike to him, Kaspar searched back for some cause. He had started out on that first trip doing exactly what he was told, treating the clerk with proper deference, as a new hand should treat his superior. And for that matter, he still treated him with an outward respect, even though he was beginning to mistrust him. Naturally he had kept his mouth shut, for a shut mouth swallows least flies. But how much more fun the whole journey would have been with somebody you could chat and joke with, someone like Gideon, the boslooper. He could have learned ten times as much from Gideon as from this crotchety clerk, who had never condescended to teach him anything.

Curiously enough, Kaspar hadn't so much as mentioned the boslooper. Except of course to Grita. Nicholas and Gideon must surely have run across each other, and in the ordinary way it would have been pleasant to discuss a mutual acquaintance.

Before his meal was over it started to rain again. Kaspar

stepped back into the shed, hauled down the hay for himself
and more for the horse to champ on, and though there was
still perhaps an hour of daylight, curled up and went to sleep.
It was more pleasant than to continue to puzzle over Mynheer Nicholas.

Early next morning, under a pale watery sun, they took
to the road; the clerk so snarly of temper and red-rimmed of
eye that Kaspar could guess what some of the sewant had
gone to purchase. To make things worse for Mynheer Nicholas, and to guard against any excuse for his complaining
again if Kaspar lagged behind, the boy drew out of the settlement ahead, slapped the pack horse to a comfortable trot,
and hawk on wrist, loped on along the trail.

And long before he expected it, came within sight of the
river; the river of the Maqua people. And on the bank quite
a substantial settlement. Smaller than Beverwyck of course,
and not for a moment to be compared with the Manhatens.
But far different from the hovels of overnight. If the cross-
grained Nicholas had wanted to press on, he could easily have
reached here yesterday before sundown, and even have had
an hour of daylight left to start purchasing beavers.

Swinging downhill, Kaspar lost sight of the place among
the trees; then coming out into cultivation, was pleasantly
surprised. The village was busy as a beehive; there seemed
as many boats on this river as on the larger one to the south.
A few dugouts, a birch bark or two glistening white in the
midmorning sun, elm bark showing almost black-green, and
what was obviously a white man's boat, broad and clumsy
beside those graceful eggshells, ferrying three cows to the
farther bank.

The sensible place to wait for the clerk would be in the
market place. Kaspar led in through the stockade, following
the road through the center of the neat little settlement.
Small patches of garden had already been hoed; apple blos-
som in red bud, and pear already white in full blow, showed

between and behind the houses. Dutch fashion, even here so far from the homeland, each house was set gable end to the road. A half-dozen narrow, thatched stalls showed where the market was, but the market was empty. Considering the buzz of activity he had heard from outside the stockade, the settlement itself seemed remarkably quiet and deserted.

Kaspar led on and out through the farther gate. And here, by the riverside, as he expected, lay for the moment the real life of the town.

It was hard to see, at first, just who was buying and who was selling. In a sense it wasn't buying at all, but swapping. An Indian would swing up the bank carrying his beaver skins, or sometimes with a squaw carrying them for him, dump the pile on the ground and stand waiting for a white man; or sometimes the Indian would walk slowly past the piles of trade goods which the white man had exposed for sale, be attracted by duffel cloth, by an iron kettle, by a set of rusty hinges, by an ax, and do part, the first half, of his bargaining there, the second half over the pelts he proposed for payment.

Kaspar offered his greetings to the few, quite few, who noted him, and was courteously answered. A pleasant change from following in the wake of Nicholas. He watered the pack horse upstream, returned, and leaning his back comfortably against the stockade, the lead rope still in his hand, settled down to watch and wait.

When you saw a number of them together like this, the Maquas, the People of the Bear, were quite distinct from the River Indians, the Mahicans; darker, their hair a little coarser, perhaps not quite so tall, and certainly a rougher, fiercer-looking lot. Fortunate it was that they had made a chain of friendship with the Netherlanders. And kept it too, by all accounts. For if they really were as ruthless as they appeared, and cannibals too by all accounts—at least they killed and ate their prisoners of war—they would be unpleasant foes. And their speech seemed different too. Here and

there a white man seemed to understand it, but mostly each
trader kept to his own native speech, without seeming to
understand or trying to understand the other; and here, as
down-river, relied on sign language. There was the sign for
"beaver" that Grita had taught him; that came in many
times. There was a sign that must mean "many" or "more":
the two hands, palm inward and fingers a little bent, came
down drawing closer together, then closing swung up and
apart. It must mean that, or something like it, for twice in
response to such a sign an Indian had added another beaver
to his pile. The sign for "gun" was simple: just the gesture
of setting a gun to the shoulder. One Indian made it several
times, averting his head in between as if unwilling to consider the other attractive objects offered him in trade, and at
last, with apparent reluctance, the white man sent back into
the village, and ten minutes later Kaspar saw the Indian pil-
ing up skins to the height of the firearm; just as a Mahican
had done at Esopus. Grita was right; it was going to be easier
to learn to talk by sign than to twist one's tongue around
these strange languages. And if she were right when she said
the same signs were understood even in different tribes, that
would give it a great advantage over the spoken word.

It grew pleasantly warm in the shelter of the stockade, and
soon an Indian woman and two children sat down on one side
of him, and a Netherlander, with a yoke of oxen and a sled,
drew in on the other, cutting off all view of the market. Kaspar felt too sleepy and relaxed to bother to move. He had
learned six new signs, or thought he had, and the next pleasant happening would be when Mynheer Nicholas arrived—
he seemed to be taking a plaguy long time—and they bought
themselves something to eat. Not for a fortune would he
untie the bag of sewant, unless the clerk were here to see.

Kaspar exchanged a few words with the ox driver, tried a
few signs on the Indian woman, though she took not the
faintest notice, and was almost asleep, when, glancing under
the bellies of the oxen, he saw a pair of thin shanks that he

recognized. Well, the clerk could hunt up the pack horse leader today, since yesterday it was the pack horse leader who had had to hunt up the clerk.

Rolling over on one elbow to get a better view, Kaspar watched with amusement. The man was glancing here and there, making curt and hasty acknowledgment of various greetings, and really seemed anxious about something. Then, catching sight apparently of the man he sought, and who certainly wasn't Kaspar, he quickened his pace toward him.

The man straightened up from tying a bundle. For a moment the fur cap and deerskin hunting shirt made Kaspar think 'twas Gideon Dolph. But this man, as he looked over his shoulder toward Nicholas, showed a short, brilliant red beard, and anyway, though stocky enough he was far too short for the boslooper.

They knew each other, Mynheer Nicholas and Red Beard —that was clear. The man untied the bundle he had just tied up, and showed each one of his pelts; mostly beaver they seemed to be, from where Kaspar lay, except for one fox and perhaps a marten or two. This man was no doubt another boslooper, doing his own independent trapping.

Mynheer Nicholas must have decided not to buy, for the man again began to tie his bundle and wrap the deerskin around it. When from a pocket the clerk took a letter, it was too far even to see the handwriting, let alone the name on it. Red Beard nodded, stuffed it into the bundle and, finishing tying, he set off down the riverbank to his canoe.

A puzzling transaction. Afterwards Kaspar blamed himself for not watching longer, but he was hungry. He gave the lead rein to the ox driver, jumped up, and plunged after Nicholas.

And Nicholas, eager to find cause for complaint, jumped to the wrong conclusions.

"So, again you have dallied for your hawking! An hour, two hours I have been waiting for you."

Did the idiot think you could fly a falcon in thick forest land?

Kaspar put on a look of innocence. "Where do we eat?"

"Eat?" fumed the clerk. "Always some excuse for delay. Now you have at last arrived, I will hire the boat to ferry us across the river. Tonight we sleep at a castle of the Maquas."

Kaspar went back for the horse, amusement struggling with indignation and an empty stomach.

Chapter Nine
The Falcon Meets
a Strange Bird

B Y THE SUN it was midmorning or thereabouts when
Kaspar, Nicholas and the pack horse came out of the
tunnel of trees into what was Indian farm land, Maqua
farm land.

Mynheer Nicholas seemed dispirited, as well he might;
his insistence, yesterday, on pushing along beyond Schenectade had led them at nightfall to a deserted hunter's shack
of bark, roofless and with only part of two walls. During the
night it had rained again. And this time there had been no
chance for the clerk to slip away and gorge himself; such
food as he had was cold journeycake of cornmeal from one
of the pack baskets.

123

Kaspar, striding easily behind, grinned to see the clerk's
short fussy gait lengthen and hasten as they came in sight
of the Maqua "castle." Perched atop a bare hill and overlooking the river it was; and, from here below, nothing of
the village could be seen, it was so hidden by the high stockade, higher, if not so smooth as the stockade of Beverwyck
or of the Manhatens. Surprising that savages, with neither
draft animals, pulleys nor iron tools, could have set those
heavy tree trunks so firmly into the ground and so closely together. Surprising too, come to think of it, that without ax or
plow or good, iron-headed Dutch hoe, they could clear and
cultivate so wide a stretch of countryside around their village.

Children, stark naked in the chill damp air, came running,
yelling shrilly. A group of youths, amusing themselves with
a rolling hoop through which they shot arrows, picked up
their shafts and with elaborate show of casualness happened
to find themselves hurrying back in the same direction as
the two white men and pack horse, which resulted in some
jostling on the narrow path that wound up the hillside. A
small child, pushed by another, fell against the horse's leg;
the child—it was a girl apparently—was frightened but un-
hurt. Kaspar picked her up and balanced her between the
panniers, where she spatted her hands and laughed and the
others joined in the laughter.

So laughing, at least four children tried to crowd through
the narrow gate of the stockade at the same time as the
horse. Since the Indians had no sleds or wagons or ox teams,
the entrance was barely wide enough for the panniers to
crowd through. But no one came to harm. And that again
seemed to be a good jest. Kaspar found it hard to believe
that these were really the fierce Maquas, the dread of the
countryside, who tortured to death and even ate their
prisoners.

From inside, the stockade differed a little from the others
he had seen. Instead of an earthen, grass-grown bank piled

up against the logs, here was only a wooden platform, a light
and insecure scaffolding; to reach it the defenders must climb
those notched poles, surely a difficult feat at night and when
carrying weapons. Piles of stones, of convenient size for
throwing, and bark containers, perhaps to hold water, were
spread around the fighting platform. But even more interesting were the houses. Of bark they were, thick wide slabs of
bark almost as flat as boards, sewn to tall upright poles with
wide strands of elm fiber; the same bark, maple it looked
like, was laid shinglelike along the sloping roofs, along the
edge of which a few grim bleaching skulls were placed; as
they also grinned from atop some of the stockade posts.

From one of the larger houses a group of Maqua men
emerged with a musket, making signs for the white men to
enter.

"Tie the horse," Nicholas ordered peremptorily. "And
bring in both panniers."

It was dry inside, dim and smoky. In the middle of the
hard-beaten clay floor a fire smoldered, its smoke escaping
through a hole in the bark roof, and around it, by the time
Kaspar had lugged in both baskets, were seated Nicholas and
a dozen or more of the savages. Handsome men they were
too; even the old ones, wrinkled as they were, seemed to
have retained their teeth and their hair and looked lean and
hard. The red earth with which they so often ornamented
themselves had left a red polish to their skins, so much darker
than the Mahicans. Except for their deerskin aprons and
moccasins, they wore no garments; the duffel or blanket
thrown over one shoulder seemed as much an adornment as
the shell- and porcupine-decorated arm bands and necklaces.

Only the younger men permitted themselves a glance of
curiosity, as Kaspar, at the clerk's direction, unpacked the
first of the loads. Custom or good manners seemed to dictate
that the remainder should sit in silence, withdrawn and apparently uninterested.

"That will do," said Mynheer Nicholas. "You may go."

Kaspar hesitated. There was a pleasant odor of cooking, and now he could see, in front of the bunks ranged along the walls, no less than four cook fires, with women working quietly about them. If ever he went out again on an expedition with Nicholas, he would first reach a hard and fast understanding on this subject of meals, and make some arrangement that would allow him to sit in on the bargaining and pick up hints. He was sure this wasn't what the director had planned or expected.

Well, there was no sense in sitting somewhere in the background, like a beggar waiting for scraps from a feast. Kaspar ducked out under the low door, parted the hovering crowd of youngsters, perched the hawk on his hat for a moment while he relieved the horse of his wooden packsaddle, and considered his next move.

The clouds were still low, but broken by glimpses of sunlight and blue sky. He would have liked to wander around and see how these people lived, but not knowing their ways he was cautious lest he infringe on some tribal custom. He glanced round him. Too many dogs and children here in the village, and the falcon was ill at ease.

But it wasn't so simple to shake off the dogs and the children. Out through the gate of the stockade and down the hill they streamed after him, their shrill voices and loud yaps making the falcon still more uneasy.

"Like to get clear of the rabble, my lady?" he asked her and flung her up into the air.

Gratefully she spread wings, swung off in a wide circle, found an updraft of air where the breeze hit the hill and was deflected, balanced on it awhile, rising a little. Then swooped off and climbed again. Around him fell a sudden silence, a silence of disappointment and dismay. No longer excited by the yells of the children, even the dogs had stopped their barking.

Kaspar looked around to see the cause. Then suddenly guessed it. These children thought he had thrown away a captive bird; had let it fly off, back to its wild state. So much the better, for after a few sad looks at the diminishing dot up in the skies, a few words of what sounded like argument, most of his "tail" broke off and drifted away.

So it was the bird that had held them! He chuckled. What a blow to his pride! A Netherlander, by himself, was apparently too much of a commonplace to interest them.

He'd give the peregrine a good chance to wait on and stretch her wings before even attempting to beat up a quarry for her; and if Nicholas wouldn't let him learn anything about beaver trading, he would just amuse himself and the falcon.

Three loyal followers alone remained, a girl and two boys, when Kaspar decided it was time for the falcon to come in. He swung his lure and called, and the all but invisible bird must have been waiting for the signal. Every good falcon, in fact every good animal, is a show-off, and Kaspar's bird was no exception.

She dived. For the space of one pulse beat she grew in size from insect to bird; for the space of another she fell so fast that you could hear, or imagine you heard, the wind whistle past her wing feathers. Nearer, nearer, till a gasp of amazement, perhaps even of fear, came from Kaspar's "tail."

The briefest fraction of time, as he held out his heavy glove, and the bird seemed about to hurtle past and crash to death. Then suddenly she was hanging on the air, every feather outstretched, and dropped gently, perhaps six inches, onto his glove.

Oh, it was a pretty sight! And didn't the falcon know it, throwing her bright glance from side to side and posing for admiration!

He stroked her, while she bowed, clasped and unclasped her talons and postured. The three children drew up closer again, shot eager questions at him. It was obvious what they were, and he answered by floating his free hand up into the air and cutting it earthward to grab the smallest of the children by the hair as the falcon grasped her prey. That evoked fresh amusement, and an evident request for the peregrine to give a performance.

The falcon tugged at her jesses, eager to be off again.

"All right, but a proper stoop and no rabbit-snatching," he adjured her.

She wheeled up, and he let her climb before starting to beat up cover to drive forth some game. With so many of these children and even adults such experts in all forms of trapping, there was a scarcity of game, and it was some time before he put up a small covey of partridge. Not much chance that the peregrine could reach them before they dived into the forest; but she must have seen the quarry, for at once she stooped. Only . . . what was happening now?

For the long, plummeting dive stretched away from the forest and out toward the river.

Swiftly he raced down the slope, leaping stumps and bushes, with his tail of children racing and squealing excitement behind him. Right out over the wide river, the peregrine struck; struck and released in an instant. A duck splashed down into the water.

As Kaspar reached the bank, a grown Indian signed to him to stop, almost threw him into his canoe, pushed off; and of a sudden, the river was full of bobbing black heads and of canoes that seemed to have appeared from nowhere.

A swimmer was first to the duck, and tossed the bird into the canoe as Kaspar came up. A call and a signal and the falcon dropped gratefully to wrist. A shout of applause from the Indians.

"Don't let it go to your head, my lady," Kaspar cautioned the smug-looking peregrine. "That last dive was a little too flat for a good stoop; more like a merlin's than a falcon's."

And here was a new and grand idea. In the home country all hawking was done on dry land; on his way upriver from the Manhatens, Kaspar had hawked over the swampy banks and islands. But in this country the rivers were so full of ducks

and geese and herons and birds that he couldn't even recognize, that they would be better hunting grounds than even
the widest swamp or clearing. And safe too. If the falcon
should, by chance, entangle her talons when she struck, and
be drawn down into the water by her falling prey, it would
be possible to rescue her before she came to harm. And after
one such ducking she would be more cautious. So many noble
falcons had met their death plunging upon a tree snag and
impaling themselves that the greater safety of hawking over
water was an additional advantage. If it could be done . . .
No time like the present for trying it.

He was attempting, by a mixture of sign language and
pointing, to persuade the man to head the canoe upstream
when a call came from the shore, from the castle itself. The
man stopped paddling to call back, in the same sort of sing-
song.

Kaspar cursed inwardly, as, falcon on wrist, duck in hand,
he was led once more to the stockade. If Mynheer Nicholas
had now thought up some excuse to interfere with spare-time
hawking, then Mynheer Nicholas would take his next trip
alone.

The crowd that now followed him—it seemed a good half
the village—waited outside.

Growing more and more rebellious, Kaspar strode into the
council house, or whatever it was, where the trading was going on. So far it was clear that not much trading had taken
place; only about six pelts lay by the clerk's side and the pile
of trade goods seemed undiminished.

"Yes?" said Kaspar, holding his temper in leash.

"The bird is sold to the chief for seven beavers," said
Mynheer Nicholas.

Either Nicholas or the chief must be weak in the mind. A
duck wasn't worth seven beavers; it wasn't worth a seventh
of a beaver.

"Perhaps I can get a beaver also for the glove," said
Mynheer Nicholas. "And that beaver shall be your very

own." His face twisted with a grimace that might have been meant for an ingratiating smile.

But why would the chief want a heavy, horsehide glove, too clumsy to be used for anything but hawking? Then Kaspar gasped, as the truth dawned on him.

"You—you're trying to sell my falcon?" he was so furious that he stammered.

"Not yours," said the clerk. "It belongs to the director, for you gave it to him."

"And the director refused the gift. So it remains mine," snapped Kaspar. He hadn't been so utterly mad since he could remember.

"Leave the hawk and go; your duties with me are ended." Nicholas commanded. "And on my return I will inform the director that you do not obey orders; the matter will then be in his hands."

Kaspar, to emphasize his refusal either to sell or to go, sat right down, falcon still on wrist. The peregrine was troubled by Kaspar's anger. He offered her the duck to deplume, but hungry as she was she refused it. He stroked her awhile till she began to be soothed. Then looked about him, to see how the Maqua elders took the dispute. Politely interested they were, perhaps even a little amused; especially the old one with face as wrinkled as old elm bark.

He said something. Mynheer Nicholas passed across to him a knife; he turned it over, tried its edge. And the long process of trading recommenced. But Nicholas was disconcerted; one could see that by the spots of color that burned on his sallow cheeks. Good! He deserved to be.

The beavers, martens and one foxskin, which were passed across for examination, were a very mixed lot; a few, one marten in particular, were beauties. But some were so poor that, by the time they reached the homeland, they would be fit for nothing. What price the clerk was paying for each skin was impossible to guess, for knives, awls, small ax heads, duffel and strings of sewant measured by the fathom and by the hand, kept being passed around, handled, discussed, and sometimes returned. There was no knowing which skins of the pile, that was slowly growing by the clerk's elbow, paid for which trade goods. Current prices, of course, were among the things that Kaspar was supposed to learn on this trip. That was why the director had sent him out with Nicholas.

Was it possible that the clerk was afraid that if Kaspar learned the business, in time he would come to supplant him? That looked very like it. But even that simple explanation of the clerk's growing enmity was puzzling. For Nicholas was always bewailing the little time he had to spend over his account books; and if anyone hated the hardships of travel, making them even worse than they need be, and got absolutely no pleasure or adventure out of them, it was Mynheer Nicholas.

Kaspar watched closely. By keeping a count of the trade goods that were handed over, and finding out, when he got back to Rensselaerswyck, their value in sewant, he could at least get the sum total paid for the skins. Not an easy task, trying to guess whether that length was a fathom and a half of duffel, adding it to seven fathoms already sold, and keeping a running count of all the other articles. As soon as he got out he would cut a stick and make notches on it to help his memory. Thank heaven he had been trained to furs, so he could remember the pelts almost without trying to.

He was still anxiously juggling eight sets of totals in his mind when the wrinkled old savage said something, and rose to his feet. That seemed to end the trading. Kaspar slipped out in search of a tally stick. It took but a moment, for the nearest and most convenient was one of the crossbars of the pack saddle.

With his knife he made long notches for tens, short notches for single trade goods. Now all he had to remember was which crossbar tallied the sewant, which the knives, and so on.

Relieved of its burden, his mind was turning to the thought of food, and not for the first time that day, when the Maqua who had taken him into his canoe beckoned him back into the lodge. To eat.

Crouching in the circle with the others, resting his gloved hand on his knee, for a falcon grows heavy with long carrying, Kaspar dipped with his right hand from the elm bowls and birch-bark platters that were set before him. Many of the flavors were new, though there were raisins and nuts and dried seeds baked into the bread, and the meat might be anything, perhaps the bear meat that Gideon said was so good; and there was a kind of boiled bacon too, bear bacon perhaps, for he knew that the Indians kept bears tied up, and fattened them for eating, as a Netherlander would a pig. He hoped that they were, just today, eating no prisoners of war, and mischievously suggested the thought to Mynheer Nicholas.

The clerk set down an appetizing gobbet of bear meat, and gulped several times before he could force himself to continue the meal.

Kaspar had finally satisfied his past hunger, but still he went on eating. With no sewant to purchase his own food, and the clerk seeming to believe that he could live on air, he would probably go hungry on the trip home; the more he ate now the longer he would postpone that discomfort. Nor did the hawk go hungry, for as he ate he let her deplume the duck and eat a good half of it.

At last, uncomfortably gorged, he rose to his feet, almost staggered to the door. A nice spot in the sun beside the pack horse, and sleep, that was what he sought. But that was not to be. He had scarcely stretched out, tied the hawk's jesses to the leash on the near-by pack saddle, when the "tail" appeared again. This time accompanied by their fathers and mothers, some of them even with their elder brothers and sisters. And what they wanted would be clear to a deaf mute, or even a blind man.

He sat up, leaned head on hand, and made signs of sleeping. He pointed to the falcon and made the same sign. Apparently that struck his audience as delightfully comical. Well, he could sit right here and entertain them, or go hawking. What he wasn't to be allowed to do, and that was clear, was to sleep.

He struggled to his feet, picked up the hawk and made for the stockade gate. He couldn't run, that was certain, not with all that food inside him. And if the peregrine managed to climb into the air at all—he grinned at the absurd thought —she would probably fall asleep on the wing. Perhaps he could borrow a canoe—he headed toward the river. Once out in the stream, with someone paddling, he could get his sleep. Perhaps.

Too dull-witted after the heavy meal to have a clear notion of how it happened, he found walking by his side the old wrinkled counselor, or chief, or whatever he was. Then a heron flew over. Without thinking, Kaspar flew the falcon.

The quarry was too low, too unsuspecting, to put up a chase. The falcon struck, a feather or two floated off, and the heron flopped suddenly down on the farm land. A dozen willing human retrievers raced after it, brought it back. Kaspar, not needing it for his own use, presented it to the chief, and noted with interest that the old man parted the feathers to see where the talons had struck. A falconer would do that, to gauge the skill of a bird, but scarce another man in ten thousand. Kaspar wished yet more that he knew the Maqua speech; a man so asute as this would be worth talking to.

And now the falcon was being coy; her head turned with too much attention or her stomach too full of food, she hung in the air and refused to see his signals or even to hear his calls. Well, let the bird go hang for a time; the main thing was to get away from this crowd. And here was the river-bank and several canoes.

The chief stepped lightly in, and Kaspar, as seemed to be expected, followed; it was a big canoe, and four other men took up the paddles. They headed, this time, down-river. They seemed to have a purpose, dropping down to some three hundred paces beyond the edge of the farm land, holding the canoe stationary against the current, and waiting there, almost under the shadow of the forest. While, from somewhere in the forest came shoutings and bangings.

Kaspar, lazily replete, eyes half-closed, summoned up just enough energy to signal to the falcon, and call. Either a cloud shifted a little or she drifted a little toward him; but showed no wish to come down. The banging and shouting in the forest grew closer; it seemed to come from a widely stretched line, not from just one spot.

The boslooper had told of a way the Indians had of driving game over a cliff, or into a trap; perhaps, Kaspar thought sleepily, they were trying to drive a deer over that sheer bank into the river. A few little birds fluttered out, swung upstream or down, and back to the bank again. The falcon paid no heed.

The chief cast a keen glance upward at the disobedient bird, at the high bank, and then ordered his paddlers to cross to the other side of the river; clearly he had some plan in mind. The falcon, as if interested, floated down to about half her previous height. Kaspar signaled her again. She couldn't help but see him now, but she continued to ignore him.

Then out from the bank shot eight huge birds, like no wild game he had ever seen before. Not geese; they seemed even bigger, and certainly darker. Directly toward the canoe they headed.

Turkeys. Those still rare birds he had seen once or twice in the homeland. But these were wild.

The first stoop missed. Perhaps the falcon, awed by the size of her quarry, deflected her aim. She swung up with the force of her dive, and Kaspar heard and even felt the rush of air driven down by her pinions.

A short stoop and this time a strike. The falcon could as well hope to bring down a cow in a pasture. . . .

Then Kaspar yelled. The all but impossible had happened. Confused rather than hurt, the turkey flopped heavily into the river, missing the canoe by less than a pace and cov-

ering Kaspar with spray. A swing of the paddles, and the
chief himself leaned over and hauled the bird on board. It
was draggled and half drowned, but noble still with its
iridescent plumage and the strange red and blue blobs or
wattles on his neck.

Kaspar thrust out his left hand for the falcon, now poised
just above his head. She dropped her fierce talons delicately
on his glove, and folded her wings, every feather expressing
her pleased triumph. He grasped the jesses; now the bird
was back she was going to stay. And anyway it was growing
too dim even for a falcon's keen eyes to mark down further
quarry.

"You bagged what is called a turkey, I think," Kaspar
told her. "And the first turkey ever killed by a Cralo bird.
Smart, aren't you!" He took out his feather and began to
stroke her.

Then the chief spoke, and in good Netherland speech too.
Kaspar almost fell out of the canoe.

"Friends," said the chief. "You. Me. Nicholas not friend.
Too much trick." And put out his gnarled old hand for the
feather.

Kaspar gave it to him. The chief stroked the falcon a few
times, and the falcon saw fit to "bate" for him and offered to
spring on to his hand. Then, to confirm his proffered friendship, the chief stroked Kaspar twice on the shoulder with the
feather before he handed it back.

That evening there was a feast at another lodge, the Chief
Aquinachoo's own lodge it seemed. And instead of facing
the long journey back to Rensselaerswyck without food, or
sewant to purchase it, Kaspar was put to the greater trial of
showing a courteously voracious appetite for the second time
within a few hours. And since he had been dismissed by Mynheer Nicholas, neither the clerk nor pack horse concerned him.

The feast, thank heaven, ended at last. Kaspar, stretched
out on one of the bunks which ranged along the wall of the

lodge, was giving his full and complete attention to the important process of digestion, when the chief called him again.

Wearily he slipped into his shoes and rejoined the group still sitting about the fire. Some strangers, men he had not seen before, were with the chief; and new arrivals they must be, for now they too were eating. Kaspar gave an inward groan. He couldn't, he simply couldn't, eat another mouthful. But that apparently was not why he had been called.

"Beavers," said the chief. "Many beavers. From the west."

Kaspar came fully awake. Here was an opportunity, a real one, to made a trade and show the director his value to the patroonship. Only . . .

"No sewant. No trade goods." He told the chief. And stretched out empty hands.

Aquinachoo seemed to have realized that. "Tomorrow, friend, you and these men after you to the white man's castle." He meant Beverwyck of course. "Friend. Friend." He indicated the newcomers and Kaspar, and said what must have been the same thing in the Maqua speech. For solemnly the newcomers gave the sign for friendship, raising two fingers upward, side by side.

A boon had been conferred upon him by old Aquinachoo; Kaspar realized that. But his mind was scarcely working. The immediate need was to turn many pounds of bear meat and yellow corn and dried fruits into something called Kaspar de Selle. An ambitious undertaking. He tottered happily back to his bunk, to give his undivided attention to the process of digestion.

Chapter Ten
A New Task
Is a Hard Task

BEVERWYCK already in sight. Kaspar had made good time; there was no chance that Mynheer Nicholas would have reached the patroonship ahead of him. First came the cleared land outside the stockade. No chickens, as far as he could see, but almost stumbling with fatigue he kicked up a rabbit, flew the falcon off his fist, let her kill and greatly relieved in mind waited patiently while she gorged.

A peregrine, like all the long-winged hawks, can go for a day without food, but two days were almost too much for any bird; two days with constant rain added to the hunger,

and a ducking when Kaspar had slipped on a boulder crossing a swollen stream. He swam ashore farther down, with
falcon still on fist. But if ever a bird looked utterly be-
draggled and furious, that was the time.

Nor had Kaspar himself fared too well, for kind as they
were, it had not occurred to his Indian hosts that a white man
might need a little provision for a long journey. The Maquas
had set him ashore on the south bank of their river and
showed him a well-marked trail, which had led, not round by
Schenectade, but direct to Beverwyck. Loping on, circling to
the north of the town stockade, he still had enough life left
to grin at his own simplicity; he had actually thought that by
stretching his pace a little he could reach Rensselaerswyck by
moonlight on the same day. Well, he had stretched his pace
all right, but half of the little streams had turned into raging
torrents, and the other half were almost lakes. When you
swung off upstream to find a less swollen ford, there was, of
course, no corresponding trail to be found on its farther side.
And no sun shone through the black clouds to give you north
and south. Kaspar wouldn't be here now if his feet, by long
practice, hadn't found a way when his mind was so tired as
to be completely befogged.

What had happened to the New Netherland river! From
the high ground where he paused, he could see right up and
down the reach. Farm land, whole meadows of it, had disappeared beneath the brown rolling flood, and the muddy
banks told that it had been even higher a day or two before.
But the Hoorn farm was safe; and the director's house still
stood, though so close to the waterside that it must have
been seriously imperiled. He straightened his left arm for a
moment, to ease its ache, and broke into a lope again to help
forget his gnawing hunger and the bone-deep chill that pene-
trated through his sodden garments. Ahead, and not so far
ahead now, lay the warm dry comfort of the Hoorn kitchen,
the reflection of firelight on the brass candlesticks on the big
dresser, Nelle Hoorn saying, "Good food is the best medi-

cine," and ladling a rich stew of meat and prunes and currants, or perhaps a steaming potage of mashed beans and butter and ginger. And there would be young Isaak who would want to hear all about his journey and what the falcon had caught and what he had said to the Indians, and Catalina and Joan . . . and Grita with her swinging black plaits and trim little lace-edged cap and long Spanish black eyes. The picture had been with him on most of his homeward run, had stayed with him as he briefly rested last night, crouched in a hollow of a tree. Soon now the warmth and the friendship would be around him, the good food beginning to quell the gnawing pains in his stomach. But before that, the director's house.

Leaping a dry stone wall that protected the house and its immediate garden, he all but landed upon the Negro, Andries, who, crouched on the wet ground, was blowing at a fire he had kindled under a three-legged kettle.

Grumbling between puffs he muttered, "You old fire, you lazy good for nothin'! Soon's I turn my back, you up and dies out again!"

"What's the matter, Andries?"

Andries turned up a lugubrious countenance. "The matter is I ain't no fish, and the river done broke into the kitchen." Then had to stint his words to blow his fire again.

Up the short steps from the high ground behind the house to the second story. A knock on the door. A voice called to him to enter, and Kaspar went in.

The council room, a stark and gloomy place at best, was dim today with the overcast skies, its four eastern windows gazing grimly down on the still-swollen river. An untended fire smoldered sullenly on the hearth. Jeremias turned round from the southern windows that faced downstream, and nodded briefly at Kaspar. He looked ill, unshaven, and as if he had not slept.

"That barn withstood the full force of the freshet. But now, when all danger seems past, suddenly it dissolves and is gone. This year again few rents will be paid, and the patroonship must find labor and money for new buildings, for repairs, and funds to replace livestock that has been swept away. Nor is that all the loss . . ."

He had been speaking to Kaspar, but now for the first time he seemed to recognize him. "Put your hawk on a chair back, de Selle. Nicholas is not with you? Nothing has happened to him?"

"Nothing, I hope. I left him at the Maqua castle."

The director seemed a little relieved, but curiously uninterested, even distracted, as Kaspar told his story.

"So he sent you home, did he? I wonder why?" Still standing, he laid a hand on the table. "Of course, he had no right to sell your falcon. Yet it is most unlike Nicholas to wish to lead a laden pack horse when there is someone to do it for him."

Kaspar, his sodden boots making black prints on the boards of the floor as he shifted his stiffening limbs, offered what seemed to be a likely explanation. "I think he did not want me to see what skins he purchased, or what price he paid for them. Perhaps he is afraid that if I learn the trade . . ." He hesitated to say it; it seemed presumptuous, "you might send me out after beaver skins in his place."

The director frowned as if he, like Kaspar, felt that there was something lacking in that explanation.

"And he took good care," went on Kaspar, "to keep me out of his dealings with that other agent of yours, the red-bearded man at Schenectade."

Jeremias pulled out a chair and sat down. "That sounds like Dirck Tienhoven. He's no agent of mine, but an independent boslooper who sells his furs directly to the Manhatens." He fell silent while his fingers drummed nervously on the table. Then seemed to come to a decision.

"I will say nothing of this to my clerk when he arrives. Nor will I mention Dirck Tienhoven. Perhaps it would be wisest if you did not discuss the trip with Nicholas, and if you pretend, as will surely not be difficult, that you are angered at his treatment of you."

Kaspar felt a sudden wave of relief, even of gratitude. Nicholas had as good as dismissed him from the service of the director. During the long chilly night in that tree he had found time to worry over what would happen when he got back to Rensselaerswyck, and whether Mynheer Jeremias would support his clerk and dispense with Kaspar's services.

In one way that would matter little. Here in New Netherlands there were more tasks than hands to perform them. If the patroonship were closed to him, there were the Company settlements and the towns of Beverwyck and the Manhatens. Wouter had offered a job—better than offered, had tried to force him into it.

But the patroonship was more than an employer. It was more than a colony. It was Kiliaen van Rensselaer himself, in his fine house in Amsterdam, saying to a small boy and his father, "It is a new world, no doubt a hard world; as a new task is a hard task, but those who have the courage and the strength need know no poverty, no hunger. In my colony alone is enough land to feed all the poor in Amsterdam. And outside the colony more land than men can use in one hundred years." One thing only had served as a comfort to him, the curious fact that at no time had the director allowed his clerk to suspect Kaspar's long apprenticeship and knowledge of pelts.

Then the director harked back: "You spoke of some Maquas who were to follow you with pelts. Since they travel faster, they are likely to be here before my clerk arrives. I shall need your help when they come."

Perhaps it was a warm rush of gratitude for the director's faith in him that made Kaspar offer, tired and chilled as he was, "Can I help Andries bale out your cellar, Mynheer?"

Again the man's mind seemed to be elsewhere. He ignored the question. "You haven't heard of course; you have not yet been to the Hoorn's?" For the first time he seemed to note

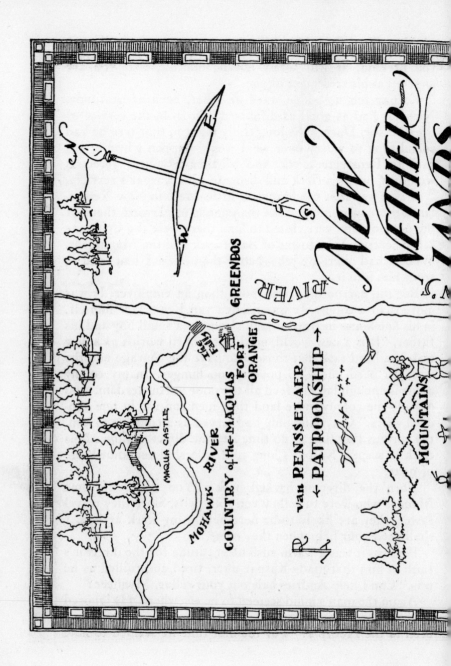

ISLAND of the MANHATENS

COUNTRY of "SEVEN BEAVER SKINS"

ATLANTIC OCEAN

Kaspar's weariness, and muddy garments. "Nelle Hoorn was drowned yesterday, crossing back from the east bank. Andries swam ashore, but neither the boat nor Mvrouw Hoorn's body have yet been found. No, let my cellar wait till the river falls and it drains itself; and go do what you can for the Hoorns." He rose to his feet, in half-dismissal. "And remember you are to call upon me for anything that they may need."

Kaspar, picking up the falcon, felt the ache drain back into his left arm, and stumped wearily down the steps. As he made his way down toward the farm he tried to remember if he had told Mynheer van Rensselaer all that had happened on the trip. And if he had, had the director understood? Back there in the council room they had been like two minds trying to communicate with each other, but each hidden by a fog, Kaspar's of fatigue, the director's of despondency; and now something of the director's mood had added itself to Kaspar's own. Nelle dead? Nelle couldn't have died like that, just swept away into nowhere since he had last seen her, so alive and motherly. That first sheer disbelief he had felt at the death of his own mother, and then of his father, came back again. It was just impossible to believe that someone should be there one day, and gone, wiped out utterly and for good, so quickly. He stumbled as he tried to quicken his lagging pace.

But the truth of it was brought home to him by the black-clad figure just closing the door of the Hoorn's kitchen. Theophilus the Miller, from the kill south of Beverwyck, raised one hand in dignified salutation, then silently climbed aboard his rawboned horse. Theophilus the official comforter-of-the-sick, not actually a minister but one who, in the absence of a minister, could, in New Netherlands as in the old country, solemnize marriages and christenings, bring comfort to the sick and the bereaved.

As Kaspar entered, the Bible from which doubtless Father Hoorn had read a chapter, lay open on the table. Mathias

still sat at the end of the trestle, unmoving, gazing vacantly
into space. But here was none of the damp grimness of the
council room Kaspar had just left; a dry warmth and a rich
odor of baking surged up to comfort him even as he closed
the door behind him.

"God be with this house," said Kaspar conventionally.

A strange woman, thin as a shingle even in her many full
petticoats, straightened up from her task before the fire, and
ladle in hand, spun round to eye him sharply. Small brown
eyes and a large beaky nose, a thin mouth, hair hidden beneath the large spotless cap with its gold bobbles at the
temples, and a chest so flat as to make it uncertain whether
her frock buttoned down its front or its back. That was Anna
Burrgh.

"You're Kaspar de Selle," she accused him, or so it
sounded. "I've heard of you, young man, and take your shoes
off before you come a step farther and your stockings are
soaking and you're wringing wet and what do you mean by
bringing that dirty bird into the house and don't stand there
with your jaw hanging down and draw up to the table and
eat . . ." She paused a moment for breath. "If you're standing there waiting for the end of the world, you've got a long
time to wait yet and a few good tasks to do. Unless men like
you expect us women to do them all."

Anna's hands worked as fast as her bell-clapper tongue,
for the bowl of good food was awaiting Kaspar, even before
he could set down the hooded hawk and pull up a chair.

"Yes, ma'am," said Kaspar dizzily and picked up his horn
spoon.

For the next week every day, rain or shine, Mvrouw Burrgh
appeared at the Hoorn farmhouse, her stout klompen on her
feet, a black shawl around her spare shoulders, a small brown
bag, whose contents were known only to their owner, in her
firm hand and a sentence already forming on her lips. Till
Grita was adjudged fit to get out of bed, Kaspar carried up

water from the river to stand and clear overnight, hauled down and split wood for the voracious fireplace, did his best to keep the children amused during the two meals which he took at the house, and listened to the ceaseless flow of wearing but not ill-tempered instruction, reproof, encouragement and advice from Anna. And, of course, had Mathias' farm work to do in addition.

'Twas as if the good man had lost the use of his legs and arms, as well as of his mind. Once a day he went down to the riverbank as though in search of something; it was easy to guess whom he sought. For the remainder of the time he sat at table; when Mvrouw Burrgh cleared away his half-finished food and set the Bible in its place, his big gnarled hands turned the pages back and forth, his eyes followed the print, but aimlessly, as if not here on the printed pages would he find the only voice that he listened to hear.

At dawn each day, after starting the fire and before Mvrouw Burrgh appeared, Kaspar took the falcon from the barn, threw her off to circle up into the skies, and by swinging the lure brought her swooping home again. Only at the price of early rising, of washed face and combed hair, were the younger Hoorns allowed to take part in this morning rite. That trick worked well, but other attempts to turn the young energy to account weren't so successful. They did their daily stints of work, for they were accustomed to these; but half-heartedly. When, on the third morning, Grita, pale and drawn of face, and still coughing, came to breakfast, Kaspar gladly resigned his care of the children.

Mathias could spare him for a half-hour, if indeed Mathias would be conscious of his absence, and there was something that Kaspar had to find out. Had the clerk returned? . . . If so, what story had he told the director? How did he account for his dismissal of Kaspar? And which would the director believe, Kaspar or Nicholas? His whole future in the New Netherlands might depend on this.

Only . . . Nicholas had not yet returned.

But the Indians, sent by Kaspar's friend Aquinachoo, were landing from their dugouts at the mud-covered grass bank of the landing place. Kaspar went round to greet them.

With a few words of the Maqua speech, and a smattering of sign language, he bade them welcome, helped them with their bundles of pelts and led them up to the director's room. In this new land how pleasant it was to greet, and be greeted by a friend, to ask after the chief, to inquire by what magic they had brought their overladen canoes down the flooded river without striking drifting trees or other snags. And how strangely warming to see the sign for "friend" used in return, and to answer inquiries by saying that the bird-on-the-hand was well and would yet catch many birds.

The director was glad—no doubt about it—to see so many beavers, and at a time of year when the market was dull. When the bundles were untied, the skins spread out, he wanted to know from what place they came.

A long way from the west, it seemed; at least twice as far from the Maqua castle as the castle was from here. Perhaps from another branch of the Maqua tribe.

Before trading began Andries, as if by custom, brought in an old silver tray bearing four small glasses and a bottle of sweet cordial. Ceremoniously the director, the two Maquas and Kaspar sipped. So strongly flavored with anise and so sweet it was, that a little went a long way; and Kaspar, more accustomed to beer and cider, found difficulty in choking it down. The tray was carried out again, Kaspar was sent up to the attic to fetch down rolls of duffel, knives, awls and other trade goods, and the business of the morning began to get under way.

In silence, for the main part, the skins were placed upon the long table and graded for size. As if size and little else were of importance. Kaspar, watching the process and involuntarily valuing the individual pelts at Amsterdam prices, wanted to offer a suggestion; only a new man at a new trade should keep his mouth shut. and learn, not try to teach.

But the director was regarding him with a half-smile. "Well?" he said at last.

Kaspar hesitated, trying to put it tactfully. "When Mynheer Nicholas was buying I wondered why he purchased poor pelts at the same price as good ones. Some of them would not fetch that price in the homeland, and were so badly cured that they might breed worms on the voyage and so damage better ones."

"So . . . ?" encouraged the director.

"If I were to value each separate pelt at homeland standards, could you subtract the cost of shipping, and the patroonship's profit, and be able to judge how much each is worth here? By offering more for the good skins and less for the poor ones, perhaps the Maquas could be persuaded to bring you only the best, and sell the profitless ones elsewhere."

Apparently it wasn't quite so simple as that, for there were dues that had to be paid to the West India Company before the pelts were shipped, and a further tax before they entered the homeland, besides insurance on the voyage. And then it was necessary to try to explain all this to the squat smallpoxed man with the single feather in his hair who seemed to be the leader of the two, though it would have taken greater facility with the language than the director's and Kaspar's put together, to launch the new idea. Mynheer Jeremias then assayed another method.

Opposite each pile of "halfs," of "kilderkins" and "wholes" and "blankets" he set trade goods. The Indians watched, curiously, their black eyes expressionless and unwinking, but perhaps a little puzzled. Then, without moving the trade goods, he set Kaspar to re-sort the skins according to their true value, and against each fresh pile he rearranged the trade goods, taking away a little from some, placing more beside others.

The Maquas looked pleased, no doubt of it, at the price set opposite the big, prime pelts; disappointed at the white man's valuation of ten ill-cured, immature and out-of-season beavers. Then for a while they consulted together. There was no question that the Indians knew good skins from bad; that wasn't the point. But the Netherland traders, in their greed for pelts, and trying to outbid each other, had been willing to accept bad skins as good, and in order not to cut their profits, had been unable to offer better prices for those that were superior. This new method could be done efficiently only where the white man could make a close guess on the home value of the goods.

But it worked. First the Indians withdrew that pile of worst skins. Then—and that was an unlooked for gain—out of some recess of their bundles they drew the best and biggest beaver that Kaspar had ever seen. And the director, after Kaspar had priced the fine dark pelt with its even coloring and texture that bespoke a winter catch, set against it a generous offer in trade goods. Generous, obviously, even in the Indian's eyes.

For lack of any coinage, other than sewant which was measured by handbreadths and fathoms, the deal was still incomplete. Some trade goods had to be swapped for others which the Indians preferred; they wanted, for instance, more blankets and less of the blanketlike duffel, and a finer kind of awl, used for sewing skins into clothes. But at last they were satisfied, more than satisfied; the director had to translate the parting words of the Indians.

"Between our chief and the director has long been friendship. Between our chief and 'Hawk-on-hand' a new friendship was made at the Maqua castle. Now, by reason of this trading which pleases us very much, both the old friendship and the new will grow warmer and stronger."

When the two men had gone back to their canoe, Kaspar found the director's eyes upon him; for the first time considering, weighing him.

"What brought you to the New Netherlands?" Mynheer Jeremias sat down at the long table and crossed one riding boot over the other. "Was it the persuasive tongue of my brother, Johannes, the patroon?" he asked. "It seems to me, de Selle, that with your knowledge of furs and your easy way of making friends, you could have prospered in Amsterdam just as well as here. Perhaps better in the end."

Kaspar, tying the beavers into bundles and making ready to carry them and the remaining trade goods back to the attic, had to stop and consider. He leaned against the table and gazed out at the sparkling waters of the wide river. "No," he said, "Mynheer Johannes gave me the opportunity and I took it." To find what had been his motive he had to reach back farther in his mind. "It was, I think, Mynheer Kiliaen, the First Patroon, who without intending it, gave me the thought that someday I must cross the water. He was talking to my father . . ."

And as clearly as if it were pictured before him, he saw that oak-paneled hallway, the wide shining stairs that led to the half-room above and the light falling through the high windows from the garden behind. He saw the kind, thin face of the old man, of the great Kiliaen himself, and heard again his voice, as a small boy, with short legs dangling from the seat of a high-backed carved chair had heard them that day, talking to Kiliaen's partner, de Vries, and to the farm manager from Cralo.

Something of this, slowly, haltingly, he told the director. And something of the First Patroon's high hopes and unselfish purpose seemed to come back through Kaspar's telling of it, as a dream will revive as you strive to recall it.

For a moment as he listened, Mynheer Jeremias seemed to kindle to his enthusiasm. Then his face fell back again into the same despondent lines. Wearily he shook his head, his thin fingers tapping gently on the table top. "That trust of my father's, we have betrayed. And, what is worse, all but forgotten. You do well to remind me, though the medicine is a bitter one."

"Oh, Mynheer, I had not intended . . ." Kaspar tried to excuse himself.

But the explanation was brushed aside. "And therein lies the value of what you have brought back to me. There have been floods, bad seasons, late spring frosts, droughts, some slight trouble with the Indians. And more, far more, friction with the Company. But it is our own people, our people from the homeland, those whom my father sought to benefit, who have done most to wreck that dream. To bring out more colonists requires money; where is that money to come from if those already here will not pay their rents? True, sometimes they cannot, but often they will not. Lies, evasions, quarrels, court processes, all have done their part to shatter the plan."

Strong words, strange words. And yet Kaspar, recalling the waste farm lands through which he had traveled, remembering the pastures and plowlands gone back, not to good forest but to scrub and brush, felt that there might be justification for them. But where, then, did the fault lie? Mynheer had said that it lay with the colonists themselves. Was that the truth?

With a sigh the director rose heavily from his chair. "Perhaps," he said, "you, de Selle, have the answer for which we are seeking. With a better price for the beaver skins we may at last, after all these years, return to the shareholders of the patroonship some profit on the money they have spent. So that they, in turn, may send out more colonists and the abandoned farms may again be put under cultivation and new crops and new hopes may put new hearts into those already here and vanquish the despair which is seizing upon us."

He made a slight gesture with one hand. "Leave the bundles, de Selle. I will have Andries tend to them."

Kaspar was dismissed. But going homeward in the warm mellow sunlight that this day flooded the hills and the plowlands, he felt that Mynheer Jeremias had not found his solution. Good land, such as this, well farmed, should need no support from the beaver trade. Nor from the shareholders in the homeland. If the colonists already here were incapable of making a living from their land, new colonists would do no better.

He heard Grita calling the children and his footsteps quickened with his mood.

Grita might have the right answer when she insisted that wheat and not beavers should be the main, the staple crop of the patroonship; she might, if only because she was closer to the problem than the director with his many cares and interests. Whoever, whatever, would decide, it was not Kaspar de Selle, as green as a raw apprentice in this strange land.

Chapter Eleven
To Train a Hawk Means
First to Train Yourself

GRITA could not force herself to believe that Mother was really gone. There were so many things that only Mother's hands could do, so much love the young ones needed that only Mother could give. Mother knew that, and God must know it too. God would not allow Mother to be drowned; she was too sorely needed. Day after day she continued to cling to the hope that somewhere downstream Mother had been swept ashore, and that word would come from some farm, some settlement, that she was alive and not to worry for she would soon be coming home again.

For awhile that hope was so present with her that she was able to work under its stimulus, and hasten over her task to have it all finished and awaiting Mother's nod of approval; as if Mother had been gone only a few hours over to Cralo, or in to Beverwyck to the market; as if at any moment the door might open and one would hear her cheery voice crying to the children, would hear her klompen slip from her feet on the stone of the entry as she changed into her house slippers before entering the sanded-floor kitchen. Before the dough, this dough she was setting, had risen, a cart would stop, and Mother would climb down—and oh, how she would be welcomed! Before the oven was hot enough for the baking—surely she would be here. Before the bread was taken out she must, she must come.

But the dough rose, overnight. The fire was raked from the oven. The loaves baked and drawn out on the peel. A hundred household tasks begun in hope were ended in despair. And still Father sat on, droop-shouldered, his big hands hanging helplessly between his knees. Food was set before him, and the bowl, scarce touched or absent-mindedly emptied, was taken away again. Grita watched him, the physical ache in her heart so great she could scarcely bear it; but there seemed nothing she could do to help.

Kaspar, almost a stranger now, since he was not inclosed within their little circle of grief, since he alone could not share the family's sorrow, came and went almost without speaking, handling unasked the tasks that Father should be doing. Joan, too young to know what death meant, called sometimes for her mother, but with her pale curls nestled into Grita's shoulder, her small arms around Grita's neck, she seemed not to mind who loved her, so long as she was truly loved. Even Catalina was not too great a problem; feeling somehow the depth of Grita's grief she tried to comfort Grita, and in comforting found, womanlike, some measure of comfort for herself.

But Isaak, after the first youthful tears, had gone off by himself, to stand beside the river. Grita would recall him to his share of the tasks to be done; and missing him a little later would find the work completed, but Isaak again slipped away. And looking out of the window would see him, his slim shoulders defiant and hating, hating, facing the wide current as he stood there, an hour, two hours at a time, gazing out over the waters. Hating, hating, hour on hour. It was not good for so young a boy. But what on earth could she do for him? She found him additional tasks, which he performed sullenly, resentfully, as if the bitterness in his heart for the cruel river was beginning to embrace his home, his family, anyone and everything, even his daily tasks. The boy would grow ill if this continued, ill in body as well as in mind. Father or some other man might discover the remedy, which not she, nor any woman, could find.

And another man it was who found it. Neglected, half-forgotten, Kaspar made pretense one morning of needing Isaak's aid to exercise his falcon. For a full hour they worked with awl and sinew and deer hide out there by the back steps. From time to time Grita could hear their low voices as she hurried about the kitchen, one asking directions, the deeper one giving them; but with no other conversation. In the end they produced a hawking glove for the boy. Then out to the barn for the falcon; this time to ride forth on Isaak's fist. Grita, watching through the window, saw Kaspar unhood the falcon; apparently that was more difficult than it seemed. Isaak put out a hand for the feather and stroked the bird and seemed to be soothing her with his voice. Kaspar retired to the barn out of sight.

Then, with a swing of his arm, the boy cast up the falcon. Head back, dark hair ruffled by the soft breeze, he watched her circle and climb, and his face, turned toward the house, was happy, excited, his eyes bright and interested for the first time in many days. He stood on tiptoe, muscles braced, lifting the peregrine upward with every fiber of his young body.

But this was only flight for exercise, not for hunting. So in a moment Kaspar came out of the barn, swinging what he called a "lure," a bundle of feathers tied into a tight ball at the end of a cord and garnished with a strip of raw meat. He whistled, that high-pitched whistle almost like a hawk's, and down dropped the bird with a speed as if it would dash itself to pieces. As it struck at the lure, Kaspar jerked the object aside and the hawk shot up again as if bounced from the ground.

Then again she struck, and this time caught the lure. Kaspar handed the hawk and lure to Isaak and the bird finished the meat-garnishing perched on his fist. If ever a boy swelled with pride and affection, 'twas Isaak Hoorn.

Grita turned away and began vigorously to polish the pewter platter. Too busy she was, she told herself, to watch a couple of boys playing with a silly bird. But twice she had to pause and mop her eyes. Kaspar was being so kind, so understanding, so—when you came to think of it—self-effacing. Oh, she had been wrong, wrong all along! He *had* felt Mother's death, he *had* been sorrowful, and she had been selfish not to realize it.

After that Isaak returned to the river once or twice; but that unhealthy hatred had lost its grip upon him. And when ducks or herons swung across his field of view, his eyes lifted from the river and followed them. Yes, the evil spell was broken, and Grita herself felt a lift in her heart.

At meals the talk now swung from the sorrowful past to a more hopeful future; Isaak planning how one day he would take a fledgling hawk from the nest and Kaspar would show him how to train her. Grita caught an air of apology in Kaspar's tones as he explained some of the difficulties of such a task.

"To train a hawk is a man's full-time task, and besides that he must never let himself grow angry, or disappointed, or make a quick jerky movement, or raise his voice unpleasantly, or even stare directly at the bird. To train a hawk means first to train yourself. And that is the most difficult part."

"Oh?" said Isaak thoughtfully and munched his food in silence for awhile.

For Grita, playing now the rôle of mother, it had been difficult not to point a moral to Kaspar's remarks. But wisely she kept her mouth shut and considered what he had said; it explained much of Kaspar. She felt now that she was learning to understand him better. Understanding seemed to be her main task these days. There was Mathias . . .

To attempt to understand Father, to try to get inside his mind, seemed at first undutiful, almost wicked. If only Kaspar, who was not of the family, could claim his interest as he had claimed Isaak's. And Kaspar, quite clearly, tried to.

He would come in from his work, raise his voice a little to make sure that Father heard, and ask, "Do you want the little black and white cow taken down and bred to the Deruyter's bull? She's calling for it." He would ask twice.

And then Father would say, "Yes, yes!" and make an impatient gesture with one heavy hand. But he had not heard a word.

When Kaspar announced that the lost farm boat had been found down-river and brought back, and was now tied up at the director's landing place, Father said, "Yes, yes," in just the same tone. Even when Kaspar told about how the people who had found her, floating bottom up, had managed also to rescue the brown hen that had been sitting on her, Father said no more; just that dull-voiced "Yes, yes."

As the days passed, Isaak was beginning to regard his father with a doubting stare, Catalina to shrink from him as from a frightening stranger; though perhaps that was partly due to a small accident that happened. Catalina had begun to model small toy animals from clay she had found in an eroded stream bank. She would roll the body of the animal out of one piece, pinch and shove the head into shape, then roll pipestem legs and ears and press them all together. It was not easy to distinguish her dogs from her cows, but in Catalina's eyes they were all lifelike, and each cow and each dog known by name.

The clay figures had grown to quite an array, and when

the table was bare the little girl would march them in a row, two by two, along its length; sometimes the cows were being driven to pasture, sometimes it was the animals marching into the Ark. The morning that the accident happened Father had gone out briefly, after breakfast, and Catalina's menagerie had paraded up, beside the Bible and even mounted its worn leather cover. Father came back, sat down, tried to turn a page, his eyes gazing not at the Book but into the distance. Catalina made a grab to rescue her clay figures, but six of them had been swept to the floor and one trodden underfoot. She could make more, of course, and Grita immediately set her to do so. But in the little girl's mind it was Daisy and Bell and Buttercup who had been swept off a cliff by Father's sleeve and killed; intentionally perhaps. With sullen, out-thrust lower lip, she kept a wary eye on Father—mistrusting now his every absent-minded move. It was not good! It was not good!

It was by sheer chance that Grita discovered how Father could be helped. To draw him from his gloomy thoughts she began to talk with him as Mother, going about her household work, used to talk. To say what there would be for dinner, to mention how many eggs she had found this morning, to speak of the blooming of the geranium in the window pot, of how soon the wheat could go into the ground, or a hazard, a forecast as to how good the cabbages were going to be this year. Perhaps Father didn't hear, perhaps he had never heard Mother either; but the chatter made a cheerful sound in the big, sun-flooded kitchen, a sort of accompaniment to the clatter of dishes replaced on the dresser, the moving of a log, the whisper of the steam from the cooking pots. Father may even have taken it for Mother's voice, for he asked, one morning—it was as good as a question—

"That barn door that's falling down?"

Grita took her courage in hand. "You're planning to go into Beverwyck and get Blacksmith to make a new hinge for it." She put it as if she were agreeing with him.

"I'm going into Beverwyck to get a pair of iron hinges for it," said Father firmly.

And he did. He and Kaspar braced the door and rehung it. Then back to his glooming again. Kaspar, waiting for the rain-sodden land to dry out and sweeten, had at last, single-handed, plowed and harrowed and begun to sow, when Grita reluctantly made her second experiment.

"I suppose you're planning to sow the three-morgen field today?" she addressed Father.

For a moment Mathias looked blank, then pushed back his chair. "That three-morgen field, it is time I started to sow it," he said, and went out.

By slow degrees she was beginning to discover the system of it. Never before had Father been quite like this; but always, now she came to realize it, he had depended upon Mother. Not so much to tell him what to do, as to reinforce his decision to do it.

As if Father and the youngsters weren't enough, Grita found herself concerned for Kaspar. But Mother used to say, "The head and the hands, only so much can they hold, only so much burden can they bear. But in the heart is always room, always strength. The good God made it so."

Returning from taking a basket of eggs up to Andries, Grita wondered whether Mother was right or whether it wasn't that Mother took so little thought for herself that she always had sympathy to spare for others. She kicked off her klompen at the door, set down her empty basket, and plunged straight in.

"Mynheer Nicholas is really angry with you, Kaspar. He got back this morning. While I was waiting for Andries to return the basket, I heard the clerk talking to the director upstairs in the council room."

Kaspar, bringing in a fresh backlog for the kitchen fire, eased the heavy section of oak onto the floor. "I thought he might be. What did he say?" The boy grinned, but not with any assurance, Grita felt.

"I don't know what he said before I arrived. But by then
he was blaming you for what seemed like a poor collection of
skins. You insulted the Maqua chief by refusing to sell the
falcon. You dallied so on the road that Mynheer Nicholas
could do no trading at Schenectade. He had to watch you all
the time to see that you didn't steal the sewant from the
packs. And you couldn't be persuaded to lead the horse at a
reasonable gait, but had to keep lagging behind or running
on ahead."

Kaspar flushed. "The last is true enough. But the rest are
lies. What else did he say?"

"Nothing much. Just that you couldn't be persuaded to
watch the trading, and spent all your time flying your falcon.
That you have no interest in skins, and will never make a fur
trader, despite all the trouble he took to teach you. He wants
you to be sent as a farm worker to a tenant of the patroonship who has been asking for help for some time."

"Kind of him!" Kaspar jeered. Then a little anxiously,
"And what did the director say to all this? He knows it isn't
true."

Grita shared his anxiety. How like a man to go out of his
way to offend so influential a man as the director's clerk; a
clerk who was always on hand to give Mynheer Jeremias a
distorted picture.

"He didn't correct him, but at least he didn't seem to
agree with him. All he said was 'H'm,' 'Ha,' 'Was that so?'
and 'Well, well.' But it was enough encouragement, so Nicholas went on to claim credit for the two Indians who came
down with skins from your friend, the Maqua chief."

Kaspar cheered up. "Mynheer Nicholas blundered there.
The director knows he's lying, as he talked with the Indians
himself while we were pricing the skins. That lie will discredit his other lies; the director is no fool."

Couldn't Kaspar be made to see how dangerous this all
was for his future? Everybody knew that Mynheer Nicholas
was a bad enemy. And it wasn't this man only whom Kaspar

had offended. There was that man down on the Manhatens. Kaspar might think the claim of debt was a practical joke, but it didn't sound like it. And the captain of the *Pigeon;* of course the captain deserved punishment for deserting both Gideon and Kaspar, but why must the boy get into such scrapes?

"Supposing the clerk gets you dismissed from the patroonship on some excuse or other? What then?" she asked.

"As soon as I've paid the seven beavers to the director, I'll be free to go where I want and do what I want." He grinned exasperatingly. "And now may I move your crane and kettle so that I can put the backlog in place?"

Chapter Twelve
The Noble,
Beautiful Clay

I T SEEMED to Grita that never, these days, could she stir
from the work of the household. To be eldest daughter
and mother as well took every living minute of the day
and even stole some from her sleeping hours, setting her
planning in bed long after she should have been asleep.

The farm outdoors, for all she saw of it these days, might
have belonged to strangers. Casual remarks from Father to
Kaspar, or Kaspar to Father, told her little more than the
hasty glimpses she could catch through door or window.
The flood had been kind, leaving a thin layer of rich silt,
not the foot-deep sand and unfertile gravel it had deposited

on some other farms. Livestock were thriving. Crops, though they would be late, so far were promising.

In other years she had found time to wean and feed the calf, to tend the chickens, to stand, balanced on the drag, and harrow before Father sowed. Oh, a hundred different outdoor tasks! This year the mare had foaled again. Father had let the youngsters christen the colt, but so far she hadn't so much as set eyes on him, not even when the youngsters raced out to watch him take his first gangling strides.

Perhaps housework would take less time once she learned to cut corners and make no mistakes that had to be corrected later. It would have to, for if she didn't get outdoors and see things happening, things growing, she would not be fit to live with. She knew it was nobody's fault but her own.

But there, as if to emphasize her resentment with being cooped up, were Andries and Nicholas, who had brought the newly imported gander and two geese, which the director hoped could be bred in safety on the Hoorn farm. And there at the barn were Father and Kaspar and even Isaak, fitting up light trammels for the birds so that they should not stray through gaps in the root fences and eat the blades of the young corn and wheat.

And here, bending as always over the fireplace, was Grita, with no chance for a closer view of the strange birds than a hasty glance through the open door.

Little Joan was as good as gold, busied under the table with some make-believe of her own which called for a vast amount of buzzing and humming. Catalina, who had a favor to beg, was also on her best behavior. But, oh dear, these ginger cakes must be ready by noontime, and if Lijntje asked just one more question, or got in the way of Grita's swishing skirts just one more time, she felt she should explode. Just plain bad temper, and she admitted it. If the brick oven would only behave for once—just for once—she'd feel better.

But now, as she raked out the embers of the fire, another large piece of brick dropped from the arch within and set the ashes pothering. It needed Mother's daylong, yearlong patience to put up with a bad oven.

Scarce daring to let out a breath, she slid in the tray full of spiced cakes, and the two little animals made with the last scraps of dough which were to be Catalina's prize for good behavior. She was setting the heavy iron door in place when Catalina's hand stretched out, and there in her palm was another animal to go in. Gingerly, cloth over her wrist, Grita reached in and set it on a corner of the tray, then lifted the door in place, with care, lest it dislodge another brick.

A quick look through the window at that tempting, outdoor world where new things happened every day, where young lambs kicked their heels and old sheep baaed, where grass was fresh and green, and the warm winds blew and men went fishing, or made trammels, or did some new tasks every hour, or everyday. Never the same old round of cook and clean up and to bed that had been her lot of late.

Father and Nicholas were making their way through the barway which led to the sheep pasture; Andries had set the empty hamper on his head and was ambling slowly homeward; his queer crooning song came in softly to her as he passed the house. Kaspar and Isaak had disappeared from sight. With the ghost of a sigh, Grita mopped her hot forehead and turned to putting away her baking things and cleaning the floor for fresh sanding. And to see also that Catalina washed her hands and settled to her stint at the lace pillow. The custom seemed to be dying out, out here, but in the homeland a maiden who had not made her own lace cap before she was eight years old would be deemed an *aislick*, a little lazy good-for-nothing; and, hard though it was to realize, someday those small fingers would be expected to fashion the hundred-yard strip for the bridegroom's collar. But as Mother always said, "Grown hands do what little fingers learned."

But small tongues can wag even when fingers and lace bobbins are at their busiest. And soon the tongue began again.

"Are they cooked yet, the cakes?"

"Not yet, Lijntje." Grita shoved the heavy loom a few inches to the right, that her mop might reach all the way beneath it. "Dirt unseen is a house unclean." Mother's proverbs were so numerous that sometimes you wondered if a number of them hadn't been made up to fit some special occasion, and on the spur of the moment. "But the dirt in view means more to do," rebelliously she muttered to herself.

By the pleasant odors of hot spices now beginning to fill the room it was clear that the worn bricks fitted less closely than ever to the oven door, and 'twould be sheer good fortune if those cakes were cooked before the oven cooled. The more you stoked the oven before setting in the dough, the more the brickwork cracked away. And the more the brickwork cracked away, the hotter you had to make your oven for baking. But midsummer was no time to ask Father to spare hours from his tasks to make repairs indoors; nor, till harvest came, would there be any spare grain or other crops to send down to Beverwyck in exchange for brick.

Catalina's mind seemed to be on her nose and not on her fingers. "Aren't the cakes ready, not even the little ones?"

"Don't be *poozly, kanaspie.* Don't whine, child." Grita chided her. But five minutes later, when Catalina asked again, she took pity on the little one, bade her fold the lace pillow in its linen cover and set it in the cupboard.

"Go, Lijntje, and look at the new geese and gander and see if they like their new trammels," she suggested. And off the girl scampered, the cakes, for the moment, forgotten.

Which left Grita free, as she hoped, to scurry around the quiet house.

But then came Father, his square head on his big square shoulders bowed a little in thought.

"It is the matter of the lambs, daughter," he said abruptly. "The director wishes to replace some of the livestock lost by the flood on other farms. Not till autumn do we lawfully divide with him the year's increase of lambs and calves. But it is only Christian that those farms which have lost the least should share with those who have lost the most."

He sank down at the head of the table, his big hands dropped between his knees, looking across the table as in the old days he would look across to Mother. The elbows of his short jacket needed a patch, and oh dear, he would soon have to begin wearing his Sabbath cap to work in, this one had a hole right through the crown.

"It is only his share of the increase that the director asks?"

"Ja." Father nodded.

Grita's back was turned; she was polishing the mantle shelf from which she was removing the dishes, two or three at a time. "Then it is better to divide them now than later. 'A debt paid is money saved,' as Mother used to say. Paying beforehand will save you labor and grass, if not money. And any that sicken or die between now and autumn will be his loss, not half his and half yours."

"Mm-m-n. Of that I had not thought," said Father. "So will we do. Moreover"—and this was the first time that Father had ever referred to it—"though much has the good God taken from us, we must be grateful to Him for you and the little ones that He has spared."

But still he sat on, unmoving. After a moment he said: "And now is another matter. Mynheer Nicholas has made clear that since Kaspar works part of the time for the director, the cost of his board with us should be paid by the director, like the board of any blacksmith or a carpenter who works for the patroonship. If he were a farm hand, working here all the year, that would be different again."

Grita stopped polishing and waited, cloth in hand. Outside in the warm June sunlight a small phœbe bird was busily carrying feed to the young in its nest perched above the doorstoep; she could see it whirr past the door, and again past. Nicholas had been here for another reason than just to deliver the geese and ask for the lambs; she had guessed it all along. There was a trick here. What was coming?

"And what does Mynheer Nicholas suggest?"

Father rasped a thumb across his stubbly chin. "The director is our friend, as Mynheer Nicholas made clear. So we should not complain to him about the board money, but only tell him that Kaspar plays much with his hawk, and is idle, and ask if perhaps a real laborer could be given in his stead."

So—*that* was it!

For a moment Grita was so furious that she could scarcely get her breath, so furious at the unfairness of the trick. Through the blood that roared in her ears she heard Father's voice continuing, in mild kindliness.

"But this I do not like. For though the boy plays with his hawk, he is a hard worker, and the hawk itself has brought us many meals of duck and partridge. No, not even for the sake of the money owed to us by the director will I do this thing."

Father hadn't seen the cunning falsity of Mynheer Nicholas. "There is no money owing," said Grita firmly. "That is only a pretense, a lie of the clerk. When Kaspar eats with us he works for us; when Kaspar is away on the director's business he does not eat with us. For more than half the time we have a laborer here at less than the price of a laborer; at no more than the cost of his food. We would do better to thank the director for Kaspar's help."

Father was pleased; you could see that. "You think so?" His head nodded in slow agreement. "Certainly then I will thank the director, and explain that the boy is working well, in case Mynheer Nicholas should say to the contrary and have him taken away."

Catalina came racing in, pigtails bobbing, blue eyes wide and startled. "They hissed at me, those geese. I'm sure they're snakes."

"Silly little girl," chided Grita. "That's just their long necks."

With the oven cloth she opened the oven door and Catalina forgot her fears, if they were real fears and not just a

claim for attention. A little anxiously Grita slid out the tray
of cakes. They had already nicely browned, almost to the
color of Catalina's clay cow. There was a cake cow; Grita
covered both clay cow and cake cow with her hand.

"Which will you have, Lijntje? Right or left? One's for
you and one's for Father."

But the little girl's sharp eyes had already marked down
the dough bossy. She pointed, her pink tongue running along
her lips.

Father laughed; and it was good to hear him. "So you
think, little one, that I cannot eat the clay one?" It was still
hot, but apparently not too hot for his calloused palm, for
he took it up, seemed to put it in his mouth, made a great
play of swallowing. And then he opened his hand to show
that it was empty.

Lijntje's eyes goggled—till his other hand produced the
clay model from behind his back and stood it safely on the
table.

Safely for the moment, for Catalina pounced upon it, and,
as it was hot, set it back hastily on the table. Too hastily, for
all four legs fell off and the head rolled away. Catalina
looked as if she were about to burst into a howl.

"But that is good clay, good clay indeed!" Father picked
up the pieces. "See, it is only where you joined on the legs
and head that it came apart. And I should know clay,"—
turned it over in his hands—"since my father and his father
were brickmakers in the homeland. Many thousands of mop-
pen and Frisian clinkers did I help my father mold and fire,
when I was little. Come now, Lijntje, let us go find this clay
of yours."

And to Grita's surprised delight, out they went, the little
girl holding firmly to the big hand and skipping beside him,
for the first time since Mother's death. Grita smiled to herself with understanding, and a little tenderly. Plan as she
might, a plan was not everything; to draw the family together again it had taken first a falcon and now a bed of clay.

Never would she have thought to find two such strange allies, or known how to use their help.

Her mood of weary despair went from her. Grita Hoorn did not stand alone in the world, carrying all the Hoorn burdens on her own shoulders. Grita Hoorn had set too much—far too much—importance on her own small doings. A bank of clay that never did a hand's turn of work or even thought a single thought had brought Catalina and her father together again after Grita had failed. And as for that proud little falcon . . .

Grita laughed aloud, for the first time in weeks. She couldn't begin to vie with that pampered peregrine. Kaspar's voice dropped to a soft cooing note when he spoke to her and addressed her as "My lady." And Isaak's adoration would turn the head of any female, even a bird.

Singing, Grita went back to her work.

A scant ten minutes later they returned, Catalina prancing ahead, Father in his deep rumbling voice saying, "Now make your animals all in one piece, little one. And set them in the sun to dry, a day, two days. And I will bake them for you in the hearth fire itself, so they will be strong as good Delft-ware."

"It is good clay, Father?" Grita asked.

"Ja. Of the best." He made the gesture of rubbing it finely between fingers and thumb.

"And would make good bricks?" Grita persisted.

"Why not? If the bricks are well fashioned and properly burned." Father sounded resentful that his clay should be doubted. "A noble clay it is, a beautiful clay."

"Beautiful clay," echoed Catalina.

Grita had to turn her face away and subdue another laugh. She couldn't, she really couldn't, be jealous of a bed of wet clay! "Noble, beautiful clay," indeed! So now there was a sect of clay worshipers in the household to add to the established religion of falcon worship.

Well-cooked meals, clothes and house kept forever neat

and clean, these were an accepted commonplace for which no praise was due or offered. But a falcon who caught birds as presumably most falcons did, was "my lady." And a clay bed was "noble, beautiful" just for being a clay bed.

Mother, of course, would appreciate the joke if she were here.

From afar off Grita could almost hear her gentle chuckle of enjoyment.

Chapter Thirteen
Kaspar Travels with
the Boslooper

ONE BREATHLESSLY HOT EVENING in late July an elm
bark canoe drew up in the shrunken river beside the
Hoorn's landing place. A large figure drove a paddle
into the mudbank to hold the canoe in place, and Isaak, a few
hundred yards upstream, wading out to visit his basketwork
fish traps, let out a yell of welcome.

Before Gideon Dolph had stepped out and shouldered his
pack, Catalina and even the baby were on their way to greet
him. Then all was suddenly mysteriously silent.

Grita, shelling late peas in the long evening shadow beside
the doorway, glanced up to see what was amiss. But nothing

was. Hands and arms were working like windmills; Isaak
and Catalina in sign language were asking questions and
Gideon, stopping to lean his musket against his stomach to
free his hands for answering, gave up the hopeless task. He
threw up both hands in despair, picked up his musket again,
bent to give Catalina a resounding kiss, and perched Joan on
top of his pack. The triumphal parade marched up the
parched, bare path to the house.

Just before dark Kaspar and Mathias, returning from a
distant hayfield, found the sign language had long ago given
out. Gideon, pipe in mouth, a sleepy Joan cuddled on his
knee, his back resting comfortably against the east end of
the house, basked before an admiring audience as he related
his adventures. The boslooper, uncoiling his bulk in one easy
movement, cradling the baby in one big arm, rose, smote
Kaspar painfully between the shoulders, gripped Mathias'
big hand with his still larger one, and roared out his joy
at seeing them all again.

"Scarcely all year have we seen you. But you come at a
good time," rumbled Mathias, squatting down on the ground
and beginning to fill his big, deep-bowled pipe which Catalina
had brought out. "After his year of idleness, tomorrow we
set the boslooper to work, eh, Kaspar?" It was too dark to
see his face, but his voice held kindly mockery.

Kaspar chuckled. He knew what Mathias had in mind.

"Tomorrow night his handclasp will no longer endanger
the fingers of an honest farmer," Mathias rubbed his right
hand, "for by then his grasp will be delicate as a highborn
lady's. Tomorrow, Gideon my old friend, from dawn to dark
you will help us with the hay."

And so it was. Next morning, even before dawn, they
breakfasted. Out in the fields platforms of saplings, supported upon rocks, were in readiness for the two haystacks.
Gideon and Kaspar adjusted the angle of their scythe blades
to suit their height and length of arm, whetted the blades to
their own satisfaction, slid the whetstones back into the

water horns slung at their belts, and began their slow rhythmical swing. Soon Isaak came running up with a third scythe he had been sent to borrow from a neighbor. Mathias took it, strode up level with the other two, and widened the swath.

Kaspar, long out of practice by reason of his apprenticeship in Amsterdam, found difficulty in holding his own. Taking narrow bites with the scythe he began to drop behind, taking wider bites he left "holidays," curving tufts of grass still standing, at which Gideon mocked.

"Think he was some kind of an Injun, wouldn't you, Mathias, leaving the scalp locks like that, all over the field!"

A halt in the still dim light to sharpen their blades again, then Kaspar began to improve. It was returning now, that easy curving swing which came from the shoulders and back and not the arms. After all, he had learned to wield a scythe when he was shorter than its swath. Now his body was regaining its old knack; and shuffling stride, deep breath and steady swing made one simple routine. He could afford to glance up, to look about him, enjoy the dawn breeze wafting over his already heated face and neck; to hear, far off, the whirr of a partridge, a fox barking on the edge of the forest. Below over the river hung a pearly bank of white, which was detaching itself into streamers, dissolving. Herons flapped heavily down to their feeding ground. Something momentarily ripped the blue mirror of the water. Fish? Otter? No way of telling at this distance.

Hay is the first harvest of the year, and this, the first cut of the haying, brought with it a vigorous satisfaction. Each swing of the scythe, if the weather held good, meant just that much more hay stored up for the winter. Each wagonload tomorrow would insure against starvation one of those horses, or two of those cows placidly grazing in the lower field. Though it might take two wagonloads in this New Netherlands, where farms lay barren for six whole months. Was it that long stretch of snow and sleet and ice, Kaspar wondered, a winter of which he had heard much but which he had not yet experienced, which handicapped and discouraged the patroonship farmers? All else, from the heat of the sun to the richness of the soil, gave them an advantage over their fellows in the homeland. If Mynheer Kiliaen had been right—and so noble a plan as his could surely not be wrong—then the fault must lie with the colonists. Perhaps Grita had put her finger on it when she claimed it was the quick money to be made out of furs and trading that tempted many a farmer to neglect his fields in early spring, and tending his traps, plant too late. Late planting let the weeds get ahead; and they all complained of weeds. Late planting, if the season were a bad one, would naturally mean that some of the corn was too unripe, by harvest time, to store well; not ripe enough even to cut in some places, so they complained.

Twice round the field now, and the morning was getting hot. Isaak brought elm-wood pail and gourd dipper, and for a moment the three drank and joked, mopped brows and stretched their shoulders. Then on again, while Isaak, with ax and knife, whittled two spare hickory hayforks in case those of last year, dried and brittle, should snap when put to the test; the boy was skilful with his tools and good at all farm tasks that were within the scope of his height and strength. It was odd, Kaspar told himself, how much he had come to feel one of the family, one of the Hoorns, and how much pride he now took in what each one did and was; from the placid good nature of little Joan to the stubborn pertinacity of Catalina. And of course Grita's courageous undertaking of the whole burden of the household, now that Nelle was gone.

Round the field once more, six bands of smooth-cut hay before them, nine bands behind. Then up cantered a horseman, Jeremias van Rensselaer.

A polite greeting, brief praise of the thickness of the hay, an expression of hope that the weather would stay fine. Then he beckoned Kaspar aside. Gideon and Mathias whetted up their blades, closed ranks and started off again.

"You told me, some time ago, that one Wouter Fries tried to hold you in the Manhatens on some claim of debt. You told me that the claim was false, and possibly some tasteless form of joke." Mynheer Jeremias checked his fidgety stallion. "In any case I should tend to believe you when you deny the debt. Also to disbelieve Fries, who was once a colonist in the patroonship and left without paying three years back rental, and owing money beside. Only, it now appears that his claim was not made in jest."

Kaspar fingered the edge of his scythe and waited, to see where this led.

"It is said in Beverwyck that a warrant or process has come from the court of the Manhatens, and that the constable, as soon as his leg is healed where he cut himself with an ax, will serve it on you. You can, if you like, answer the process, but must then go down to the Manhatens to be judged, since the cause arose outside my jurisdiction. Or you can be away," he smiled a little, "when the constable arrives."

Kaspar looked at the director in puzzlement. Probably the director was right, for no one in his senses would go to the trouble and expense of prolonging a very poor joke by taking it to court. A Netherland magistrate would fine the joker heavily if the trick were discovered. But if it wasn't Wouter's idea of humor, the other explanations were far more difficult to believe. Wouter would as soon expect to get blood out of a stone as money out of a newly arrived colonist. And as to using the threat of his false claim to hold a man in the Manhatens, and to set him against his will to work for Wouter as a fur expert, that was idiotic. All that would be necessary would be to appraise the pelts so badly as to cause the employer loss instead of profit, and so get kicked out again.

Perhaps the director, being a magistrate, would have some suspicion of what lay behind the false charge. But if he had, he made no mention of it.

"If the court process had come to me," he was saying, "it would have been wrong of me to warn you. But since I have

only heard gossip, as anyone might hear it, I suggest that
you make yourself scarce till we can learn more of what may
lie behind this."

So the director too had his suspicions, had he?

"I suggest that you go away, to buy beavers; not that
many can be found at this time of year. In two weeks, in
three weeks, or perhaps a month we may have an answer to
Nicho—to Wouter." If that was a slip, it was intentional,
for the director was smiling.

"If you need sewant, or trade goods, send someone to me,
but do not come yourself." He swung his horse and leaped a
low hedge. With a wave of his riding crop to Mathias, he
was gone.

When told of the projected fur trading, Gideon Dolph
roared with laughter. "If Gideon comes back from the forest
because there are no beavers to buy, then there are no beavers
to buy!" he insisted. And the jest amused him for the remainder of that day.

But at nightfall when Kaspar was in the barn feeding the
falcon he came out and joined him. "Mathias says that he
and Isaak can finish the haying," he stated bluntly. "And we
travel in my canoe. Where do you want to go?"

Kaspar had no idea.

"Then we will portage the big falls that lie a little above
Beverwyck and paddle up the western river through Maqua
country. That is the direction where beavers, if there are any
to be had, will be found." Then a thought struck him. "The
Maquas sent a peace party up the northern river to treat
with the Mahicans, at a place called Saraghtoge. The Mahicans have already passed upstream—I met them yesterday
morning—but we may still be in time."

At dawn next day they went down to the boat. To travel
with the boslooper should mean adventure, something quite
different from tagging along behind, or in front of, Mynheer
Nicholas. His vast and cheerful energy would be a wonderful change from the sour ill-humor of the clerk.

Isaak was off with his father, milking, or turning the cattle into new pasture; for at this early hour the night's mist would have left the hay too damp to rake and gather. Catalina was helping Grita put a new cheese into the press, and salt and turn those waiting on the shelves of the tiny stone-floored dairy. But Kaspar and the boslooper were not to depart unseen. As Kaspar, sleepy falcon in hand, leaned down from the bank to lay his bundle in the canoe, the bundle stayed in his hand. For something stirred beneath a blanket. And there below him in the boat a small Indian boy, no bigger than Catalina, sat up and rubbed his eyes.

The boslooper let out a roar. "I thought I left you with your mother and father in Beverwyck."

The child took precisely no notice, but started in businesslike fashion to roll his blanket, then tug on the paddle that pinned the canoe to shore.

"You go right back home, Tawyne," shouted the boslooper. "Right now. Come, Tawyne, get out of that canoe and start trotting."

With careful deliberation the small urchin washed the mud off the paddle blade.

"Perhaps," said Kaspar unthinkingly, "he doesn't know our speech."

"If he doesn't, I don't either," said Gideon. "But what I'd really like to know is, how he found out we were starting this morning." And that was an interesting detail they never did discover.

The urchin had even brought along a small-sized paddle of his own, which, as soon as they were stowed aboard and had pushed out into the current, he applied with a monotonous skill and apparent ease, hour after hour.

"Where did you get him?" asked Kaspar at length.

"On the east bank, halfway down to the Manhatens. I thought that he was lost. I asked every Mahican for a good fifty miles up and downstream, but they'd none of them heard of him. He was like your falcon; once I'd got him I

had to feed him and exercise him. That was a year ago."
Effortlessly the boslooper's paddle dug whirlpools in the
river. "When I came back to Beverwyck he disappeared and
I found out where his parents lived. And that he was named
Tawyne, the Otter. But that didn't do any good. I stopped
in to see the old man when I went off trapping last winter, to
get him to promise me any beavers he could get hold of. I
left the boy there, of course. I was most of the way to the
Maqua river when there, ahead of me in the snow, stood
this same little limb-of-Satan."

"I'd a heap rather have my falcon," said Kaspar. "She's
more useful."

"Oh-ho, don't you believe it. This one can steal food where
there's none to be found. You keep an eye on your falcon or
you'll find her feathers sticking out of his mouth someday."

And the brat was indeed useful. When they came to the
Falls, even at this season of low water a magnificent sight,
where a whole wide river crashed and roared, foaming in
angry white over a rock face far taller than the tallest pines
around it, the Indian knew exactly what to do.

If Kaspar and Gideon supplied the motive power, it was
the urchin, kneeling right up in the bows of the frail canoe,
who impassively steered their course among the boiling
eddies and whirlpools, right up into the spray of the Falls
itself. They drew in to the rocky shore and unloaded the
boat, Gideon lifted it to his shoulders, Kaspar swung the
boslooper's heavy pack of trade goods to his back, and
reached down for his own small bundle of food and blanket.
But the Indian boy had already shouldered it and started up
the steep trail, worn smooth and slippery by the thousands
of moccasined feet that had gone before.

Tawyne said something in the Maqua speech. Gideon set
down the canoe in a quiet eddy at the head of the Falls, and
walked back to examine the trail.

"Likely enough the boy's right. But it might be any
Maquas, not the ones we're after. Then again the peace

party may have cut overland. We'll paddle on to their castle."

But that proved unnecessary, for a dugout coming down was hailed, and reported that the three canoes carrying the peace party were probably on their way, the members having been held up for a final council. Nothing to do then but wait, either here or back at the bottom of the Falls; one place would be as good as the other. So once more they shouldered their loads, and, more difficult than climbing up, slipped and slithered their way back, down the spray-covered rocky shore.

This time, at the boslooper's suggestion, they embarked and paddled upriver a short way to a low bare island. "Mostly," the boslooper explained, "I wouldn't trouble, for there'd be no danger. But when there's peace in the offing you never know what to expect. There are always a few young braves looking for a last scalp or two, while they've still got enemies to take them from. But we'll be safe enough here, and the Maquas can't pass without our seeing."

They made camp, nothing much since they might be off again before nightfall, just a small fire of driftwood to smoke a little and advertise their peaceful intentions. A war party kindles no fire.

Kaspar, resting his gloved hand on his knee, became aware of the beady black glance of Tawyne, the Otter, and felt himself, after a while, begin to fidget under that unblinking stare. He hooded the hawk anew, clipped the leash to her leather jesses and with a tinkle of her bells, set her to perch on a branch.

"What is it?" his hands signaled the small boy.

"Bird lean, not good to eat," came the answer.

"Not eat. Fly," Kaspar signaled back.

"Better show him," said Gideon. "Then your falcon may live to a greater age."

She needed flying anyway. Gideon preferred to lie stretched out with his short pipe, so Kaspar and the Otter took the empty canoe and paddled off, the falcon, unhooded,

perched on a stretcher. Up on the Maqua river the falcon
had killed over water, and each time had had her quarry recovered for her and had been allowed to gorge on it. So if
she had any sense she would kill over water again, and not
drop the game over the dense forest that here lined the
riverbanks.

Even so it was a gamble, whether to fly her off the fist, like
a short-winged goshawk, or let her climb and wait on in
readiness for her stoop, as a long-winged falcon should. Well,
there ahead were some black spots on the water. Kaspar
tapped the Otter on the back, to draw his attention, slipped
the bird's leash, and cast her up.

Proudly she circled, up and up, the Otter's eyes and head
circling with her. Kaspar dampened his finger and held it
up to judge the wind. But the falcon herself had made its
direction clear, circling farther over the eastern bank in
readiness to stoop down into the wind when the time came.

A careful silent paddling around the small island so as to
take the ducks by surprise and put them into the air. Again
Kaspar tapped the Otter on the back and pointed upward.

A splendid stoop it was. You could almost hear the wind
whistle past the closed wings; you could hear the thud of the
strike. Then the falcon had shot up again, was diving on
another quarry before the first had even hit the water. And
the Otter, with a yelp of delight, was digging holes in the
river with his paddle.

They picked up the first two birds and Kaspar swung the
lure. But the falcon refused to come in. Away upstream
she raked, while Kaspar cursed under his breath and urged
the slow canoe after her. Only a moment though, and high
overhead she came shooting back again. This time there was
something being driven before her, something that began to
circle. A heron, slow in flight but quick in climb. But the falcon outclimbed her, swooped and rode the bird down, almost
to the water level. And came in to fist, even before they had
the quarry aboard.

The Otter wanted to go on, wanted to catch every bird on the river. But the three good flights were enough for one day, as the falcon showed, with her open beak and hard breathing.

With the fire already kindled on the island, they cooked the heron and a duck and reserved the remains of the second duck for the falcon in case she did not kill on the morrow. Tawyne ate most of the heron, whose meat was too highly flavored for Kaspar and the boslooper.

Nightfall was close; the sun cut off by the tall forest on the western bank left the river in gloomy shadow. Its bright sunset reflections now vanished, it flowed silently, as dark as steel. Then from downstream appeared three canoes. The Otter noted them first, as mere spots in the distance, but it was Gideon who identified them as Maquas.

"Why Maquas?" Kaspar asked. "Have they a different way of paddling?"

"It's the course they steer; since the Mahican party went ahead, other Mahicans would know that the banks had already been scouted and were reasonably safe. But the Maquas are traveling plumb in the center of the river. Men don't struggle against the current just for the fun of it, but to keep out of the reach of chance arrows from the bank. I don't like the look of things at all."

Gideon took his pipe from his mouth, set it back, took it out again. "In peace or war a man knows how to look out for himself, same as he does on dry land or in water. But this isn't peace or war, but a kind of mixture, like a bog or quicksand that's neither land nor water. Half-minded I am to turn back tomorrow."

Chapter Fourteen
Kind of in Luck
Either Way

OUTSIDE the narrow circle of firelight the night was
black, the island melting into the invisible river, the
cliff-high forest on the banks now no more than coal-
black walls supporting a faintly luminous ceiling of dim starlight.

The faintest rustle of water rippling against canoe bows
came to Kaspar's ears, a more whispering cautious note than
the open murmuring of the river itself. The boslooper, taking no precautions, was telling the story of a knife fight with
a wounded bear, and in a voice louder even than usual.

Kaspar signed to him for silence.

182

"Too dangerous!" roared the boslooper in reply. "If they're Maquas, we're safe. If they're Mahicans we may be, though it's not so certain. We couldn't defend ourselves if we tried, not in the dark, when one invisible bow and arrow is worth ten blazing muskets."

Well, if that were true . . . Kaspar reached out, stirred the fire to a brighter blaze, and leaned casually back again. But he found it difficult to listen as Gideon took up his story again; his eyes tried to stretch out into the darkness, his ears to shut out Gideon's voice and the crackle of the fire.

The boslooper finished his story, and offered what perhaps he thought was encouragement. "There's one thing about it, we aren't likely to be captured and taken home to the tribe for torturing; the elders of the tribe would be against it, seeing they're out to fix up a peace. And if a young brave steals upon you in the darkness, you won't even know when his club crashes down on your skull and crushes it in. So we're kind of in luck, either way."

Luck! Kaspar felt the remains of the duck turn around in his stomach, and in spite of the warm night, with a good fire at his feet, he shivered. He envied the Otter, who, curled up in his blanket, seemed to be asleep. This was a most unpleasant way to meet danger—to have to sit still and do naught but hope.

At last, a new sound—of feet wading through shallow water. A dark shadow, now reddening in the gleam of the firelight as it came silently closer. He held his breath; in a moment the suspense would be over.

"Don't suppose you could fly your falcon by night and kill some more birds, could you?" Gideon asked. "We're going to have guests."

And sure enough, from the darkness a voice said, with a note of pleasure, "Hawk-on-Fist and the Man-Without-a-Lodge!" And with no more concern than if he were in his own castle, Aquinachoo, the Maqua chief stepped into the firelight, and sat down.

Other Maquas followed—Kaspar was able to recognize some of them—and made the sign of friendship. In the darkness, canoes were swiftly unloaded and lifted from the water. A few casual courteous inquiries, more wood brought in and placed beside the fire, and one by one, where they sat, each man stretched over backward, rolled in his blanket and slept.

Next day, before full dawn, all the canoes were in the water again and moving upstream. And again, Kaspar noted, keeping as far as possible out of bowshot from the banks.

At the Maqua castle he had marveled at the amount of food one Indian could eat at a sitting. Now he was surprised at their apparent indifference to hunger. At the chief's request Kaspar flew the falcon again and again until the bird was wearied. The game was hauled aboard, but no attempts were made to eat the meat raw, as Maquas were said to do on occasion; still less to halt and kindle a cook fire ashore.

In the course of that day he learned more about the peace expedition. There seemed no doubt that the Mahican chiefs and sachems were in favor of it. The Iroquois group, to which the Maquas belonged, had, for some years, driven back the Algonquin group, of which the Mahican's were a member tribe. But whatever terms of peace were offered, they would be sure to stick in the craws of the younger warriors, whichever side they belonged to. Kaspar found himself learning much. The Mahicans, it seemed, had once controlled this northern river, right down to the Manhatens, and it was from them that the Hollanders had purchased the mainland and the islands around Beverwyck. But the Maqua chief was now ordered to demand that such purchases should in the future be made from the Maquas.

That part was simple enough. But harder to understand was how still another tribe, the Indians from the north as they were called, the Hurons, came into the picture. It was only after Gideon's careful explanation that Kaspar began to realize that Indian wars were almost constant, and that when two tribes made peace, it was usually so that each could be free to fight against some other tribe. Both Iroquois and Algonquins were menaced by the Indians from the north, who were now helped by, and strongly allied to, the French. With the muskets purchased from the Netherlanders the Maquas could now hold the Hurons in check, so that temporarily a sort of truce seemed to exist between them. But the Algonquins, less fiercely warlike perhaps, and less well armed, had suffered a number of defeats. That might be the turning point which would make the chief's peace terms acceptable. But, Kaspar gathered, it would be touch-and-go.

There was no halt, to eat or rest. If a man was thirsty, he dipped up a handful of water from the river, scarce halting his paddle. Even in the heat of the day the canoes drove onward, north. By noon Kaspar's shoulders were aching as they had never ached before, but Gideon and the Otter seemed as untiring as the four paddlers in each of the Indian canoes. By midafternoon it was only by keeping his eyes on the swirl that was made by his blade in the water that he could insure that he was doing his share of the work, for his arms seemed to have lost all feeling.

Nothing could have been more welcome than the chief's request that he fly the hawk again. Though when he threw her off, his weary hand wouldn't rise above the level of his shoulder.

It could scarce be called hawking, up here, where not even a fowling piece had taught the ducks to keep their distance. The falcon climbed, stooped and struck; climbed and struck again, as if stooping to a lure. And of her own accord, without calling, came to fist to rest and eat.

That evening, as they halted early beside a rapid, the chief had a request to make. "You know, Hawk-on-Fist, the purpose of our meeting with the Mahicans. Though it was agreed that only three small canoes from each side should meet, our enemies have taken six at least. And more Mahicans, it is

thought, have come from the east, overland. We cannot turn
back, or the young men of our people would laugh at us. So
we must go forward."

Kaspar, stroking his complacent bird, listened closely,
Gideon translating when the chief, in his earnestness, lapsed
into the Maqua speech.

"If we, the elders on both sides, are allowed time to show
our reasons for desiring peace, and to open and examine the
presents which each side will bring for the other, then all may
go well. But the young hot-heads will do their best to prevent
the meeting."

It must, Kaspar felt, take real courage, knowingly to risk
your life for the good of your tribe. Clearly the chief was
about to ask for help of some kind. Difficult to see what, for,
unlike the boslooper, Kaspar was unarmed. Whatever it was,
it would be dangerous. But courage, like friendship, is con-
tagious, and Kaspar found himself offering his aid.

The chief seemed pleased. "Thus speaks the tongue of
friendship." And developed his plan. If, for a time, he could
hold the attention of the young Mahican warriors, he and his
party might cover the distance from their canoes to the council rock in safety. The Mahicans, he averred, were like
women in their curiosity. Would Kaspar sell him the falcon?

Kaspar looked at the falcon, and back again at the impassive Aquinachoo. It was a hard, almost an impossible decision
to make. Next year, at breeding time, he could catch an
eyas in the nest and train her. But it would be a different
hawk. And this peregrine that he had bought at Cralo, had
nursed through the long sea voyage, and brought in safety to
this wild country, was a piece of the homeland. She had been
his companion, his friend, as no other hawk, no other person, had ever been. Yet he could see the chief's need.

The chief perceived his struggle to decide, and seemed
to sympathize.

"Could I lend her to you till the council is ended?" asked
Kaspar, seeking a compromise.

"No, for that would be as if I went with borrowed name, or borrowed ornament." Seeming to suggest such a proceeding would be unlucky, or perhaps arouse the contempt of the Mahicans, if they guessed the bird were not his own.

Kaspar picked up his glove, placed it on the chief's hand, took the bird from her perch and clasped the chief's gloved fingers over the jesses.

"And the price?" asked the chief.

He hadn't thought of that. One price was as good as another as far as selling a friend was concerned. "Seven beaver skins," he said, at random, because that sum had so long been in his mind.

The chief nodded agreement. "And for the glove and the long leather by which she is attached?" He meant the leash. "And the ball of feathers which sometimes you swing to call her down from a height?"

"Nothing," said Kaspar. What did they matter?

The chief made a sign to one of his followers; and from among the peace presents seven beavers were selected; the best, Kaspar could swear, of the lot. Blankets, as the biggest were called, each a prime, as Kaspar's expert eye assured him. He wished now that, if he had to part with the bird, he had given her as a free gift.

But it was too late for that, and he did his best to mumble adequate thanks.

"And this," the chief lifted from his neck a string of bear's teeth and slid it over Kaspar's head, "for friendship."

Next morning, though Kaspar understood the journey was nearly ended, they made the same dawn start. And this time at his own request the chief took a paddle in the boslooper's canoe, and as soon as the dawn flight of birds to their feeding grounds began, Kaspar taught him some of the art of hawking. Then on again after that brief halt, keeping each bank of the river under closest scrutiny.

During these hours Kaspar learned more of the complications of peacemaking. The true place of the council should have been, it appeared, an island below Beverwyck. For that was the "council hearth" of the Mahicans. But since that island, among other lands, was under dispute between the two tribes, the sachems of the Mahicans had wisely suggested another place. An island, of course, for the reason that the open river, flowing on either side, stood for openness and honesty and, more practically, provided some safeguard against treacherous attack.

At midday the island came in sight; and when they drew near, at Kaspar's suggestion the chief flew the falcon. Neatly as a hawker trained from boyhood the old chief detached the leash, unhooded the bird. With a glance, as if of gratitude to Kaspar, he swung up his fist and released the jesses. The bird's long knifelike wings took hold of the air almost before she was launched. Was there ever such a noble peregrine before!

A moment of bitter anguish as Kaspar forced himself to realize that the falcon was no longer his. That never again would he pet her, praise her for her skill, or hold her on his fist. As far as he was concerned she was gone for good.

Then he turned his attention from the bird to the Indians. No doubt as to the effect on the Maquas in the three canoes, each head was tilted back, each pair of eyes peered upward. And the dozen or so Mahicans on the island, all who had so far shown themselves, craned upward too, puzzled, curious as to what new art this was that the dreaded Maquas were displaying. And not those dozen only, Kaspar's sixth sense told him, but perhaps a hundred others still in hiding were following the falcon's flight. Not a bowstring twanged, not an arrow gave its faint, deadly whistle.

So far the sale of the peregrine to Aquinachoo was serving its purpose.

The bird circled up and up, while the four canoes waited. Then stirred by some movement on the island a partridge tried to cross the narrow stream that separated island from riverbank.

The falcon stooped.

Then for a moment the whole purpose of the exploit stood in peril. If she killed over land she would have to be left there while she consumed her quarry, and gorged. Or else the chief and Maquas would have to go ashore and risk an encounter with an enemy ambush.

The falcon struck and rode her quarry down. And not till she disengaged her talons was it certain that the partridge would fall into the water. A leisurely eddy of the stream brought the bundle of feathers closer to the boslooper's canoe. With a yelp the Otter dived overboard and triumphantly held the quarry aloft with one skinny small arm.

Among the trees on the riverbank there was a murmur that was not of the wind's making. And the Mahican elders, waiting on the island, forgetting their dignity, had come down to the water's edge. Their curiosity about the falcon had made them bridge that dangerous gap between waterside and council hearth.

The falcon returning, alighted on Kaspar's bare fist. Swiftly, for appearance' sake, he transferred her to the chief's glove, where she deplumed her dead quarry and started to eat it. The canoes drew in to the shore; the boslooper's with the chief in it, leading. Maqua leaders mingled with Mahican leaders, and a treacherous arrow could scarce kill one without the other. The difficulties of a first meeting had been overcome.

Kaspar was stepping into the shallows when Gideon tapped him on the arm and signed him to come back.

"I don't like the look of things. Not even now," he murmured. "The old ones mean peace, for I can hear voices of women and perhaps children at the other side of the island. But that bunch on the mainland will make trouble if they can."

The boslooper might be right; after all he had had years of experience with these people and their ways. Kaspar knelt down again in the boat and took up his paddle.

"Shall we wait here in the middle of the river and throw out a fish line to show our peaceful intentions?" he asked.

But Gideon had a better notion. Where there were women there was bound to be trade. He gave a pull to his paddle and they headed for the north end of the island.

And quite a little camp it was, with hearth fires and brush shelters and even a few naked children and scrawny dogs. Beside the women, whose voices they had heard, a half-dozen men, not important enough for the council, were busy hauling in a seine net.

The boslooper sounded relieved. "It's going to be all right after all." And leaving the Otter with the canoe, he and Kaspar went ashore and opened the bundles of trade goods.

But business was slow, slower than Kaspar had ever known before; Gideon had nearly smoked his pipe through before a skein of scarlet worsted was exchanged for a bundle of inferior muskrat pelts. The boslooper must be right, because he knew the ways of the Mahicans, but to Kaspar it seemed that the people were either sullen or else afraid. They hung back, lingering about their fires, scarce glanced at the spread-out wares, even made pretense to be needed in hauling in the small seine net. Perhaps they didn't know what a good start the peace council, at the other side of the island, had made. Perhaps they, like the Maquas, were afraid of some last minute trick being played. That, of course, would account for their reinforcements on the mainland.

Or it might not.

"If they won't trade," Kaspar suggested, "why not go back to the canoe and fish, off the south end of the island, where the chief can find us if he needs us?"

The boslooper agreed. "Anyway I'll begin to pack up. That may start them trading. These river Indians are all the same: if they think you want to buy, they don't want to sell; if they think you don't want to, they come clamoring."

But he was wrong this time. Impassively the Mahicans watched them pack and carry the bundles back to the canoes.

Then suddenly a high, thin scream rose from the other end of the island.

Kaspar and Gideon, about to step into the canoe, straightened up and listened.

Kaspar first caught the ominous sign. His falcon, the peace falcon, swinging up high into the air. Then a Mahican came racing into camp, and shouted what sounded like a command.

Gideon grabbed up his musket. "You stay with the canoe," he ordered.

But that, that was impossible; it would be cowardly. He paused to give the canoe and the Otter a shove, which sent them to the safety of deep water, then turned and raced after the boslooper. He passed him, tearing his way through a thorny thicket and led him to the easier going of the open shore line.

Fighting with clubs and with stones, all apprentices did that. But this fight would be to kill or be killed. What did the boslooper intend? One shot from his musket and he would have no time to reload. Then it would be knives, his and Kaspar's against the Mahican clubs and hatchets and arrows. Hopeless odds—but Kaspar patted the knife at his belt to make sure it was there, and raced on.

One advantage only; if the young braves had managed to swim or wade across from the eastern shore, the last thing they would expect would be two white men charging in from the north to reinforce their Maqua friends. Just that one advantage—surprise.

Kaspar missed the trail again—only afterwards did he realize how lucky that was—and, avoiding the dense thickets, led the boslooper still farther out on the mud flats. A rock, flat-topped as a table, loomed up near the tip of the island on his left. That, from the description, might be the place of the council party. He swung inland toward it.

A brief struggle through tall reeds. Then he gripped the trunk of a tree, swung up it, scrambled by moccasin- and finger-hold up a crack in the rock. And stopped, shocked into immobility.

Four bodies, huddled in death; another Maqua still drawing up and straightening his legs in final convulsions. Somewhere in the shadowy thickets a fiendish yelling told that the remaining Maqua elders were being hunted down. A shot roared out—from a Mahican musket since the Maquas had come unarmed.

Kaspar bent over the body that had been the old chief. Yes, he was dead. The back of his skull crushed in by a club.

A voice, Gideon's, shouted, "Get out of it, boy! Save your own scalp! There's nothing we can do." And a shove from behind started his feet moving again.

Down off the rock, by the easy way which the elders had climbed such a short time ago. Down to the waterside. And at Gideon's best pace, Kaspar picking him a trail through the mud and rock, they circled back northward toward their now distant canoe. 'Twas that or swim, and with little hope either way. For by now the Mahicans must have seized both the canoe and the Otter.

But downstream came the canoe, shooting swiftly with all the Otter's small force behind it. And behind that another canoe, the cause of his haste. In it was a single Mahican.

The boslooper raised his musket. A shot roared out. The man in the pursuing canoe pitched overboard and the boat seemed to take water. The Otter, more by instinct than by plan, headed in as they splashed out to meet him.

Then on downstream, driving their paddles for very life. Something swooped down out of the skies. Without thinking, Kaspar stopped paddling and thrust out his fist. Even as the talons pierced his bare skin, he took up the leash and threaded it through the jesses. Then, perching the bird swiftly on the canoe stretcher, back to furious paddling; he could not help but notice that her feathers were splashed with bright blood, the blood of the chief. From the east bank came yells of furious insult and challenge.

The Otter answered it in a shrill bloodcurdling war whoop. A half-dozen arrows "thucked" into the water, but short, for the range was too great.

Suddenly Gideon pointed back. The canoe swung round and, close under the west bank, picked up a swimming Maqua. None too easy a task to get him aboard. A cut had slashed open his mouth, but disdaining both pain and blood, he grabbed the Otter's paddle and plunged it in with fierce angry strokes. The small boy, keeping watch over his shoulder, reported no pursuing canoes in sight.

"But that can't last," the boslooper grunted, "and with six paddlers to a boat they'll overhaul us long before nightfall. They won't let anyone escape to tell what happened, if they can help it. And besides, I've killed one of them already."

In short breathless sentences, little more than gasps, he consulted the wounded Maqua elder. And even the Otter. Kaspar had no thought to spare for what they were saying; he was too busy getting every ounce of thrust into his paddle. Then Gideon passed forward his paddle to the Maqua, the Maqua passed his small one on to the Otter, to give the bos-looper time to reload his musket.

Soon, for a brief moment of bliss, it was Kaspar's turn to hand over his paddle, drop his weary arms to his side and gulp in deep lungfuls of breath.

Gideon, or the Maqua, drove the canoe on toward a group of small islands that appeared in midstream. As a refuge it could be only temporary, for scouts following them on the eastern bank would mark them down; and when the Mahican canoes shot downstream in pursuit, it would be the end.

In among the islands, down through a narrow passage of water, then, masked by the same islands, a sharp turn in to the western bank.

The boslooper hurled his pack ashore as the Maqua lifted a boulder and loaded it into the canoe. Kaspar barely had time to snatch up the falcon before Gideon's foot thrust through the frail, bark bottom of the boat. And that evidence sank out of sight below the mud and water. Then up the steep bank, the Indian leading, the Otter close to his heels; taking every advantage of cover, here running at a crouch, there crawling for a few yards, till they reached the safety of the forest.

Temporary safety only.

"We've thrown them off," gasped Gideon, at a stumbling run beneath his heavy pack. "They'll search the bank as soon as they can cross; there may even be a few on this side now. If they don't pick up our trail till nightfall, we're safe, but that's too much to hope."

Thick bush by the riverside gave way to more open ground. To a deer trail. But Gideon with his load was holding up the retreat. He knew it too. With a curse he hurled it off the trail.

"No time to cache it," he told Kaspar. "But mark that clump where it fell."

Kaspar did. His beavers were in it, the beavers that would pay his debt to the patroonship. If either he or the boslooper survived, that debt could yet be paid.

Chapter Fifteen
Man-Without-a-Lodge and
Hawk-on-Fist

THE SUMMER was passing. Grita could count it in the deepening of the leafy green of forest, in the whitening of dandelion heads, the unfolding of the tiny green nests of the wild carrot bloom, in the hatching of the second brood of phœbes that had built beneath the overhang of the house thatching. But most of all she could tell it in the length of time she had been missing Kaspar.

Never, she told herself, as she sat sewing patches onto the seat and knees of Isaak's second pair of leather breeches, never would she have guessed that the tall lad from the homeland would have sent his roots so deeply into their

195

Hoorn family life. And so short the number of weeks he had
been here too. But constantly, as she hurried about the
kitchen, or bent weeding in the bright hot cabbage patch,
she would find herself glancing up, hoping to see him striding down the path from the director's house, his hat cocked
rakishly over his laughing blue eyes, hawk perched on his
gloved fist, and a whistle on his lips.

The first few days after his departure with Gideon she had
felt no regret. Far from it. Just a natural feeling of relief
that there were two less places to lay at table, two less beds
to make each morning, five instead of seven people to cook
for, clean up after. But swiftly the sense of relief had turned
to a vague sense of loss, of something missing in her days,
something missing from the house, from the family. Not
Gideon, for the boslooper could come, eagerly welcomed,
and go, unregretted. He had often done so. No, it was Kaspar, she realized, whom she missed so much.

And with this realization began to grow concern for his
safety. What could have happened? Snake bite, sickness,
some accident, some quarrel with an Indian? The dark depth
of the forest held so many unknown dangers that she dare
not let herself begin to imagine them.

But two men were safer than one. And Gideon was a
friend wholly to be trusted. If anything had gone wrong,
she comforted herself, one of them would be sure to return,
or send word back to the director. So nothing could be amiss,
nothing.

Another week passed. There was so much she would like to
tell him, tell Kaspar. "Have you noticed how much the pig-
lets have grown, Kaspar, since you went away? They're so
strong and heavy that Father can't keep them safe in the
pigsty any more. As soon as he replaces one of the broken
bars of their pen they push out another. Have you noticed
Catalina's menagerie, Kaspar? She has modeled pigs now
too, and the new geese; and after they dry Father bakes them
for her in the hearth ashes. See, there they are, lined up on

the very top of the kast. You can scarce mend the fire these
days without Lijntje's rushing up to rescue another of her
clay pets." And later, "Kaspar, couldn't we make small bricks
that way, to repair the oven? I've tried daubing the broken
pieces with clay, but the clay falls out as soon as it dries. If
you don't come back soon, you'll find there's no bread. I've
come to baking half-sized loaves and even quarter loaves,
small as they are, and they only just bake through."

She was even cross with him, she told herself, for remaining away so long. She needed his help; she would go and ask
the director how soon she might expect him back. Yes, that
was the thing to do, go ask news from the director.

So, one afternoon, with a fresh-cut cabbage and one of the
new batch of sage cheeses which had turned out very well
indeed, and a clean napkin folded over the top of her basket,
she strode purposefully along the shore trail, to the house of
Mynheer Jeremias. A little breeze from the river ruffled her
hair, blowing the stiff edge of her white cap, pleasantly cooling her warm cheeks.

Andries was languidly sawing wood behind the house. He
gave her a wide smile of welcome and used the excuse of her
coming to drop his saw and amble forward.

"Don't stop work for me, Andries," she told him firmly.

But Andries as ever was equal to the occasion. "Maybe if
I was to carry that heavy basket for you, Jufrouw Hoorn,"
he suggested hopefully. "It's a mighty hot day for carrying."

"And for sawing wood too, I suppose," she laughed at
him. The old fraud; if once he got in out of the sun he'd stay
there a good hour. "Is Mynheer Jeremias in his room? I'll
go right up."

But she didn't go up. Once in the kitchen she heard voices,
and paused. The director and Nicholas? No, another voice.

"Well, Mynheer Director, since you're bent on knowing
the truth, I can pay my back rent but I ain't minded to. Not
without you'll give me the loan of new saw blades for the
sawmill. I've fixed to cut me boards for a bigger barn."

Why, that was the voice of Symon Bleeker from down beyond Normanskill; she knew his surly tone. A slack farmer
he was, and gossip had it he was years behind on his payments
to the patroonship. What would Mynheer van Rensselaer
say to him? What would his answer be?

She could feel the director hesitating. Should he risk more
of the patroonship's money, or lose for certain what was
already owing?

"So, it's this way, is it, Bleeker?" and his voice sounded
tired and embittered. "The patroonship supplied you with
farm land, house, barn, livestock and seed. And even paid
your passage from the homeland. Your farms get worse with
every season because one year you're busy fishing the river,
the next hiring out as a carpenter in Beverwyck, and now it's
a sawmill. The last thing you think of is the tares in your
wheat and that the milk cow has dried up for lack of good
grazing. Some people have the effrontery to tell me to go
whistle for the rent. But you have the effrontery to go one
stage farther, and demand more equipment."

"That's so," said Symon Bleeker calmly. "I've been talking
it over with my neighbor Garrity and we're both half minded
to pick up and move out anyway. No sense to paying rent
when there's all the land between here and the Manhatens to
be farmed free."

"If you buy it from the Indians first," snapped Mynheer
Jeremias, "and then build your own house and barn and supply your own stock and seed. . . . Well, there's no sense in
arguing with you. I'll come with my clerk tomorrow to list
the stock and tools that belong to the patroonship. Perhaps
you're right, and Rensselaerswyck is well rid of you."

A chair scraped on the floor above as the director rose to
his feet. Symon Bleeker's voice took on a whining note. There
wasn't, it seemed, so good a site for a sawmill within many
miles, not with the same all-year flow of water and handiness
to the town of Beverwyck. And maybe he had been a bit
hasty about saying he wouldn't pay his back rent.

Grita dumped the cabbage and the cheese on the kitchen table and hurried away down the path. Her cheeks were flaming with indignation, her heart heavy with unhappiness. Poor Mynheer Jeremias! This was the sort of thing that he had to face over and over again. Though never before had she heard it first-hand, never before realized it so clearly. In the end he'd probably give in to Symon Bleeker, or at least let him go without suing him for the back rent. And, whether he stayed or went, there would be another neglected farm going back to weeds and valueless brush. The Honorable Shareholders of the Patroonship, back in the Netherlands, could have no idea of what happened over here.

It was some days before Grita, urged by growing anxiety for Kaspar, found courage to go again, and this time she went in the evening, after the young ones were in bed. Her bare feet felt their way along the worn cattle tracks beside the water; cool and pleasant the earth felt, and soft sweet scents borne on the damp evening air wafted up to her nostrils. The river, brightened by star-touched ripples, stretched like an upside-down sky to the black wall of frowning forest on the far shore. The chorus of crickets told that summer was passing, a crescendo that would rise and rise till frost came and stilled it. Off there ahead in the darkness a tree crashed, with a long rending sound, and a wildcat screamed in the darkness. Such a little narrow strip of tamed New Netherlands; seeming to exist on sufferance of the indifferent Indians and the tall illimitable forest. Unconquerable forest and savage Indians stretching farther than any white man had ever gone, likely farther than he would ever go. Her footsteps quickened on the path.

A bat's squeak, high and thin; a ghostly owl on silent wings drifted across, almost brushing her face, so intent it was on its hunting. Then the pleasant homely odor of tobacco on the still evening air announced that Mynheer Jeremias was sitting, as often he did, smoking his long porcelain-bowled pipe, on the small wharf above the quiet river.

"Mynheer . . . ?" She made herself known to the dark shadow whose head turned at her footfall on the boards. "It's only Grita."

"Grita Hoorn? How pleasant, child. Come and sit down."

The thick-sawn planks of the wharf edge were dry, and still held the noontide heat, and it was restful to reach down and find that her toes could still touch the water at its late-summer level. Not in daylight would she be so lacking in dignity; but here, in the darkness, and with no children for whom she must set an example, she could drop a few years and restraints with her household duties.

"Lone thoughts are sometimes troubling, and you are welcome." The director spoke a little sadly. "But what brings you, child?"

"To ask news of Kaspar de Selle," she said directly. "He is now away for many weeks, more than a month; and he left in such haste. Have you had word from him or from Gideon Dolph, Mynheer?"

"None, I'm afraid. But the lad should be safe with the boslooper."

"Where did you send him?" she asked, trying not to make the question sound too blunt.

He asked a question of his own. "Has de Selle told you of the man in the Manhatens who claimed a debt of him, possibly as a stupid joke? . . . He did? Well, when the boy first told me I'm afraid I doubted his story. Particularly the possibility—if it were not a joke—that Wouter Fries wanted him because he was a fur expert. Just a silly story, I thought, concocted by a sharp, young, city-bred apprentice to try to impress a new employer, and the 'joke' part thrown in, in case I would not believe him. But it seems I was wrong, for later I heard that the court of Beverwyck had been ordered to find him, find Kaspar I mean, and send him down to face the claim. So I warned the boy to make himself scarce till I could get further news of the matter. He has been a good worker and an honest one; it is my duty to protect him."

In the dim light she could see his face, kind and anxious above the white blur of his lace collar; his hands, a little restless, tapped on the arms of the wide, high-backed chair, or occasionally raised the big pipe to his lips for another puff. Her feet gently stirred the cool water; a fish plopped, making a ripple against the reflection of a star.

But the case was more serious, Mynheer the Director went on to say, than he had thought at first. When, as the magistrate with jurisdiction over the patroonship, he demanded to see the court summons, he found it legal and in order. Moreover, the man Fries, in swearing to the complaint of the debt, had added the names of three witnesses. According to Kaspar's story, as the director pointed out, Wouter's first claim was for a debt incurred on shipboard; but the witnesses had not been out of the New Netherlands for the last ten years, as the director had discovered. Why, the director asked of the darkness, had four men taken the risk and the trouble to hatch up a false charge against the boy?

"For revenge? Scarcely. For de Selle has had no opportunity to do them an injury. For profit? What profit could they get from an almost penniless lad who had just landed here?"

Grita tossed a braid over her shoulder. "Only if Wouter really did want to keep Kaspar down at the Manhatens because of his knowledge of pelts."

"I think they want not so much to keep him in the Manhatens as out of Rensselaerswyck." The director put forward the suggestion. "You are a friend of the boy, and serious for one of your age, or I would not tell you of my suspicions. Now Wouter Fries receives beavers from the red-bearded boslooper, Dirck Tienhoven, and it seems now that Tienhoven has dealings with my clerk, Nicholas. For two years I have had my doubts of Nicholas."

So that was why Kaspar had been sent to buy beaver skins with Nicholas? Or at least one of the reasons. And that of course . . .

But Mynheer Jeremias spoke almost her own thoughts. "When I sent de Selle out with my clerk, the clerk, instead of being grateful for his help, did all he could to get rid of him. Are Nicholas' double-dealings so profitable that it is worth the while of Wouter Fries, and others, to go to the trouble and expense of trying to get de Selle out of Nicholas' way? If so, the patroonship has lost much money through my clerk's dishonesty and my own carelessness. But I have checked the number of skins he purchased against the number of skins we sent down-river. And still I cannot find what trick he has played."

"Then must Kaspar spend the rest of his life dodging this false claim of debt?" she asked, trying to keep the indignation out of her voice. "Of what use will he be, even to the patroonship, if he must hide like an animal in the woods?"

"Patience is needed!" His tone was mildly reproving. "Mynheer the Honorable Peter Stuyvesant, the Governor of all New Netherlands, has asked me to find a match for his English carriage horse. In three weeks, or perhaps a month, I will go with the horse to the Manhatens. There something further may be discovered concerning Wouter and his witnesses. Perhaps if I add my knowledge to that of the governor, we may find an answer to our problem."

And with that Grita had to be content. Until the next day.

She was sitting in the doorway breeze, her cap off, her arms bare to the elbow, churning butter, driving the long plunger vigorously up and down in the narrow wooden churn, when the director stopped his horse at the gate, dismounted and came down the walk. She stood up to receive him, concerned at what might have brought him here, startled at the deeper etching of the lines on either side of his mouth.

"There is bad news," he said quickly and without preliminaries. "But still hope. The Mahicans have all crossed to the east bank in fear of the Maquas, and news has come that they have massacred a Maqua peace party, somewhere upriver. With the peace party were two friends of ours; but it is not known that they were killed. Not for certainty. But their names are Man-Without-a-Lodge and Hawk-on-Fist."

"Gideon and Kaspar!" That was all that Grita could utter.

"Yes, but we must not yet despair. A Maqua raiding party of forty canoes has been seen traveling upriver, and another party is said to have gone by land, to avenge the crime and the insult. When they return we can hope for more news. We must wait, child; wait and hope."

Dully she went back to her churning and watched the director climb heavily to his horse and ride toward Beverwyck. She must, she told herself, do as he said, keep on hoping. And she must not let word of this reach Catalina and Isaak; she would warn Father of that this evening in case he heard the story in Beverwyck market.

But the day's work had to be gone through, no matter how your heart ached. When Mother was drowned, duty had to come before sorrow. Now Kaspar was missing, the rule of life still held; and lest, between dawn and dark there should be a moment's idleness in which to think and consider and weaken in her purpose, Grita found herself an added task. Brickmaking, to repair the faulty oven.

Her first idea was to shape bricks of Catalina's clay, as one shaped dough, or butter, by hand or between wooden paddles. But Father, coming upon the scene of her experiments, pointed out that in this way the bricks would turn out of unequal sizes and be difficult to fit together. He and Isaak could knock together wooden molds into which the clay must be squeezed; and even before that could be done the clay must be worked with water to rid it of sand, or rootlets from the bank above. Also, he pointed out, they must be careful not to dig too deep, but take only surface clay, since that would have been weathered by sun and rain. There was more to brickmaking than she had first thought possible, and in spite of her troubles her interest grew.

Since it was easier to draw the clay down to the riverside than to haul water up to the clay, she and Isaak planned the brick-molding close to the landing place. Kneading the clay by hand, as if it were dough, turned out to be a slow process. Amused, when he discovered them at it, Father had a more practical suggestion.

"Use a washtub, daughter. Or the pig trough that Isaak made. Clay is healthy stuff and will not harm either pig or human."

Barefooted, stamping the clay and water together, till it was soft enough to mold, was a new and amusing occupation and gave the young ones a fresh interest in the task. Even Joan was big enough now to try to be of help, and, without trying, to splash clay up to her eyebrows. By the time the clay was ready, Isaak had made the first molds: a strong shallow box partitioned into four, without tops or bottoms. While he pinned together the second mold they laid the first on a wide flat strip of slab-side, shoveled in the clay, pounded it down, and scraped it level with the top of the mold.

Even as they worked Grita found her glance straying up the shining length of river. Somewhere to the north was Kaspar; someday down that river he might be returning. Oh, surely he *must* be returning!

The first four bricks were a failure, for in their impatience the youngsters removed the mold too quickly, before enough water had oozed away or the clay had properly set. The bricks, sagging out of shape, had to be shoveled back into the trough and worked again. But now there were two molds, and once they were both filled Grita decreed that they should be allowed to stand until Father judged they were dry enough.

Then came another delay, tantalizing beyond measure to the eager Catalina. After the shaped bricks were out of the molds Father explained that they must wait still longer, drying in the sun before they could be fired. Meantime, more clay could be trampled, and the molds refilled—till forty whole and shapely bricks-to-be lay spread out on the bankside above the river. Dried on the top to a creamy tan, they had to be turned, to hasten the drying of the dark damp underside, and finally be stood on end to air yet more. Some days of anxiety when rain threatened. But the rain held off and the sun beat down. And at last Father, going down for a morning inspection, declared they were ready to be fired.

Then he frowned his perplexity. "In the brickyard there are kilns made of fired brick, in which to fire the new raw brick. Still, we will do our best."

Under his direction a square yard of ground was smoothed off and the bricks built up on it in the shape of a little squat chimney. Not solid, but with as much space as possible left between each brick and its neighbors. Inside the chimney Isaak dropped pine cones and other kindling, dried ax chips and larger pieces of wood. Catalina brought an ember from the kitchen hearth.

"Not too much at first, boy," Father counseled. "First a gentle heat to drive out the steam; then hotter when the bricks are fit to bear it."

The pine cones crackled, the wood caught. Smoke oozed up the small chimney, seeping out through the cracks. Minutes of open-mouthed anxiety lest the soft structure crumble.

It was then that Nicholas arrived. He came scuffling round the end of the house with his short, busy-seeming stride, fussing down the path, pausing to peer back as if to take stock of everything from house-thatching to pigs, orchard to cabbage patch. Of course, the director had to have someone to tell him how his farms were being run, but Grita had often wished that it wasn't this Nicholas; his long inquisitive nose got too much enjoyment out of the business. Now she felt an inward chuckle. Father and Nicholas, that was always an encounter worth listening to.

"Gideon Dolph is here." The clerk's usual accusing tone made it sound more like a statement than the question that he intended.

Father took it that way. "Is he?" He turned his blue gaze from the smoking chimney to Nicholas.

"I said, 'Is Gideon Dolph here?' "

"No," said Father. "That you did not say."

"Well, I ask now, 'Is Gideon Dolph here?' "

Grita bit on the inside of her lip while Father's head turned slowly, surveying the landscape around him. "No, Gideon Dolph I do not see. Perhaps he is not here."

"Nor Kaspar de Selle?" Nicholas was careful to make it a question this time.

"I do not see him either," said Father firmly.

Nicholas took a swift glance at Grita, at the children, even at the improvised brick kiln, as if hoping somewhere to find a more certain answer. Failing to get any he snapped out, "See that your thatch is repaired before winter," wheeled angrily, and strode off.

Isaak let out a rude whoop of laughter, but smothered it with his hand as Grita frowned at him. Nicholas might have heard, he probably had. All the same she wanted to laugh too, her heart felt suddenly so light, so unaccountably light. And why was that?

Father put it into words, "So he has news of the boslooper and Kaspar, and thinks they have come back here." Perhaps Father's kind eyes had seen more of her worry than she had imagined. "They are safe, then, our friends." He said no more, but bent his attention again to the brick kiln.

Next morning that hope was confirmed. Their neighbor Mvrouw Burrgh descended upon the Hoorn farm right after her morning marketing in the Fuyck, in Beverwyck; she had not paused even to drop her filled market basket nor change to her house cap and apron, so fresh, so warm on her tongue was her news.

The news might not be of Kaspar at all. But only yesterday the clerk, Nicholas, had heard something; and that, whatever it was, would naturally be current in the market place this morning.

"The price of eggs, has it fallen again?" Grita temporized; for the woman's bony birdlike features gave no clue.

"Ja, all things from the farm are cheaper still. Soon it will not pay a farmer to send his boy and wagon to the town, for it is better to ship his corn down to the Manhatens. And my potatoes that I took . . . but of this we can talk any day." She spread her wide skirts on the hearth settle, and leaned forward eagerly.

It was coming now; Grita snatched up the sock she had been knitting; her fingers began to work furiously.

"That Gideon Dolph and that newcomer from the homeland who stayed here, whose name I do not remember, they were not killed but are alive and trading in the Maqua country. Yes, girl, of this I am sure."

Grita's needles dropped a stitch, but she went on knitting. Her heart was hammering so hard she could not utter a word. But with Mvrouw Burrgh it was not necessary to ask questions; her words flowed out without encouragement to fill any silence they came upon.

"The good news should have been known a week ago, or more; for then it was that the Indian boy was sent to deliver it. But only yesterday did his father hear that there was any message. Today it is all over the market. Everyone is talking of it. You too would have heard had you gone into the town. It is good news even to those who did not know this Gideon and this Kaspar, for where two white men are killed others may also be killed; but where the two are found to be safe there is greater safety for others . . ." Her voice rattled on and on and on. But it was music, every word of it.

And after Mvrouw had left, that was not the end of good fortune. For the brickmaking showed signs of being a success. Father had to rebuild the openwork chimney so that the unburned ends of the bricks would now get burned. And none broke in the rebuilding. After the second burning, while the children watched, he tapped brick after brick lightly with a hammer, testing them by the sound. Nearly all of them rang true. "It is something you learn when you are young," he explained to Isaak.

Next he sent Isaak with the team and wagon to Beverwyck for a schepel measure of lime, and found sand down in the river and washed it free of mud. And one day he announced that Grita must do all the baking she would need for several days to come. Gladly she struggled through that day, baking and reheating the oven and baking again, in spite of the temperature of the summer day. Tomorrow they would tear down that brute of an oven and rebuild it.

Perhaps Kaspar would be back before the oven was ready to bake the wheaten bread, which, like all true Netherlanders, he enjoyed so much. Broken bricks littered her kitchen floor, gritty dust settled on cupboard and kast and mantleshelf, so that every dish must be wiped before food could be cooked in it or served on it. Isaak, under Father's instructions, made a curved wooden form to hold up the new brick arch until the mortar set; another day and the form was taken down, so that cracks between the bricks could be freshly pointed up with mortar. Often she glanced out at the road, hoping that Kaspar would arrive to share the family triumph, hoping almost that Kaspar would not come while all was so upset.

At last she cleared out the last piece of dropped lime, the last dusty footprints. But still no sign of Kaspar. Tomorrow, Father promised, she could light a few wisps of straw in the oven, the day after kindle a few twigs. By the end of the week it would be safe to use again. And still no Kaspar.

She set her dough one evening by the warm ashes. The next morning heated up the oven, raked out the embers and set the bread to bake, the finest, lightest loaves she had ever made. Surely that was a good omen, wasn't it? Surely Heaven would be kind to her, and send her more good fortune.

It was when she went outside to call the children in to share her pride in the new baking, and in the new oven which all had helped to build, that she saw the two men approaching.

All thoughts of the new bread slipped from her mind. For the tall one striding along the path from the director's house was Gideon Dolph. And beside him, not Kaspar, but Mynheer Jeremias.

Too far away as yet to see the expression on their faces, or to judge by the tone of their voices whether the news they brought was good or ill.

Suddenly she turned back indoors. She could not, she dare not meet them.

For on Gideon's fist rode the falcon. Kaspar's falcon.

Chapter Sixteen
Beyond the
White Man's Reach

KASPAR'S left arm felt strangely light and empty as his loping stride carried him on toward Beverwyck. A falconer without a falcon feels naked as a Netherlander without breeches. Not, he chuckled to himself, that there was much left of his breeches either. But no respectable burgher or his wife was likely to be encountered out here, on a forest trail, in the darkness of early morning.

In less than an hour now he would see the falcon again, be stroking her, talking to her, in the Hoorn barn. Gideon, a day's march ahead, would have found out from the director if it were safe for Kaspar to remain within the patroonship, or if it would be wiser for him to start straight out again. This time, if he had to go, he would accept the director's offer of some trade goods; it had been tantalizing to see the boslooper turning good profit, day after day. Not that he could really grudge the boslooper his success; no one could, who really knew him. The finest companion in the wilds, in rain and shine, in safety or danger, that a man could have. Danger and hardship showed what a man really was; there had been plenty of both in the past weeks.

That race for safety from the riverbank and the pursuing Mahicans; the need for utmost caution—for there might be Mahicans ahead as well as behind—contending with the urgent need for speed. Not till they stumbled across a Maqua hunting party did Kaspar get rid of that feeling of a barbed arrowhead about to bury itself in his spine. Brrr . . . he could almost feel it again now. And how unwillingly he had forced himself to turn back with that slight escort, to recover Gideon's pack and his own seven beaver skins.

When at last they reached the village of the Maqua chief, Aquinachoo, Gideon Dolph had difficulty in forcing his legs to take him up the last slight slope to the stockade; the Otter, much against his will, was being carried. Kaspar's muscles, hardened by much falconry, bore through to the last; but there in the lodge his mind seemed to go blank. Apparently he had fed his falcon and himself and listened while Gideon told the news of the disaster to a hastily summoned council; had been questioned and had replied. But he could recall nothing of it.

Next day he came to life, stretched out on the ground in the sunshine, bare as a newborn child, and being rubbed and pounded and pommeled and turned over and rubbed and pounded again. Two aged squaws were painfully working the stiffness out of him, while one still older, the sister of the dead chief, directed the process. With a few words in the Maqua speech the older squaw dismissed her helpers and addressed a question to Kaspar.

He almost caught the meaning, but the woman's intonation made the speech sound strange; and anyway his mind was still dull with the dregs of fatigue. She brought him garments, first no more than moccasins and the buckskin apron such as the braves wore in summer. Then with a twinkle of amusement in the sharp old eyes added trousers and a fringed hunting shirt embroidered with dyed porcupine quills.

As the sun was hot in the dust-covered yard, he followed the squaw back into the lodge. No sign of Gideon here; the bunks along the sides were empty. The whole village, he was now aware, seemed strangely silent. The women pursued their tasks, pounding corn, grinding meal, carrying trayfuls outside to winnow in the breeze, or brought water from the river below, but all without the usual cheerful babble of gossip. Even the voices of the children, playing outside, seemed muted, subdued; all with a sense of waiting. And not a man of warrior age in sight.

Kaspar, being served with a bowl of thin gruel compounded of meal, berries and crushed nuts, grasped of a sudden what had happened. This was women's food. The hunters, before going off on their long man hunt, had filled up on the last of the bear meat and venison. He made the hand sign of "war" and "question."

The squaws, perhaps because they remained more at home, were less adept at the sign language than the men. He could not read the old woman's answer, but from the expression on her face he judged that he was right, or nearly so. If not an outright war between the Maquas and the Mahicans, then a heavy punitive raid; and it looked as if Gideon had gone with them.

What ought he to do? Kaspar shoved aside the half-finished bowl of gruel to consider. As a friend of the murdered chief, he felt the need to avenge him. Killing and war were bad, but to lie in wait for, and ambush a handful of men brave enough to come unprotected to treat for peace, that was cowardly, barbarous and utterly unforgivable. With a hot hatred such as he had never known before, willingly, with his own hands, would he have killed one of the treacherous band that had slaughtered the peace party.

But of what use was he? What could he do? Unarmed, unskilled in Indian warfare, he knew he would be a burden, even if, on inquiry, he found which route the raiding party had taken, and by hard running caught up with them.

As his quick anger cooled he saw that as a Netherlander he had no right to involve his people on one side or the other. Both Mahicans and Maquas had been friendly to the white people; and when it came to that, from Gideon's account, the Maquas in the past had been more cruel, more bloodthirsty even than their neighbors. The bleached skulls that topped the stockade attested to that.

He finished his meal, and sick at heart, made the hand sign for "hawk." The woman pointed. And there in a dim corner of the lodge perched the falcon, the leash properly secured around her jesses with Kaspar's own knot, which no one else would have imitated. So he hadn't forgotten her on the previous night. And there was her "casting" below the perch to prove she had been fed. Half-heartedly and without enjoyment he took her out and he gave her her morning flight, let her kill, after a couple of misses, and sat waiting beside her while she deplumed her quarry. And, since he had no heart to fly her again today, let her gorge herself to the full. Then back to the lodge, with the half-formed notion of resting today and tomorrow starting back to Rensselaerswyck.

But in the lodge was Gideon. Eating prodigiously, rubbing the sleep from his eyes and chatting with the chief's sister as freely as, perhaps more freely than, he would gossip with a white woman.

"She says," he translated for Kaspar's benefit, "that we are welcome to stay. In fact she is urging us to. Only it's this way; when they bring back the chief's body, her brother's body, if they can find it, they'll divide up all his goods. And if

we are here, we'll be expected to accept a share. It would be
insulting to refuse, but I couldn't take it, all the same. If I'd
had the sense to hang around the peace council, one white
man with a musket might just—I don't say he would—have
prevented the massacre."

Kaspar sympathized. He felt that way himself. Though
one man with only one shot to his musket would have done
no good; he was sure of that. All the same, like Gideon, he
felt the responsibility. Unreasonable as it might seem, the
death of the chief still hung heavy on his conscience.

"I'd rather clear out," said Kaspar.

"Good." Gideon approved with a nod. "The weather's
warm and fine and I've still got my trade goods. We'll strike
out west; there may be a few beavers and there may not, but
we'll kind of beat a trail and make a few friends toward the
future."

There was one more thing to be done, and Gideon could
help him. The dead chief had purchased the falcon; with
seven beaver skins, pelts of the finest and largest. Would the
sister of the chief accept back the same seven skins and let
Kaspar keep his bird?

With growing anxiety he heard, but scarcely understood,
the discussion that followed. The old squaw, politely at first,
then almost angrily, was refusing. Gideon did his best, you
could see that. But at last he flung up a hand, as if in accept-
ance of defeat.

"She won't agree. Not for a moment."

Kaspar's eyes turned to the falcon. "But couldn't you explain to her that the falcon is useless without somebody
trained to fly her? And that I didn't really want to sell?"

Gideon's deep laughter roared through the lodge. He said
something to the woman, whose face broke into a thousand
wrinkles of amusement. Then still shaking with laughter he
turned back to Kaspar.

"She says the bird wouldn't even make a meal. All she's
refusing is to accept the seven skins."

The old woman spoke again.

"She says that the skins and the bird are both yours. Nor is the friendship between Hawk-on-Hand and Aquinachoo to be measured in beavers. She says you are her son and that there is always food and a fire in her lodge for you."

Kaspar tried to say something, stammered out his thanks. But he hadn't the Maqua words for his deep gratitude, nor did he know the sign talk for it. It was only later that Gideon explained just what this friendship might mean; that among the Maquas, descent was traced through the mother, and not the father. That, like several other women in the tribe, this woman was a hereditary chief of her own clan, just as her brother, by marrying into another clan, had become first a leader of war parties, than a leader of his clan.

When Gideon, preparing for departure, bethought himself of the Otter, it was the chief's sister who had him hunted out and brought to the lodge. When Gideon and Kaspar decided to dispatch him to Rensselaerswyck with the reassuring news that Kaspar and Gideon were still alive, it was only the authority of the chief's sister that made him start off, instead of hiding and following the white men on their journey west. Or so it seemed, for the Otter started out all right—they saw him go.

The trip from one Maqua castle to another, farther west along the Maqua river, would last forever in Kaspar's memory. Gideon was right; there was little trading to be done. But something about the boslooper's burly good humor went straight to the Maqua heart. Kaspar learned to play a number of their games, and the falcon never failed to interest them. But it was Gideon who could take them on at feats of strength, casting a huge rock over his head and usually outmatching by a yard or more the throw of the strongest man in the village. It was Gideon who wrestled as well as any Maqua; and when he was downed, which was seldom, roared with laughter and gave his triumphant adversary a small present.

Streams that in the springtime would be roaring torrents
were, in late summer, easily waded or crossed dry-shod;
trails, which in midwinter would be choked with snow, were
smooth as the path between the Hoorn house and the Hoorn
barn. There were lakes, small and large, thick with wild Indian rice, harboring more fish and birds than even the great
river at Rensselaerswyck. Traders had rarely come all this
way; and at the end of their journey they reached country
where, instead of Netherlanders, it was Frenchmen from the
north who, for the past years, had purchased most of the
beavers.

Gideon promised himself, and the Indians, a return visit
next spring. He could, he told them, offer better prices than
the French, for his trade goods and his skins would have less
distance to travel to reach the sea. And even for the same
price the Indians said they would save their skins and trade
with him instead of with the French; for the white tribe to
which Gideon belonged was the friend of their allies, the
Maquas, and the French were friends of their enemies, the
Hurons of the north.

"They think the French voyageurs are spies for the Hurons," Gideon explained, "and that where the French penetrate the Huron, raiders will follow. Indians set great stock
by friendship and enmity; even with animals. Did you know
that the beaver is the special friend of the Maquas and their
allies, in fact all the Iroquois group?"

"Then why do they kill them?" Kaspar asked.

"Death, itself, doesn't count for much among these people. They say the beaver gives them his skin and his meat to
help them, and dams up the streams for their fishing. So all
the beaver bones are saved and taken back to bury among
the beavers—something to do with life after death—and
you'll never see an Indian giving beaver bones to the dogs."

Kaspar was learning more all the time. He was learning
the language too, as well as the thought of the people, though
the speech seemed to vary, anyway in pronunciation, from

place to place. Even the Otter taught him much. For to their mingled annoyance and amusement they still had the Otter with them. The young scoundrel had played his usual trick, and four days westward of the old chief's castle had met them in the forest just as casually as he might have run across them in the Fuyck at Beverwyck.

No, the Otter hadn't gone to Rensselaerswyck. No, he had taken no message. He admitted, he even boasted as much. Gideon accepted defeat with a laugh and the Otter was again one of the party. Kaspar felt a little differently about it.

If he had known that the Otter was going to play this trick, he would have tried to find some other Indian, someone he could trust, to take a message. Or, if necessary, he would have asked Gideon to delay the trip west for four days while he himself risked the journey to the Hoorns and back. He hated to think of the concern they must feel when news of the massacre spread round. Of course, they would have tidings, too, of the escape of the two white men, uncertain tidings; but what would the director think, what would Mathias think? Even more important, what would Grita think and feel when week after week passed and no further news arrived? No use now sending the brat back on their outward journey; he would only hide again and pop up on their return.

But thereafter Kaspar, to his own exasperation, found that whenever he looked at the Otter, dirty and rascally and a thorough nuisance, he thought of Grita. Not that there was the slightest resemblance. Grita, with her gay integrity and inner wholeness, her long black Spanish eyes with their full-fringed lashes, the way she had of tossing one dark braid impatiently over her shoulder, the pretty quick gesture of her hands, so unlike a Netherlander girl's. She had once told him that her father was Spanish; she had told him, too, how hard she tried to be like Nelle and Mathias. As if he wanted her to be like them, good simple souls though they were. No, it was her laughter and her twinkling fun that he recalled, and what a joy and zest she put into all she did. He even found himself missing her. But why the urchin Otter should continue to remind him of her, he couldn't say. Unless it was a growing fury with the Otter, that his disobedience should cause Grita Hoorn to suffer even a moment's concern or anxiety over his own whereabouts. For he knew that she would feel concern, even as he felt it for her.

As, at long last, they turned back and started for home, Kaspar came near to a quarrel with Gideon. The Otter, he pointed out, was Gideon's follower, not his. So it was for the boslooper to send the boy home. If he were only a few days ahead of them in arriving at Rensselaerswyck, it would at least break the news and insure that they weren't taken for ghosts! Or anyway that they didn't cause more shock than was necessary.

Gideon agreed. "But do you think I'd have had the Otter with me for the best part of two years if I could find a way to get rid of him? Oh, he's been useful at times, but he's like your falcon, a heap of trouble. I've tried beating him, I've tried cutting him off without food. I've threatened his father with everything short of death if he doesn't hang on to his son. Now what are you going to do?"

Kaspar waited till evening, when he and Gideon and several elders, gorged with meat, were sitting about the fire. "What," he asked, "is a good name for a girl? One who is idle, one who is disobedient, one who sticks close as a burr?"

Kaspar had thought out his sentences long beforehand, but even so it was difficult to get the proper intonation, and the Indians clearly understood but little.

"A squaw name?" one of them asked. "There are many." He gave a few.

Kaspar picked one out, not knowing what it meant. "That," he said, "will do. It is easier to say than Tawyne."

A quick interest showed in the Otter's face.

"A squaw is safe to travel alone, for none would molest her. But since the Otter, or, as we shall call her now . . ."

and he gave the new name, "is dressed as a boy, that may be the reason why she stays always with the white men. She is afraid to journey alone, back to her people."

Gideon caught the point. Swiftly he enlarged on it. "It will be safer then," he asked Kaspar, but in the Maqua speech, "if we dress the Otter in the clothes of a squaw?"

Now the grave faces of their hosts began to show an appreciation of the jest. Kaspar dare not glance at the Otter just yet, although he knew what he would read in that usually impassive little face. The furious indignation, the outraged dignity, with perhaps a trace of dread.

"She is a dirty one, this little squaw, seldom washing even the feet after a journey," Kaspar carried on with Gideon's suggestion. Besides, he had suffered much from the strong odor of Otter on this hot summer's travel. "So the clothing need not be costly, for that would be waste."

Now some women were leaving their duties to come up and hear what was amusing their men. One of them removed a thin necklace and tried to put it around the Otter's neck. With a squawk of protest he dodged. Another woman made a clutch at him, calling him by the new name. There was more laughter. Said one of the men, mock-seriously, to another, "First it would be better that the women do the young squaw's hair, after the manner of women."

"And perhaps," offered another gravely, "at first being accustomed to the apron of a boy, she will not like the skirt of a woman, and it will be necessary to tie her hands on your journey home."

Kaspar took a glance at the small boy. In a moment now the boy would bolt. "Of course," he said deliberately, "if it were found that he were not afraid of traveling alone, and that he went home to his own people and gave the message that he was told to give, we would know perhaps that he really was a boy. And not a young squaw. In that case in Beverwyck he would still be known as the Otter, and not by the name of a woman."

It was sufficient. Next morning the Otter could not be found. Nor, to Kaspar's relief, did they find him again on the homeward journey.

The way home was just as uneventful and perhaps even more pleasant. The last half, paddling lazily with the current in a canoe that Gideon bought, was a triumphal progress; for at each stop now they were greeted as old friends. At the last Maqua castle the burial ceremonies had long since been completed and a few fresh heads upon the stockades showed that the Maqua raiding party had taken its revenge. Then on again by canoe.

Close to the Netherlands settlement of Schenectade, the time came to decide a problem they had discussed a number of times before. If Kaspar was still wanted for that debt, he would have to take precautions. As a newcomer, not many people, probably none in Schenectade, would know him by sight. But they would recognize Gideon. And because of the story that Gideon and Kaspar de Selle had been companions at the peace party massacre they would guess who Kaspar was if the boslooper were seen with him. The falcon, too, would make his recognition certain. Clearly Kaspar and Gideon must part, and Gideon must take the falcon.

Kaspar offered, in exchange, to carry on to Rensselaerswyck at least half of Gideon's pack of pelts. For some reason that seemed to amuse the boslooper.

He burst out in his usual guffaw, and said, rather puzzlingly: "Since when did the laws of the cities concern us bosloopers of the forest? We don't risk our scalps to fatten still more the fat burghers of Beverwyck or the Manhatens! You leave the skins with me, boy; I know what to do with them. You won't be a day behind me as I reckon, and I'll see that Isaak feeds your falcon till you come."

Kaspar had stepped ashore, waited in a thicket of sumac till nightfall, and, his left arm feeling strangely light and empty for lack of glove and falcon, started on his lope for home.

Chapter Seventeen
Bait a Trap with Bread and
Catch a Netherlander

IN SAFETY, still in darkness, Kaspar circled the sleeping
town of Beverwyck, and came at last to the Hoorn barn
as the line began to brighten over the eastern hills. In a
sheltered corner the falcon was well, and, he would swear it,
pleased to see him; "bating" as soon as she heard his voice,
jumping from her perch to his hand just as soon as he came
within reach of her leash. So Gideon was back. He stroked
the bird a moment and considered. Whether the summons
were still out against him or not, for an hour or two he would
be safe while Beverwyck officials yawned themselves awake
and dressed and stuffed themselves with breakfast.

Replacing the reluctant bird upon her perch, he strode across to the house, picked up the water pails left last night outside the door, set the carrying yoke on his shoulders and went down to draw water from the river.

In leisurely fashion he threw out first one bucket, then the other, on the rope and drew them, filled, to shore; welcomed the remembered feel of the yoke across his shoulders as he straightened under his load. After his long wanderings in the wilds this daily chore brought with it a touch of reassurance, of friendship. Unlike the life of the wilderness, here on a farm a man need not stand alone, surviving only by his own efforts. There was satisfaction, of course, in independence, but there was satisfaction, too, in this life where each member of the family worked for the whole; the pleasure of doing things for others, of having them do things for you. Was that what people meant by "civilization?"

He smiled with enjoyment as he anticipated Grita's surprise at finding her water buckets already filled; she would toss back that long braid over her shoulder when she saw him, and say, "Oh!" and then "Kaspar!" And that dimple in the corner of her mouth would flicker an instant. In just one word, just her simple speaking of his name, the welcome would be complete.

But the surprise didn't quite come off. As he turned back to the house in the cool growing light, he noted that a thin feather of smoke was already rising from the chimney. The top half of the door, that had been closed when he took the pails, was open now. And as he slipped from beneath the yoke, the bottom half swung open too.

And Grita ran out, grasped his hands and said, "Oh, Kaspar!" Just as he had known she would. Only the pigtails were gone, tucked out of sight beneath her cap.

"Grita!" and it was all he could do not to add "Dear!" So glad was he to be back again.

Still holding both his grubby hands in her clean cool fingers she drew him into the house, in wordless welcome, and stood off gravely to consider him; from his straggling uncut hair, now worn Maqua fashion in two rough braids, to the bare toes protruding through the ends of his tattered moccasins. He must, he knew, be a horrifying scarecrow.

But she seemed not to mind, and gave a soft laugh of relief and reassurance at what she noted. "Poor Kaspar, you must be nearly starved. Gideon lost more flesh than you had on your whole body when you started out. So I was prepared to see your backbone through your ribs."

Then came to his nostrils the most delicious odor he ever expected to smell again, this side of heaven. Bread. Wheaten bread. Fresh baking in the oven. It drew him into the kitchen.

Grita's cap bobbed as she scolded him. "Raw meat I suppose you've eaten, all these weeks. And bark of trees. You men! What is the use of feeding you, when you run off, come home half starved, and need to be fed all over again?" But she was laughing at him. "Well, I've been up for hours, and the bread is nearly ready to take from the oven. They say bait a trap with bread and catch a Netherlander!" She pushed him into a corner of the settle and began to bustle about the hearth.

Hungry he was, after these long weeks of meat and more meat, for good wheaten bread. But hungrier still, though he had not guessed he would be, for the sight of Grita's kitchen. His eyes wandered over it: its puncheon floor, scrubbed and sanded, its wide stone hearth, with the heavy crane, and kettles kept warm in the ashes and already simmering. As the first light of dawn stole in through the open window, picked out the bright blossomed plants Grita had nourished there, it struck, clear and sharp, on the polished brasses from the homeland that stood along the mantle shelf, shone back more gently from the silver-blue pewter platters and pitchers that were ranged along the dresser. All was so clean, so orderly, so ready for instant use. And Grita herself, moving deftly, swiftly, lifting a lid to stir the bubbling corn pudding with a long-handled spoon, fanning the flame a little, rearranging a pot on the fire; she was the very spirit of this kitchen, of this household, of the civilized as distinct from the savage. Wholesome, good for the soul as for the body.

But troubling in her strangeness to one who had seen only the boslooper and the Maquas for so long. Enigmatic, a little bewildering in the competent manner in which she pursued her craft—handed down from woman to woman and incomprehensible to a man—the mysterious rites of home-making.

Puzzling in some other way, too, she had become. Was it something to do with her hair? Kaspar's eyes followed her about the kitchen, curiously, happily. Grita no longer seemed a girl; sometime during his absence she had joined another tribe, the tribe of women. Yes, that was the change that had puzzled him, the new assurance visible in all her movements, the new mother-of-the-household air.

Her voice roused him from his reverie. "Almost ready now." The oven door swung open; she lifted the long-handled oven peel. And the sweet maltlike odor of the baking richened the air. Kaspar's hunger seized his full attention.

An elm bowl of milk, cool from the dairy room, was placed before him. His knife sliced the fresh, spongy loaf. His teeth bit into it. Oh, this was very heaven!

Grita watched him a moment, her head cocked to one side; she gave a little nod of satisfaction and went back to sliding out the remaining loaves, talking as she worked. She began to give him news of the household, of Isaak's prodigious growth and his increasing skill with tools, now his strength was more suited to them. Of his greater patience with the livestock. Of Catalina's waning interest in her clay menagerie, and her growing ability with the needle and the shuttle. Of baby Joan learning to spin, and Father teaching her her letters from the book of Genesis. But when she came to speak of Mathias she hesitated; she began to talk of the oven, and of the new bricks that had repaired it. That was puzzling. Bricks?

"Here are blackberries," she said, "and fresh cream. Perhaps you had blackberries with your Indians, but I'm sure no such cream," and filled his bowl again.

"Bricks?" said Kaspar. "What about bricks?"

"The Hoorns," said Grita, "seem to be going back to their family trade of brickmaking. We started with forty or fifty. Just enough for the oven. Then Father made more, to repair his pigsty. Then someone in Beverwyck wanted a half-hundred, of a special size, and the brickyards would not trouble with so few; so Father made them for him instead. Now Father has already shipped a load down to the Manhatens. The director is getting worried because of our wheat and the way father seems to be losing interest in the farm. I'm getting worried because of the way he's been burning up our winter firewood for the brick kiln. But fortunately he can't make any more bricks this year; he's used up all the weathered clay on the surface of the claybank and will have to dig out more and pile it to weather through the winter."

Kaspar stretched luxuriously and propped his elbows on the table. Through the wavery glass of the window he could see Mathias stomping off to the barn to milk. Odd to think of that good stolid man bursting forth with so much energy, so much unsuspected purpose of his own, into a new trade. As Mother Hoorn would have said, "Not from the bark can the strength of the tree be told."

"But bricks are something that can wait," Kaspar protested. "The director is right, the wheat harvest can't wait. And the price of the first wheat will be high, for the crops have been bad for two years, and the freshet damaged so many of the riverside farms."

"I know. And it's not so much this year's crop that worries me as Father's losing interest in his farm. It's next year and the next and the next that matter. But what can we do? The director himself has talked to Father about it; he wants to ship two hundred scheples of wheat to the homeland. And the governor, Peter Stuyvesant himself, has asked for as

much wheat to be sent to the Manhatens as the patroonship
can spare. They want wheat even as far down as the Company's settlement in Curaçao."

"So it's wheat against beaver skins?" Kaspar was beginning to see why Grita was so warmly concerned for the
future. "If people want wheat as badly as in the past they
have wanted beavers, and there's a surer profit in growing
wheat . . ."

"Of course! Then we'll have good farmers and good
farms. And there'll be beaver dams again and the floods will
do less harm. And the Maquas will get fewer firearms for
their bloodthirsty wars. And . . . Oh, can't you *see*, Kaspar?" She swung round to confront him, a note of entreaty
in her voice.

"And it all depends on this year?"

She turned and began to gather the bowls and horn spoons
to set the breakfast table. "Oh, Father will get in this season's crop; he's promised the director. Anyway, no farmer
could leave such a wonderful crop ungarnered. Have you
seen it yet, Kaspar? It's the finest and cleanest we've ever
had, so thick and tall and strong, you've never seen the like."

"And if this wonderful crop and this year's heavy demand
don't bring prices that will tempt Mathias and others to
grow more and better wheat, then your hope is gone. Is
that it?" Kaspar's voice grew tender without his being aware.

Grita nodded, close to tears. She might have said more,
but Mathias himself appeared at the door and, seeing Kaspar, set down the pails of milk and hurried forward, still in
his wooden klompen. His hands were outstretched in welcome.

"Almost we believed you were killed. Grita here, she—"

"Here's Isaak," Grita broke in hurriedly and in odd confusion, "and the children."

Then the kitchen seemed filled with a horde of welcoming,
and also hungry, youngsters. So much they wanted to know;
such chattering and questions, and such eagerness to relate

their own personal news. When Gideon came down the ladder from the loft above the kitchen and Mathias drew out the seat in front of the big Bible, removed his hat and read, with slow-moving lips and following finger, the morning passage, it seemed as if time had stood still, as if nothing had happened between now and the last time Kaspar had sat here.

And at this same hour, at this same time, all over the New Netherlands, folk were sitting down to breakfast, each to a table of such plenty as was seldom known in the homeland save to the wealthy; a table on which the corn meal and wheaten bread, the pea gruel and boiled cabbage, the haunch of roast meat, the fish and cider and milk and beer could be offered without stint, could be shared with any passing stranger. For all this abundance came from the forests, the rivers, the rich soil of New Netherlands itself. Bad seasons there might be, but with health and strength a man and his family could lay by and provide for these.

Yes, this was as Kiliaen van Rensselaer had seen it, long ago in Amsterdam. As a small boy Kaspar had seen it too, and had dreamed of it all these years. But if people continued to neglect their farms, as Mathias himself was beginning to, who would be left to produce this store of plenty? A man and his family could not live on pelts, or on the money pelts brought, unless food could be bought.

Gideon's rich roar of laughter broke through Kaspar's half-dreaming reverie.

"Beavers . . ." said Gideon, and between huge mouthfuls launched into a story to amuse the young ones.

Beavers. He must get his seven beaver skins from Gideon; as soon as this meal was finished. If Gideon and Mathias judged it to be safe, he would go straight to the director and pay over the skins. Already he was a part, a small part, of Kiliaen's great plan; but, till the passage debt was paid, not more, in his own mind, than a servant of the director, to do as he was told, to go here and there as he was sent. Once the

payment was made, he would be a free associate in the enter-
prise. Free; more free in a way than the director himself.

Freedom, yes, freedom was the very principle of the
dream that he shared with the first patroon. Not the garbled
"freedom" that was so often in the mouths of the laziest,
most useless prentices of Amsterdam; but an honest freedom.
Freedom to live and work under the conditions imposed by
sun and rain and health and sickness and good luck and bad.
The freedom that suited a man who had the courage to fight
back and defend himself and others in his care. Not the
puling "freedom" which demanded to be freed of all responsibility, even for himself, and cast a man's burden upon some
master or patroon; that was no more than a form of slavery
or infancy. A real man should stand square to fate and the
elements and fight his own battles with them. That was the
only true freedom.

Yes, the purpose of the First Patroon demanded free men
to fulfil it. For only a free man could understand the dream.
The first step, small as it might seem, was to pay those seven
beavers to the director.

Chapter Eighteen
Susskooks Again

THE MEAL FINISHED, the family scattered to their various chores. But Kaspar, drowsy with much food and good companionship after a night of travel, sat on, while the boslooper filled his short wooden pipe and blew contented rings at the ceiling.

"And what will you two loafers do now?" asked Grita cheerfully, handing Catalina a bowl of scraps to carry out to the chickens.

"I plan to see the director, to find out if it's safe to stay here, or whether the summons is still out against me."

"I do not think it is safe. Three times while you two were away people have come, asking for Kaspar de Selle," she warned him, a note of concern in her voice. "And by this time of day Mynheer Nicholas will already have come from his house in Beverwyck to work in the patroonship's counting house."

Kaspar's sense of satisfaction at his return, even his sense of safety, was beginning to fade. "Then I'll see the director this evening and spend the day hawking; the bird needs exercise."

But he was dissuaded even from that. As Gideon pointed out, Isaak would be glad of the chance to fly the bird, and Grita suggested that it would do Kaspar's appearance no harm if he slipped down to the river, under cover of the banks of the dry kill, swam for an hour, and let her cut his hair when he came back.

"You'll need your good clothes, to visit the director. They're in the kast in the loft," she added.

A lazy comfortable swim, upriver and almost across to the east bank; back to the house again, apparently unobserved. But more and more his feeling of security had dissipated. Back in the loft, dressing, Kaspar realized that he would wear his homeland garments only until he had seen the director and paid the price of his passage out. Then he would be under no obligation to the patroonship and would be free to take to the forest again and become a real boslooper. Of one thing he was quite sure, he had no intention of risking six months, a year, in prison; for the laws here were as they were in the Netherlands, and a debtor, once convicted, might remain behind bars as long as his debt remained unpaid—and while he lay in prison would, of course, have little chance to pay the debt and the mounting charge of his board and lodging. Or in some cases the court could decree that the debtor be sold as a bound servant to anyone who was willing to pay the creditor. That might be worse.

Clean and dressed, Kaspar found Gideon still in the kitchen.

"Where can I find those seven beavers?" Kaspar asked.
The boslooper looked surprised. "You don't want the skins themselves?"

"But of course I do. They are to pay my debt to the patroonship, for my passage from the homeland."

"Oh, they're not lost or stolen or anything," Gideon assured him. "They're on their way to the Manhatens, with mine. You'll get a better price there, and you don't have to pay the patroonship tax to the West India Company. Not the way I sell mine."

Gideon's words were plain enough, but Kaspar had to make sure. "You mean they're to be smuggled out of the country?"

Gideon let out a shout of laughter. "Why, of course, boy! Do you think the beaver cares, once he's lost his hide?"

"But the law," Kaspar still protested.

"There are laws, boy, and there are laws. There are laws to protect people from harm, from murder, from stealing. And they're fair enough. But when a law is made to allow people to steal, it runs against my conscience. Isn't it stealing when the West Indian Company takes from me the value of one skin in twenty? They're my skins, aren't they—the whole twenty of them? Why should I hand one over to the West India Company just because they say I must?"

Then sensing Kaspar's dismay he capitulated. "Ho there, boy, you look as if you'd waked up to find your scalp gone. If the pelts mean as much as that to you, we'll get them back. Look here, there's a sloop leaving Beverwyck tomorrow morning. Likely enough with this good wind, she'll overtake the canoe with the pelts aboard before they reach the Manhatens."

The plan was simplicity itself and worked without a hitch. That evening the Hoorn farm boat ferried Kaspar, again in his worn deerskins, over to the Ostwal, the east bank where he could wait safely enough, since the Beverwyck jurisdiction did not extend here. Shortly after dawn, when the sloop, following the usual custom of earning some extra styvvers as a ferryboat, disembarked a handful of passengers, Kaspar, yawning and rubbing his eyes, stepped on board. Gideon, refusing to take no for an answer, had insisted on paying his fare down-river and had already preëmpted a comfortable corner of the deck among the fragrant sawn lumber and sacks of corn.

A quick easy trip, with the current and the breeze favoring. But they did not, as Gideon had hoped, catch up with the canoe that carried the pelts.

If the one-eyed captain and his part-Indian wife who cooked and helped him, had any suspicion who Kaspar was, or that he was wanted by the law, they kept it to themselves. But as soon as the farm land in the Manhatens came in sight, the boslooper took an additional precaution. He paid the fares and, saying something about "saving steps" and on his way in looking over some farm land which he intended to buy, had the captain disembark his two passengers well north of the stockade.

Kaspar could scarcely recognize the place. It was here that he had hawked on his first arrival. But then the land had been bare and brown. Now every foot of the countryside was good rich pasture or sown to tall, ripening wheat or corn. And by the look of the ears of wheat, by the black tassels on full corn ears, the grain down here was ten days, perhaps twenty, in advance of Beverwyck. Yes, farther south the season would be longer, and perhaps on this high ground no freshet would threaten early sowing.

In an open field two men were loading a farm wagon with hay. Gideon neither called greetings to them nor answered their hail, in fact seemed rather to avoid them. A clang of cowbells as a herd passed them, going home to be milked.

"We'd best wait till the gates of the stockade are about to be shut, when everyone is trying to crowd in at the last minute to escape the fine," the boslooper suggested. "The less these burghers take note of Gideon Dolph the better."

That suited Kaspar well enough. If Wouter Fries, or the fat or the thin constable, caught sight of him he might not get away as easily, this second time. Kaspar's safety lay in the fact that this was the last place Wouter would expect to find him. What risk it was that Gideon ran he could make no guess; he couldn't very well be an actual smuggler, since smuggling would have to be done in the port itself. It might be that, as a man of the wilderness, he was shy of towns and townsfolk and covered it up in a veil of mystery to make it more romantic.

It was late and almost dark when they let a stream of wagons, young livestock, and returning townsfolk carry them in through the gate; with sufficient dust, whip-cracking, shouting and confusion to hide a small raiding party of Indians, if there had been one. Trees, heavy with fruit, lined the broad de Heere Street, and over to the west between road and river stood the summerhouse, in its formal orchard, where Kaspar to his horror, had all but run into Governor Peter Stuyvesant and his escort of drummers.

Then Gideon tapped him on the arm and in the growing dusk they followed a herd of goats up a side street, leaving the dust, and the main flood of lowing, bleating and shouting to pour on to its homes and byres and pens and stables. A few windows glowed with candlelight, scents of cooking perfumed the evening air, here and there a burgher sat peaceably on his stoep smoking his evening pipe, a tall pewter-lidded beer pot by his side.

"Where now?" asked Kaspar. It was time this mystery ended. Also these smug and orderly houses and streets were making him ill at ease in his patched deerskins.

"To get your beavers, of course." Gideon, with musket, powderhorn and bullet bag, looked just as incongruous in this peaceful town, his shuffling swinging stride more suited to forest trails than to cobbled pavement. He may have felt that too, for he added, "Just as soon as we lay our hands on them, we'll get out of this, stockade or no stockade, and likely enough find Dirck Tienhoven and his canoe at the usual place upriver."

Between two houses they turned through a gate to a side door, hidden from the street. The boslooper raised the knocker. "This is the agent who buys our beavers," he said to Kaspar. "But seeing he's a friend of yours, you'd best stand back in the shadow behind that clump of sunflowers."

"A friend of mine?"

"Yes, Susskooks . . ."

"But . . ." Kaspar was about to protest that he knew no such person when the top half of the door swung open. And, silhouetted against the candlelight behind, a fattish, slovenly figure, Wouter Fries.

Kaspar stepped back hastily. But was it too late? Had Wouter Fries seen him? If he had, the man gave no sign, his expression hidden in the shadow. He opened the lower half of the door, said something reprovingly about, "Late . . ." and "Neighbors . . ." Then Kaspar was left outside, alone in the deepening twilight.

The chances were, he decided, that he was safe. Unshaven, soiled, no longer in homeland garments, and above all without the falcon, he would scarcely be recognized for the new colonist, straight from Amsterdam, that Wouter had known. But all the same he felt anger with the boslooper. If Gideon hadn't, as usual, made such a childish mystery of everything, and had said the name of his agent, it would have been just as easy and twice as safe for Kaspar to have stayed outside the stockade; he would still have been near enough to identify the skins if there was any mix-up about them. As it was, it would do no harm to keep a wary eye on Wouter.

No light showed in the front window facing upon the street. Kaspar moved down the passageway between the two houses and saw the glow of candlelight in the back window, and what, in the dusk, seemed to be a small garden. The window was unshuttered, the casement ajar, but Kaspar had to make the choice between crouching under the window to overhear as much as possible, or standing far enough away to watch, with safety, what went on inside the room. He chose the latter.

Even so, the boslooper's loud tones carried out from time to time to where he stood.

". . . Dirck must have cut out Esopus and paddled straight on. Hardly expected . . . yet . . . When did the redhead get in?"

Wouter's mouth opened and closed, but his words were inaudible.

"Well, I sent down seven blanket beavers . . . get them back before they're sold . . ." Gideon moved farther into the darkness, away from the window.

Even in the light of the two candles, the room looked rich and oddly out of keeping with the dingy exterior of the house; brass and pewter, even a bowl of silver, gleamed on the carved dresser and kast top, and the table carpet looked deep and costly. An oil painting in a gilt frame hung upon the farther wall.

Wouter, drawing a chair to the table, seemed to be protesting mildly about something.

"You haven't?" Gideon's roar came clearly to the garden. "Then who has? Those skins weren't mine to send; they slipped in by mistake." Then. "Of course not. I've offered the owner money. Do you think I'd come all the way down here just for the fun of it?"

Kaspar hadn't expected this additional complication, but it was plain enough that if Wouter had ever received the skins he didn't have them now.

As he watched, Gideon was becoming more emphatic in his demand, and Wouter, after a bit, seemed to agree with him. He got up and moved out of sight for a moment, came back with brass inkstand and goose quill; and having shoved back the table carpet, wrote a brief note, sanded and folded it, rang a small brass hand bell and handed the message to the slatternly woman servant who answered the summons. A

moment later Kaspar heard the passage door close and,
peering cautiously round the corner of the house, saw her
waddle off through the gate. There might be some time to
wait, but it looked as if Gideon had had his way, and Wouter
had sent for the skins. Good!

Yes, clearly the two men in the room were just filling in
time. Gideon had leaned his musket against the wall and
dropped his bulk into a chair. A little time passed, and
Wouter disappeared again and returned with a tray, a bottle
of some cordial and two small glasses. Kaspar shifted from
foot to foot and sighed; the talk inside went on, but he could
hear almost none of it now. He didn't envy Gideon that
strong anise-flavored cordial, but those olleykoeks, brown
and crusty, they were biting into now looked almost as good
as Grita's. The time dragged on.

"Susskooks," Gideon had called the man. Where had he
heard that name before? Ah, yes, it was the unknown Indian
word, repeated several times by Gideon, on that first trip
upriver. Susskooks in the Manhatens, the person to whom
he was dispatching Indians with their beaver skins to sell.

But Kaspar knew more of the language now. Susskooks
was not a complimentary name; it meant "snake," someone
who was deceitful, treacherous. Did Wouter know that?

Sounds drifted in on the evening air: a child's high wail,
the closing of shutters, the locking of doors for the night.
The shot of a gun, touched off perhaps by accident, or intended to scare a suspected intruder from a fruit garden.
Then the first call of the rattle watch, coming closer, fading
off again into the south. Almost an hour had passed. Kaspar
was squatting on the grass, but the night air was chill, and
he shivered.

Someone down the street was playing airs from the homeland on a flute; Kaspar's thoughts, drawn by the tune, had
wandered right back to Cralo by the time he heard steps in
the alleyway. A bang at the knocker, and the woman's voice
saying, "It's me, Mynheer Wouter. They've come."

They've come? Did she mean she'd brought the skins? Curiosity led him to move toward the house corner and peer around.

By the side door several people, the woman and two men. And his movement had caught their attention, for they turned toward him. Oh, well, just look innocent, walk slowly past them out into the road, go a little distance, wait in the shadows, and return when they had gone. Even if they thought he had been stealing pumpkins, the fact that he was carrying nothing would make them pause for a moment before shouting for the watch. Besides, he might have been just a neighbor taking a short cut.

Boldly he strode toward them, whistling one of those airs that the flute had played. Not shrinking too much to one side, to pass them in the narrow passage, for that might . . .

"Stop!" A hand grabbed his arm. "Let's see your face!"

He knew the voice. With a jerk he threw off the detaining hand. But a blade glinted in the light from the suddenly opened door as the short sword pressed against his deerskin shirt.

"That's the one; that's Kaspar de Selle!" Wouter shouted from the doorway. "Hold him. Don't let him go!"

With a bellow of wrath the boslooper charged out from behind Wouter, hurling the man aside against the long, thin constable. But the fat one, Hendricks, still held Kaspar helpless at his sword point. The thud of a heavy blow, of Gideon's musket butt, and the sword dropped with a clatter to the planked path.

Kaspar crashed, shoulder to belly, into Wouter, heard the man's whistling gasp, and knew he had put one enemy out of the fray. Then Gideon yelled, "Don't fight! Run!"

Still dazed by the suddenness of it all, he turned and bolted. But for a moment in the wrong direction. Gideon wasn't following. Kaspar glanced back to see why, and discovered his error. The boslooper, the thin constable hot on his heels, was bolting out of the alley, into the main road.

Two men lay in the alley, and Kaspar, turning back after the boslooper, had to leap them.

He felt a hand grab him by the ankle, then he hit the ground. His head, shoulder and knees were stabbed with a sharp shock of pain.

Chapter Nineteen
A Cell in
Fort Amsterdam

ROUGH HANDS threw Kaspar face down in his cell. Before he had time to look about, the jailer's lantern was gone. Black darkness. And the stench! The bang of the door, the clank of a bolt shot into its staple outside, and a faint retreating gleam of light visible through the barred grille. A little painfully Kaspar got to his feet.

He fumbled his way around the heavy log walls; no other door, no other window; not so much as a crack between the heavy squared timbers. He might as well be philosophical about it; he was caught. And the next thing to do was to stretch out on the solid puncheon floor, rub his bruised knee-

caps, and crook an arm as a pillow for his aching head. No
one, nothing, could trouble him here. There might be more
comfortable quarters, but none safer than a cell in Fort
Amsterdam! Kaspar de Selle might as well sleep.

Reluctantly, slowly, he came awake. Gray light filtered
through the bars of the grille; a wooden bowl with wooden
spoon stood just inside the door. So that was what had waked
him. He picked it up, stirred the thick grayish mess. But it
smelt better than it looked and gladly he wolfed it down. He
could have managed a quart of cider, however stale and hard,
but prisoners, he realized, can't be choosers. And by way of
passing what might be the first of many long weary days of
waiting, he set himself to puzzle out what had happened the
night before.

It was all too clear now, with the wisdom of hindsight;
Wouter had recognized him at once, but had cunningly shown
no sign of it. Then, under pretense of sending for the seven
beaver pelts, he had dispatched the woman with written instructions to call the constables; while Gideon, all unsuspecting, had chatted and sipped cordial.

And what would happen now?

The boslooper had done his best and would now be on his
way upriver. Kaspar couldn't blame him for that. For now
that he had attacked a constable he too would land in jail,
if he were seen around the Manhatens. If he had sense, of
course, he would go straight to Jeremias van Rensselaer; if
he didn't, no doubt he would tell the Hoorns what had happened, and Grita would certainly go to the director. That at
least was one gleam of hope in a gloomy world.

But that would take weeks. And even then, what could the
director do?

Kaspar got up and went to the grille, pressed his nose
against the bars and looked out. Nothing to be seen except
a narrow passageway, with a bare patch of sunny dusty-look-
ing ground at the end, that might be a corner of the fort
parade ground. The steady creak-creak of a windmill and

a babble of sound, of voices, betokened a market near by. He was choosing a clean patch in the floor to stretch out on and maybe catch up with his sleep, when he heard the stamp of approaching feet. The bolt creaked back and the door swung open.

And a stranger stepped into the room. A prosperous burgher he was, from wide lace collar to ribboned shoes. Impatiently he signed to the jailer to withdraw, and he and Kaspar stood considering each other. A townsman; he might be a magistrate, he might be a lawyer seeking a case and a fee, though that seemed hardly likely; the mere sight of his client, begrimed and bruised, would have made him decide there was no money to be had here.

"Kaspar de Selle?" The man's voice was pleasant, his manner courteous, and his narrow face and thin lips became more assuring when he spoke. He thrust his thumbs into the wide Spanish leather belt and glanced about him as if for a seat. Then back at Kaspar.

"I am Oloff van Cortlandt."

Oh, yes, the agent for the patroonship; the very man he had tried to see last spring, when first he had arrived.

"A boslooper, Gideon Dolph, aroused me in the early hours of the morning and told me the story of your misadventure. I advised him to show a clean pair of heels and to leave your problem to me. Now how much do you owe? And what is the value of the seven beavers? Perhaps we can set one claim against the other."

"I don't owe a styvver," Kaspar mastered his indignation. "Except—except to the patroonship for my passage. And those seven skins were to pay the director."

"Then why does Wouter Fries lay charge against you? Forgive my seeming to doubt you, but if I am to help you, I must know the whole story."

Van Cortlandt called back the jailer, demanded a couple of chairs. In greater ease Kaspar told what he knew, and added also what he guessed lay behind it.

The man pursed his thin mouth and considered awhile, his thumbs in belt, fingers drumming thoughtfully. Then, "You were trained as a furrier?"

Yes, that was true.

Mynheer van Cortlandt pursed his thin lips again. "You must know by now, or at least suspect, that Wouter and doubtless several accomplices are smuggling furs out of the country. Do you know any of them? Can you give us any certain information that would help us catch them?" He paused. "I see you would rather not. That is a pity, because, though of course a countercharge against Wouter would not be a defense against his claim of debt, yet if he and his witnesses against you were to be convicted of smuggling, it is doubtful if the magistrate would believe their evidence against you."

Kaspar was thinking hard. This man was really trying to help him; what could he do to help himself that would not put Gideon in danger?

"If we could find where the blanket beavers were," he suggested, "I could identify them. They wouldn't, of course, be smuggled, but they might be among furs that were smuggled, or at least intended to be smuggled."

Van Cortlandt looked up sharply. "You are sure you would know them? Remember that any marks you have made on them are probably scraped off, and new marks, possibly Wouter's, will be in their place."

Kaspar smiled.

"It's no laughing matter, boy . . ." Van Cortlandt began.

Kaspar shook his head. "It's not that. It's the skins, identifying them. You don't have to read the collar on your dog to know the dog is yours. It's the same with skins; they're as different as one dog from another."

Mynheer van Cortlandt stood up. "Very well. I came here to say that I'd have food sent to you, and a few small comforts. And if I liked your looks I considered standing surety, on behalf of the patroonship, for your debt. But now I have something better in mind." That was all. The visitor wasted no further words but recalled the jailer to unlock the door and departed. Kaspar was left alone. But not for long.

Either impressed by Kaspar's visitor, or liking Kaspar's looks better by daylight, the jailer turned considerate and affable. Water, soap and a towel were brought; and the man, taciturn as he had at first seemed, turned out to be a friendly, gabby bore, who had a long tale to relate of a wicked neighbor who constantly robbed his lobster pots out in the East River.

Lobsters, he said, still ran to two or three feet long on occasion; and went on to tell of larger ones he had caught in earlier years. Kaspar, unable to escape the flood of reminiscence, suspected that the man had a special reason for taking on the duty of town jailer. It might be profitable; it might even carry with it a special social standing, from his point of view; but, above all, the value of the job would lie in the free listeners it provided, listeners who couldn't back away beyond the four walls of the cell, or plead that now they must get on with their chores, or that wife or dinner were awaiting them.

Would the man never stop! Kaspar ached to be left alone and puzzle out his situation. At last dusk came and the man regretfully had to go to the guardhouse to eat his evening meal and then fetch Kaspar's. Kaspar took off his moccasins, stretched out on the borrowed pallet, and, his ears still buzzing, tried to concentrate his thoughts, and at least make some sort of a guess as to his fate.

What could be the possible motive behind Wouter's claim of debt? At first, back last spring, it had been no more than a threat. Just a blunt "work for me here as a fur expert or I'll clap you behind bars!" Then, like a fool he had dismissed it—almost—from mind as a poor sort of jest. A reassuring idea, but quite out of character with Wouter as he knew him now.

Was it possible that, all along, Wouter's aim had been not so much to keep him in the Manhatens as to prevent him from going to the patroonship? The same in result, but the purpose different. Yes, it began to tie together now. Wouter dealt with the red-bearded Dirck Tienhoven, among other bosloopers. Dirck Tienhoven—Kaspar had seen with his own eyes, at Schenectade—dealt with the patroonship's clerk, Mynheer Nicholas; though Mynheer Nicholas, when employed full-time by the patroonship, was naturally expected to have no private dealings on the side. Just one slip Wouter had made; he should have sent earlier warning to Nicholas that the new arrival had been trained in the fur trade. Then the clerk's methods might have been less crude.

Wouter's mistake was easily explained. Nobody in this country, where people seemed to be Jack-of-all-trades, appeared to realize what it meant to be properly trained in one. They wouldn't believe, he was sure, that a not very smart apprentice could see a raw fur as it came into the Netherlands and recognize again the same fur when it came back to the Netherlands, months later, after being prepared and treated in Muscovy. They couldn't understand that no two pelts, just as no two human faces, had ever been alike, exactly alike, since the world began; and—Kaspar grinned to himself at the thought—a pelt had an advantage over a human face; it had two sides and you could recognize either one of them.

And now, since Wouter had failed to keep him in the Manhatens, had failed to keep him out of Rensselaerswyck, what was his purpose in pressing his charge? Was he hoping to discredit Kaspar with the director, so that he would be sent back to the Netherlands? The patroonship was full of debtors; everyone seemed to owe everyone else, so even if Wouter thought that the director would believe the claim, he would scarcely expect the director to waste good money sending Kaspar back again to the Netherlands. No, that couldn't be it.

Revenge? No, Wouter had nothing to avenge, no quarrel on shipboard, nothing.

Kaspar sighed and gave it up. Supper was long in coming. He was just drifting into sleep when there, in his prison cell, stood the jailer with his candle lantern. And—two soldiers. For one wild moment he wondered if the man had come back with a couple of his friends to talk all night.

"I've orders," said the jailer, "to deliver you to the military escort."

Kaspar shuffled into his moccasins, stretched and stood up. Resignedly, still drowsy, he marched out with them, one guard in front, one behind.

Out through the fort gate to the north; and how pleasant was the taste of the soft, fresh, evening air to mouth and nostrils! Around the corner of the fort, and south through an open space dotted with empty market booths. Where could they be taking him, and at this time of night? And what had soldiers to do with a civil case of debt?

Down, now, almost to the waterside. Had Mynheer van Cortlandt bribed the guard and the soldiers to smuggle him aboard a ship? To escape? Or was this some trick of Wouter's to crimp him aboard a home-bound ship and get rid of him that way? No, that was all much too dramatic and fantastic.

Tall houses on the right, made of brick in tapestried pattern, and finer than any he had seen on the island. On the left, the river lapping softly against the docks and piles. Nothing else lay ahead. He had as good as decided that after all he was to be put on board a ship, when the soldier ahead of him started up the high stone steps of the big four-story residence. And the soldier behind gave Kaspar a shove, as order to follow.

The door opened. The voorhuis, the foreroom or wide hallway, was lighted with many candles; that was his first impression after the night outside. At a huge carved and polished table set four burghers, one of them van Cortlandt.

Another, even with his wooden leg hidden by the table, Kaspar would have known anywhere, would have recognized by that hawklike nose alone. His Excellency Peter Stuyvesant, the Governor of the New Netherlands.

A mere flicker of a glance, and the governor said, "We have met before. But then you carried a falcon. Where is the falcon now?"

"In Rensselaerswyck, Excellency," Kaspar blurted out.

"A pity. Falcon and falconer should never be parted, or both will mope. But for the moment we will speak of beaver."

The governor consulted with Mynheer van Cortlandt; the other two burghers, officials of some kind they seemed to be, with their papers and quills and books, were referred to and replied. It would be bad manners to listen and try to overhear. Kaspar, until he should be addressed again, kept his attention on the room and its furnishings.

And gorgeous it was indeed, with deep-fringed hangings, two sets of each, at the tall, leaded windows which seemed to be of painted or stained glass. The great bed in one corner of the room was draped in red damask, and the tiled floor covered with fine carpets. Many paintings decorated the walls. The carved benches, polished till they shone in the candlelight, were deep-cushioned. And the great kast and china cabinet held such a display of silver and fine chinaware as he had not seen since Amsterdam. This could be no less than the governor's own house. But why had they brought him here, a boy thrown into jail for a claim of a few guilders? The situation was becoming more and more fantastic.

"It is said," the governor addressed him, "that you are trained to a knowledge of furs and pelts. But of this we must assure ourselves beyond doubt or question. What pelts have passed through your hands while you have worked with the director at Rensselaerswyck?"

"Do you mean 'how many?'" Kaspar asked. "I don't know, as I can't remember figures well."

He saw a glance pass between the governor and Mynheer van Cortlandt. And the glance said impatiently, "No use! The boy's a fool."

"But I can tally off each pelt if someone will count them." And as the governor seemed to be waiting, he began, "Beaver, beaver, marten, beaver . . ."

He closed his eyes to make his recollection clearer, to see himself back again, valuing the pelts on the long table at the director's house. Valuing them silently, to himself, not wishing as a newcomer to get on the wrong side of Mynheer Nicholas by too much show of knowledge. "Beaver, fox, beaver blanket, an Indian robe of twelve beaver skins, much worn but excellent for castor. A bearskin, but badly cut with knife or tomahawk . . ." He went on for a bit, and added, "That was all in the first parcel." Opening his eyes he noted that one of the clerks had been tallying them off on a list.

The governor held up a hand. "One parcel will do."

The clerk read out the totals, the second clerk leafed through a ledger, came to a page, ran his thumb down it. "That parcel arrived on the twenty-seventh of June. Mynheer van Cortlandt paid the duties, and the skins are by now in the Patria."

"The count is correct?" asked Peter Stuyvesant.

"Correct, Excellency," said one clerk. "Correct," said the other.

The governor's searching glance probed Kaspar's face. "You say you cannot remember totals, boy?" he asked.

"No, Excellency. Only pelts." He hoped the governor was not disappointed again. But it was the truth. "I was trained as a furrier, not as a clerk."

His Excellency seemed amused. "Then I think, my friend Oloff," he told Mynheer van Cortlandt, "our stratagem may succeed. Now, boy, back to the jail, and get you a good night's sleep. You will need all your wits about you in the morning. And let me add that I think you will soon return to your falcon."

Easier said than done, to get a good sleep. With nothing
but the governor's vague reassurances that soon he would be
back at Rensselaerswyck, Kaspar built and demolished again
a dozen wild hopes.

Peter Stuyvesant had said he would be wanted again in
the morning; so with the first light of dawn, sifting grayly
through the bars of the grille, Kaspar was washed and
combed and ready. Breakfast, when at last it came, was difficult to eat, for instead of breakfast should have come the
two soldiers. When the two soldiers did come, he had resigned himself to, at least, the failure of the governor's plan,
to another long day in prison.

Out into the full light of a glorious autumn morning—and
how grand the sun felt, how wonderful the taste of freedom,
if only for a few hours! An embarrassment of attention was
accorded him as, with his guards, he traversed the length of
the Het Marckvelt, the market place. This time the booths
were occupied; Indians as well as whites gazed at him curiously; children ran after with clattering wooden klompen,
hoping no doubt to see at least a good hanging; the dogs
barked; a woman called to the soldiers, "Hold on to the
scoundrel; likely enough he knows who stole my melon!"

Down to the waterside, into a boat where two other soldiers waited on their oars. Then, on a choppy cross-tide and
current, out to a ship that swung at anchor in the stream.
The *Homelander,* two-masted, built high in stem and stern
to batter her way across the rough Atlantic seas, and already
half-loaded, Kaspar judged by her waterline as he hauled
himself up the ladder.

A brief glimpse of the deck, with its coils of ropes, its
bright polished brass cannon, its creaking windlasses, its
bundles and crates not yet stowed, then down into the shadowy hold, with horn-faced lanterns hanging overhead from
the low timbers. Hot it was and smelled foully of dried skins,
sassafras, timber, and all the other miscellaneous items of
cargo. The *Homelander* must have lain long in the stream,

waiting to make up her full manifest, which, now the main beaver season was over, would take some time. Shirtless men, their shoulders glistening with sweat, were shifting cargo, restowing it in such a way that the bundles of pelts, some merely tied, some sewn up in coarse cloth, were accessible.

Two men with lists were checking, one man, by his weathered face and high, greased leather sea boots, obviously the ship's captain. The other one of the clerks he had seen last night at Whitehall, the governor's house.

A throbbing sound in the distance, growing nearer, resolved itself into drumming. Chairs were brought down to the cleared space in the hold, and his Excellency the Governor, in slashed velvet doublet of bright brown over yellow satin, a lace falling-ruff, and bright plumed helmet, stumped, still agile despite his wooden leg, down the stairway. Impatiently he twitched his vermilion cloak aside, hitched his sword to a convenient position and sat down. The bands of silver on his peg leg were only less gay than the red silk rosette and red-heeled calfskin boot on the other.

It was quite a retinue that followed. Two important-looking burghers whom Kaspar heard referred to as schouts, magistrates, took seats, one on either side of the governor. Mynheer van Cortlandt swung himself to a wooden crate, overlooking the others; two more clerks, one carrying a heavy volume apparently of court minutes, which, as it happened, he had no occasion to open. About six other men; and with them, a look of anxiety, or at least perplexity, on his unpleasing face, was Wouter Fries.

The hot dim space below decks was full of wide beaver hats with bright nodding plumes; light from the open hatch above reflected back from swords and polished cuirasses as figures moved and shifted; there was the white of wide ruffs and collars and lace bands to point up the blue and red of cloaks, the brown of leather and homespun and good Netherland cloth.

A sharp rap from the governor's silver-banded peg leg
upon the decking, and the buzz of conversation ceased.

"Well, Captain Claes, have all your pelts paid duty at the
Weighhouse pier?"

"Your Excellency . . ." it was the clerk of last evening
who spoke, "there are fifteen bundles which do not corre-
spond with the Weighhouse books. We have set those apart,
here."

"Good. Now we have before us two cases, neither of
which will we try, both of which we will examine." The governor addressed the two magistrates. "Mynheer Wouter
Fries brings a claim of debt against Kaspar de Selle. Kaspar
de Selle denies it. Stand forth, Wouter and Kaspar.

"Also, Kaspar de Selle brings claim for seven blanket
beavers against Wouter Fries. Wouter denies this. Watch
closely now, for something more grave than two small claims
of debt will, I think, be proved before you. Kaspar de Selle,
take what help you need, and search the fifteen bundles for
your seven blankets."

It had come now, the test; whatever the test might prove
to be. Supposing he failed? It would be easy to fail when you
didn't so much as guess what you were expected to accom-
plish, when you hadn't the slightest idea of what lay behind
all this.

And, he told himself, if he should fail in front of the
patroonship's agent, two magistrates of the city and the
redoubtable Mynheer Peter Stuyvesant himself . . . His
mouth went dry at the thought. But summoning up an air of
confidence, he bade the sweating seamen untie the bales and
bring them, one by one, under the open hatchway where the
light was the best.

Kneeling on the deck, swiftly he searched through the first
bundle. No blanket beavers there. Rather a poor lot of skins.
The batch was set aside, another brought to him.

Easy enough to find them if they were here. But again,
they were not.

As fast as the men could bring him the bundles, as fast as his fingers and brain could work, he skimmed through the remaining thirteen. And with mounting anxiety.

He stood up. "Your Excellency, the blankets are not here!"

"Wat duivel is dat? What the devil is that?" snapped the governor, his face flaming red with annoyance. "They must be!"

"Excellency, there is not a blanket, scarce a prime skin in the whole fifteen bundles; some are hardly worth the shipping."

"You recognize none of the skins?"

Kaspar had no notion where this was leading; all he could do was tell what he knew.

"Two bundles, or most of the skins in them, come from the patroonship. But it is as if the director had sorted them, for these are only the poorest. The best of our purchases have been taken out, and others, which I have never seen before, have been put in to replace them."

He shot a chance look at Wouter. And under the wide hat Wouter's expression, smiling, almost triumphant a moment ago, showed traces of uneasiness.

The governor's anger had dropped as swiftly as it had risen. He leaned forward with quick interest. "A good point, and easily checked. Clerk, examine the undersides of the skins as the boy hands you those he says he recognizes."

Kaspar sorted deftly. Out of one bundle of a hundred he set seven aside. Of the second bundle twenty or more. "Those I have put aside I have never seen before. The others belonged to the patroonship."

The clerk, reversing the skins, ran through them too. "All these also bear the mark *JvR*," he reported.

The governor frowned. "For the moment I do not understand. Have they also been marked at the Weighhouse?"

"All," said the clerk.

"Ha! That is interesting." The governor sat back suddenly, setting his bright plumes to nodding. "Then if all those other bundles, that agree with the captain's manifest, have paid duty, and the separate skins in the fifteen bundles not on the manifest, have also paid duty, there is a thief at the Weighhouse. How say you, clerk? Have you received duties and not entered them in the Company books?"

"Your Excellency, never!" protested the clerk. The man sounded frightened; but angry too, that anyone should doubt his honesty.

Kaspar was looking not at him, but at Wouter—Wouter who seemed pleased again, his full loose mouth slightly smiling.

"Perhaps, Excellency," Kaspar ventured, "though the sealed bundles which we have not examined bear the Weighhouse seal, some of the skins inside do not."

"Ha!" The bright plumes nodded again. Then his peg leg stamped down on the deck planking. "Of course! Any but a fool would have guessed already! Why do we search for the seven blankets among the fifteen bundles? Of course, they are among the others; the others already sealed. Put back these fifteen," he commanded, "and bring out those that are sealed and that are marked on the outside *JvR*. You see now?" Triumphantly he challenged the two magistrates.

"Yes, Your Excellency," they agreed. But never did two faces look so blank.

Chapter Twenty
Seven Fine
Blanket Beavers

ALMOST at once Kaspar uncovered the seven blanket
beavers. There was no mistaking Aquinachoo's skins.
He set them aside.

The clerk, at a sign from the governor, turned them over
to show the backs. They bore no owner's mark, no mark of
duty paid.

"Your Excellency, never have I seen those skins." Wouter
burst into protest. "Never! Whatever the boy says is a lie!"

The governor shot him a glance and he subsided.

Kaspar scarce noted the interruption, for something else
had caught his attention. And dexterously his fingers were
sorting the remaining skins of the bundle into two lots. It

253

was then that he heard the voice of the director, Jeremias van Rensselaer, at the stairhead. Heard greetings pass between him and the governor, and some query as to a carriage horse.

And with the director was Mynheer Nicholas.

Dimly Kaspar was beginning to comprehend the trick that Wouter and the other smugglers had played. He caught the governor's attention.

"These other skins, Excellency, that I have sorted out, truly belong to the patroonship."

Eagerly the clerk bent to examine the backs. "A mark has been erased from each of them. No one would erase a custom's mark. So these must be the marks of the owner that have been scraped away. These, then, must have been stolen."

The magistrate nodded sagely. That was a piece of reasoning simple enough for their judicial minds to comprehend.

A chair had been set for the director. Governor Peter Stuyvesant turned to him and began to explain. "Your fur expert serves us well, Mynheer. Already we have discovered the trick played by the smugglers. Their fifteen bundles of pelts, we shall find, are placed in the wrappings and under the seals of yourself and other honest shippers. And your pelts, which bear the Weighhouse mark, are bundled separately. Thus anyone who checks, unless with the full book from the Weighhouse, or the captain's own manifest, finds fifteen bundles which apparently have lost their seals, as might easily happen. But each skin in it bears the Weighhouse mark. And the remaining bundles are all sealed with the Weighhouse seal, and so would normally be above suspicion. Doubtless before they reach the homeland, a confederate on board ship finds means to change things back as they were before. So that the smugglers' pelts, in your sealed bundles and marked with your name, are not sent to your warehouse in Amsterdam."

Was that it? Kaspar wasn't the only one to receive enlightenment. The magistrates behind the governor's back were exchanging nods. How simple it was, now that it was all explained!

"The boy has shown himself worthy of belief. And since, before he had means to know that his seven beavers had been smuggled, he claimed them from Wouter Fries, it now lies with Wouter Fries to show how these seven pelts came to be among the other dishonest pelts. Now Wouter Fries must have confederates, whom he trusts." This time, Kaspar felt, the governor was explaining to the magistrates. "Those whom he would trust in one matter, and who would trust him, would also be his accomplices in another matter. It would be profitable to inquire into the occupation of those witnesses whom he called in his claim of debt against this young man."

Kaspar had almost forgotten his own danger. But the fear must have been inside him, nagging at him all the time. For now, of a sudden, at the governor's words he felt a burst of confidence, of happiness. Again how simple it was when the governor explained it.

Wouter would never, now, dare to call those witnesses. Or if he did, they would almost certainly fail him.

Peter Stuyvesant was still summing up. Quite casually, as if everyone else understood, and merely for the sake of the director who had come in late on the proceedings. "The smuggler's ring, though perhaps few in number, seems to reach far. It embezzles or steals, as well as smuggles."

Kaspar grasped the governor's meaning before his next words were out. And his glance was in time to see Mynheer Nicholas' fingers clench to whiteness, even though his face showed no sign of guilt.

"Somewhere, between the time when you buy them, and the time they reach the Weighhouse, your mark, *JvR,* is scraped from the best of your skins and they are taken by the smugglers. Inferior pelts are marked with your mark and put in their place. If you send a hundred beavers to the homeland, a hundred pay duty and a full hundred arrive there. But those which arrive may be only half the value of those which you sent. I am sure, Mynheer Jeremias, you will have no trouble in finding who is the knave who has played you this costly trick."

The governor's glance touched lightly upon Mynheer Nicholas.

"But come, my friend, the rest is for my magistrates and my clerk to uncover. You must take a glass of wine with me at Whitehall, and we will talk of the horse that you have brought down for me. Moreover, this Kaspar de Selle will wish to return to his falcon."

The light was dim under the stretched tarpaulin, the gray light of before dawn. On the rolled-up blanket pillow, a few feet away, the back of a red, tasseled nightcap showed that Mynheer Jeremias still slept soundly; though by the creak of the mast, the gurgle of water past the yawl's bow, the *Pigeon* must be under way. Kaspar rolled out from under the awning, stood upright and stretched.

Daylight was not far off; the western shore, in soft autumn haze, was distant, dreamlike, and patched with strange bright hues, reds and yellows. To starboard, now dropping well astern, the village of the Manhatens lay toylike, silent, slumbering. But a faint breeze brought the smell of wood smoke, of tanning and of a cow byre near the water's edge. A cockcrow echoed out across the water. The tide setting more strongly inland, the captain put over the tiller and swung the *Pigeon* farther offshore, into the main current.

Again Kaspar rubbed his eyes; this time the stocking growing on the captain's busy needles was blue instead of red; this time the cargo was more neatly stowed, the passengers were different. But the same boat, the same water, the same offshore odors, and yes, even the same scent of food wafting down occasionally from the bows, reminded him of that first voyage up this mighty river.

Captain Strycker lashed the tiller, groped his way forward past the tarpaulin. A gentle bump. And again, as last time, a burst of angry words from the *Pigeon's* skipper.

"Gek! Idioot! You, Jan Lansing, get out of my way."

Jan Lansing! Kaspar craned round the sail as a pair of skinny, freckled hands worked their way aft along the gunwale, fending off a clumsy rowboat. And to make things complete, the owner of the hands had to be, was, Jan Lansing.

The face came opposite Kaspar's, the skinny hands, in their surprise, almost let go their hold.

Kaspar grinned down at the face. "Is this where you live, Jan, in mid-river?"

"De hemel! It's the fool with the falcon!" Jan grinned back. He was longer than before and if possible more skinny and freckled.

"Not fool enough to take the smoke of every fire for an Indian signal!" Kaspar protested. "And how did you like the flavor of heron?"

Jan made a face and spat disgustedly. He passed a short length of line around a cleat on the *Pigeon* and sat back in his rowboat to enjoy the tow. "Where you bound for now?" he asked.

"Back to Rensselaerswyck. Ask for Kaspar de Selle if you ever get upriver."

Jan's face struggled very hard not to betray its surprise. "You the fellow spends one day in jail and the next as the guest of the governor? And look at your funny clothes," he jeered, boylike. "Think you can do any work in them slashed open sleeves and that white collar? And I'll bet you got red posies on your shoes!"

There would have been more, only that Captain Strycker came stomping aft, and Jan Lansing, knowing from experience just how far it was safe to hitch a tow, cast off and dropped astern. A few parting, friendly insults and he was gone.

Kaspar, perching on the gunwale, glanced down at his shoes; red heels they had too. He laughed. Well, it had

needed Jan Lansing to whittle him down to man-size again.
Yesterday . . . ! He could grin now when he thought of it
instead of throwing a chest!

How proudly he had insisted that the director accept the
seven blanket beavers instead of seven ordinary beavers, in
payment to the patroonship. Mynheer Jeremias had been
pleased, and, most clearly, surprised, at so handsome a dis-
charge of the debt. He had spoken aside to Mynheer van
Cortlandt, and when director and governor had gone direct
from the wharf to Whitehall, Kaspar found himself being
taken to eat his noon meal at the van Cortlandt's house.
And there Maria van Cortlandt had laughingly stood him in
the middle of the room, turned him round once or twice, and
run upstairs to the attic with purpose in her eye.

He bathed; Mynheer van Cortlandt lent him his razors.
Then down from the attic tripped the footsteps of Maria.
Outside his door a whispering and Mynheer van Cortlandt
came into the bedroom, his arms draped with assorted garments, a pair of red-heeled, red-rosetted shoes in his hand.

"My daughter," he said, "judges that we are much of a
size. She says moreover that as you are invited to dine with
His Excellency it would be well for you to attend in—shall
we say?—more conventional garb than ragged deerskins."

Now the garments, shoes and all, were justly his, by right
of purchase. For Mynheer Jeremias, as it seemed, insisted
that he should pay for all this finery to balance the extra
value of the blanket beavers. Jan Lansing might jeer, but
how Grita's eyes would sparkle when she saw him in this
brave array. Kaspar hoped that she wouldn't laugh too!

Kaspar sighed contentedly. Now it seemed that he had
friends all up and down the river; from His Excellency the
Governor on the south tip of the Manhatens, to the sister
of Aquinachoo right up in the Maqua castle; from the large
boslooper to that skinny little Jan Lansing; his gabby acquaintance the jailer to the clerk of the Weighhouse, who,
impressed by Kaspar's knowledge and memory for skins, had

asked if he wanted to remain and work in the Manhatens. And the Hoorns. But they were so much more than friends; they were like one's own family.

Of course, he had made enemies as well as friends; the head of Mynheer Nicholas peering forth furtively from under the tarpaulin reminded him of the unpleasant fact. Noting Kaspar, the pale light eyes shifted, the face achieved, though with obvious difficulty, what might pass for a smile. It was too much, perhaps, to hope that the clerk would bear him no ill will; but for a time at least the man clearly intended to be pleasant. And if it came to another test, if Nicholas tried any further tricks against the patroonship, there were always those notches on the pack saddle which he had made at the Maqua castle. And the saddle was now in the director's attic, ready to check against the clerk's entries in the director's account books.

As the yawl went about on another tack, the odor of cooking came more strongly, more appetizingly, from the small fire in the bow. Good cooking too; Andries' cooking. Not that the Negro was either stirring the pot or tending the fire. Lounging comfortably against the side of the bow he was lending his presence, his encouragement and his toothy approval to the real cook, the captain's son. All the same, the meal, when it came, would prove to be of Andries' cooking. Kaspar recalled with a chuckle one of Grita's comments, "Oh, Andries is smart enough; don't let that manner of his deceive you for a moment. I'm always a little surprised when I see the man doing his own work, instead of sitting by and nodding approval and letting the director do it for him!"

A good breakfast it was, when it came. And a pleasant one. Mynheer Jeremias, more cheerful and unworried than Kaspar had ever known him, perched on a wicker hamper eating from a gourd bowl, the clerk crouched angularly and somewhat uncomfortably on the boards, and Kaspar found himself a seat on the rolled-up tarpaulin. The autumn sunlight was pleasantly warm, the breeze crisp, water gurgled

past with a little song of contentment; and they were going
north, going home. Kaspar had never felt so happy. Though
it was difficult, when he stopped to think of it, to know just
what made him feel that way. His future was surely as uncertain as it had been six months ago, maybe even more
uncertain.

Freed for the moment from his official cares, the director
set down his finished bowl, borrowed tobacco for his china
pipe from the captain, and line and hook from the captain's
son. Perched carelessly on the gunwale, he trailed his line
overboard and seemed as content as Kaspar himself with the
sun, the river, the white flecks of cloud overhead and vict-
uals pleasantly digesting. As carefree and pleasant a companion as the boslooper himself.

His talk harked back to the happenings of yesterday. His
Excellency had been pleased, Kaspar knew, with the carriage
horse selected for him, and with its moderate price. But more
than a small and successful deal lay at the bottom of the
director's satisfaction. The patroonship and the West India
Company, so common gossip had it, were bitter rivals. But
yesterday the director and the governor had met as friends,
and as allies. Between them they had accomplished what perhaps neither would have done separately; they had brought
to light the smuggling trade, and caught the principal vil-
lains, who for years had been depriving the Company of its
revenues and the patroonship of its profits. Perhaps it was
that simple example which had helped to heal the feud. Company ships were to be placed more freely at the disposal of
the patroonship; and the dependence of Beverwyck, the
Manhatens, and even distant Curaçao upon the wheat and
other produce raised in the New Netherlands, had been em-
phasized by the governor. Could the patroonship, he had
asked, raise more supplies? There followed a long discussion of prices, qualities, of roadways, of wharves and shipping, of lumber and sawmills, of brickworks and tileworks.
All of which had meant little to Kaspar, and meant little

now, when the director again referred to them. In time all sorts of things might spoil these noble schemes, undoubtedly would. He remembered that even yesterday the director and governor had grown heated, then coldly courteous, over some matter of the patroonship boundaries; and later over some matter of the jurisdiction of the Company magistrates in Beverwyck.

Long days drifted by on the leisurely current of the quiet river. And drifting down in midstream, their rags of lugsails scarce large enough to give them steerage way, came every homemade contraption that would float.

A raft of logs, small haystack in the bows, midships and aft fenced in with pens of sheep and—actually—pigs. A giant's coffin, its rough sawn planking pegged and tied together, bore three puzzled-seeming cows. Larger haystacks, seeming to float directly in the water but with an invisible boat of some kind under them. Better boats, at least looking more watertight, but with no better lines than those of a housewife's wash trough, carried cargoes in baskets and in sacks plaited by the Indians. Kaspar knew the contents to be grain, early wheat most likely, for unthreshed wheat was also being ferried down, the heads of the sheaves turned inward into their golden shooks.

Hay for the governor's carriage horses, straw for plaiting and for bedding, meat for the market, and grain for the windmill beside Fort Amsterdam. Even the boats, or most of them, would be sold for the value of their planking. That was a reason, now Kaspar came to think of it, apart from simplicity of building, why so many boats were square as boxes. Straight planking would sell better than planking curved or warped to shape.

Such haste to get the first harvest to market while high summer prices still held! Boys no bigger than Jan Lansing steered, with a long oar over the stern, rafts big enough to build a house on. They were all that could be spared, for in every field within view of the river, men, women, girls and toddlers were still harvesting. Here and there rose the dust and chaff of winnowing, and the cadenced thump of flails. To a farmer's ear the cadence told how many flails were swinging, when new sheaves were thrown on the threshing floor, even the kind of grain. Wheat, of course.

The weather held good. Long days followed, with halts at Esopus, and at Klauverack, where Andries and Mynheer Nicholas went ashore to purchase more provisions. It was while lying off Klauverack that the director brought up the matter of Kaspar's future.

Kaspar, he pointed out, was now free, and under no obligation to stay on in the patroonship. Did he intend, when the trapping season again opened, to go down to the Manhatens, through which passed all the pelts of New Netherlands, where his training could be turned to better profit?

Kaspar himself hadn't quite faced the future. But the Manhatens, no. "I thought perhaps I could go out with Gideon Dolph and learn trapping and spearing through the ice. Then when the season was over, I could sell my pelts for trade goods, and go out again west of the Maquas, to buy in more pelts; and sell through the patroonship, if you would let me." He put it hesitatingly; for the plan was reasonable enough, but somehow it didn't appeal as it would have done a few months ago.

And the director didn't even think it reasonable. "Why learn a new and difficult trade which Gideon and the Indians, who have done it all their lives, can do so much better? You already have a trade, a trade in which you have served your full apprenticeship."

Yes, that was true enough. But outside of the Manhatens, Kaspar pointed out, the need for an expert in furs was very limited. He could hardly make a living at that alone.

"I wasn't referring to furs, to beavers," Mynheer Jeremias paused to refill his pipe and light it with an ember from the cook fire. "No. I meant farming. Your father was a farmer before he was farm manager. You were brought up on a farm, one of the best in the homeland. Mathias Hoorn tells me that you have an eye for livestock and crops and are not afraid of honest work."

Kaspar waited, saying nothing.

"And there's also Mathias to consider," the director continued. "I cannot afford to let his farm grow back into wilderness while he neglects it to make bricks, badly though bricks are needed in the growing towns. But if another tenant takes the farm, Mathias will not have his clay. Also the new tenant would want the Hoorn house for his own family." He tamped down his pipe. Still Kaspar waited.

"Well, why not take the home farm? I offer it to you under two conditions. The first, to let the good Mathias work his clay bed; that much the patroonship owes him. The second . . ." A faint smile curled around the director's lips, "that you leave the Hoorns in possession of the Hoorn house for as long as they wish to remain."

"Well," the director said, after a moment, "I think I will walk ashore for a while, till the others return."

Kaspar was left alone to think it over.

A few days more and they were in sight of that island where the captain had run aground in attempting to save his own skin at the expense of Kaspar and Gideon. If the captain recalled it, he gave no sign. Perhaps he didn't even recognize the place, since, with the shrinking of the river, the flatts were now joined to the mainland. That same afternoon, with the river valley filled with an odd smoky mist that made the towering golden maples and flaming beech along the banks fantastically dreamlike, Kaspar sighted the slow turning sails of the Beverwyck windmill; and knew that this evening his knees would be beneath the Hoorn table, that his next meal would be of Grita's cooking.

The *Pigeon* held on past the Beverwyck jetty. Andries began to tie up bundles and strap the director's traveling trunk. The last slow leg of the journey, with little current against them at this season of the year but little breeze to fill the sails. Kaspar felt himself urging the boat forward. His eyes searched the bank for some familiar figure. But no Mathias to welcome them, no small Catalina racing the boat as he moved slowly along parallel to the bank. Though there was the little house, just north of the director's, squat and sturdy and homelike under its giant shading beeches, its thatched roof and log walls all of a piece with the earth that it hugged so closely. Its door, as he could see even at this distance, waiting open, wide and welcoming, and homelike.

Home. Why that was what it was! Home! Kaspar felt his heart quicken with excitement as they drew slowly nearer. His eyes sought for the flutter of a skirt, the white patch of a cap among the trees. Or perhaps for another figure running to greet him, hawk on fist: young Isaak. Yes, what he sought was the falcon; of course. The governor was right; that was the reason for the stir of excitement within him. A good falconer, he was anxious to get back to his falcon.

Chapter Twenty-One
The Kiliaen Guilder

H IGH UP in the apple tree Kaspar straddled one bough,
leaned his back against another, and reached up for
the perfect russet fruit, full and ripe, just above him.
Plucking it, he began to munch. There was a tree of apples
back at Cralo with this same flavor, sweet and tart and sun-
warmed, which crunched crisply between the teeth; his mind
swung back to the homeland with a touch of nostalgia. But
even that faint sadness seemed but to emphasize the flaming
misty glory of the autumn day, much as Grita added the
sharpness of hard cider to bring out the sweetness of her
mincemeat pies.

No one had a right to be at once so happy and so idle. Mother Hoorn would have quoted at least a couple of sayings to prove that idleness and wickedness were one and the same. But the sin of sloth would sit light on anyone's conscience on a day like this.

Blue lay the river under a blue sky, scarlet and gold the hardwood, patterning the dark pines like a rich embroidery. Grita was right; it was as if the hills were aflame, burning with a soft fire under the smoke of autumnal haze. What a noble, vivid thing was this season, over here! How unlike the brown rainy sadness of the dying year in the homeland. Here all was triumph; a shout of exaltation at harvest; a hope, a promise, not a condoling melancholy. Kaspar bit deeply into the apple.

Winter, they told him, was a fulfilment of this promise; the ground so deep frozen that whether he wished it or not the farmer had time on his hands. It was the season of visiting along the river, just as it was along the canals of the homeland. But here, each year the river froze hard and fast for month after month and most of the way to the Manhatens; there would be skating; there would be fishing through deep holes in the ice; Isaak was counting on that. Mynheer Jeremias and many others would get out their ice sleds, set calks in the horses' shoes and there would be such racing, such excitement, such overturning of sleds on sharp river turns, such bonfires and outings as not even the homeland had known. And Kaspar was in a mood to look forward to it all.

Perhaps it was the toil of the past weeks that had given him this added appetite for play and for leisure. Not a muscle in his arms and back and thighs but had groaned, daily and almost hourly. But the wheat was cut, the sheaves had been stooked, the stooks had been threshed or stacked, the stacks thatched, and a fine boatload of grain had been sent down-river. What remained, now prices had broken, could be threshed as occasion offered and be held till next summer when prices in the Manhatens rose again. Indian corn, the second cut of hay, root crops, all were safely garnered; a good part of the roots were stowed in layered straw in the root cellar. The Hoorns were safe for another year; no famine now could touch them or their livestock.

And Kaspar, he was safe too. He tossed the core away, swung a foot idly from his high perch, considering what had happened. With the conviction of Wouter Fries and two others for the crime of smuggling, Wouter's claim of debt had been quashed by the magistrates at the Manhatens. Kaspar could live openly at the Hoorn farm or go into Beverwyck without fear of arrest and imprisonment. He could take his part in work and play with anyone else in the whole community. Not till he found himself free had he realized quite how much he had fretted at the prospect of being a runaway, almost an outlaw.

From the house down the slope a small figure emerged from the open doorway, paused a moment, then moved purposefully up through the orchard. The sunlight made patterns of light and shadow across her white frilled cap and on her neatly patched fresh apron, slanted with the spattering of freckles across her upturned face.

"Kaspar?" called Grita. "Where are you, Kaspar?"

He waited a moment, till she was almost beneath his tree. Then asked innocently, but with laughter in his voice, "Did you want me, Grita?"

She had a sack over her arm. "Fill this for me with good apples for the house, before you shake down the others of this tree for cidering." She bundled the bag and tossed it up to him. "Tomorrow we must hand-pick enough fruit to store in the attic."

He filled the sack, while she waited, dreamily watching the flow of the river. He reached it down to her, then standing upright he shook the tree lustily.

She dodged back, laughing as the ripe fruit pelted round her, and, while he climbed to a farther bough to shake that also, she began to gather the falls into a heap, ready for the wagon when Mathias should return with it from Beverwyck. Five more trees they shook and gathered, in pleasant easy comradeship.

Even the orchard was bearing well this year. Big trees; Mathias must have planted them when he first cleared the farm land and—up to the past year or two—well pruned. But now they needed the knife and saw again.

"I think it was really Mother who was the farmer," said Grita surprisedly, "not Father at all. Perhaps that was why he asked her advice so often." She finished a pile and went on to another tree.

"Oh, he was a good farmer!" she continued. "With his hands, but not with his heart. I wish there was someway he could be two people; one to make bricks and the other to plow and sow." She sighed. "The director is right; the farm must be tended and Father will have to choose between his bricks and his farm. Why isn't Isaak five years older!"

There was another way, a simpler way. But it concerned Grita herself, and Kaspar felt that he must be more sure. He said nothing, but went on stooping and bending, gathering apples into piles. It was pleasant here in the warm shadowed orchard.

When he broke the silence he said: "I can see Mathias' reason, can't you? The farm, to him, meant Nelle; he can't think of them apart. When your Mother was swept away by the flood, it was as if the farm was swept away too. His feet will follow the path to the barn, his hands will milk the cow, but it's all habit; he scarcely sees either path or cow. If it hadn't been for finding the clay, something might have happened to him. Oh, I don't know what; he might have drowned too, without his intending it. Or he might have lost part of his mind."

"I know. But—but the director is right. A farm must be farmed; it's as simple as that."

Then came a welcome diversion. Kaspar from up his tree

caught sight of them first. "Here come the youngsters, back from school. And sitting still all day doesn't seem to have cramped their legs."

Dignity required that Isaak shouldn't run just to keep up with his younger sister. Catalina had no such scruples. Her short plump legs bounded ecstatically, her petticoats flew out, her klompens patted little puffs of dust along the road. They arrived, making a neck-to-neck finish of their race, Catalina calling, "Don't tell! Don't tell! Oh, let me tell first!" But so out of breath with her final effort that the task fell to Isaak.

"Honeybees, that's all it is." Isaak made a gallant effort to sound uninterested. "The Irishman has some. His son sits next to me on the bench, and he's whispered about them so I had to go and see them."

"And they buzz and they sting." Catalina had found her breath. "Look," she showed a swelling on her ankle. "It hurts still, but I didn't cry."

"They make honey. And beeswax for thread to sew shoes and harness."

Grita's smile took Kaspar into her confidence. "Someday we must really keep bees, Isaak. But you must learn to finish one journey before starting another. As soon as Father comes back with the wagon, we must all start loading these apples for the cider press."

Isaak picked out an apple and bit into it with decisive young teeth. "Kaspar," he asked, "may I exercise the falcon first? I had no time to before I went off to school this morning."

Kaspar was about to give permission when he caught Grita's glance. "I think I'd better fly her myself before I forget all about falconry. Or get too fat to run."

Good. Isaak took that all right.

"And what about getting your chores done?" suggested Grita. "The water pails are empty and I need more wood."

The youngsters trotted on down the hill; Grita turned to Kaspar. "Thank you for taking my hint. You see how fast

Isaak is growing; he's so thin and reedy that I don't think it's good for him to go racing off after the peregrine. If you're going to fly her now, I'll just run down and see that supper's stewing, and meet you in the north pasture." And salved her conscience with an afterthought. "I must go see what chestnuts we're going to have this year and try to forestall the squirrels."

The peregrine on her perch greeted Kaspar with pleasure. How dreadfully he had neglected her! Not physically; she had all the flying that she needed, all the attention, with the bath Isaak had built for her, the padded perch; and as much carrying on Isaak's or Kaspar's fist as a favorite hawk in a king's mews. No, the neglect was in his mind. There had been so many things to do at harvest time, so many things to think of, so many new judgments to make and new responsibilities to assume, that more often than not he fed the hawk, or even flew the hawk, his mind on other matters.

As Mathias with his farm, so Kaspar had been with the falcon. Only now for the first time did he notice that a feather had gone from her right wing. No sign of it under the outdoor perch; perhaps then it was inside the barn.

It was in the barn that Grita found him, bending over to search more closely in the dimness.

"The peregrine's lost a flight feather," he explained.

"Does that matter?" asked Grita. "Surely she'll grow new ones when she molts."

Oh, yes, she would, Kaspar agreed. But without the support of all the old feathers, new feathers were liable to grow in warped or crooked. At Cralo, of course, all molted feathers were carefully kept and labeled, in case they were needed for replacement.

"Replacement?" Grita sounded bewildered. "How? Do you sew them on?" They had given up the search and started up toward the north meadow.

"Yes, with a special needle, a three-sided imping-needle. No, honestly it's true. Isn't it, my lady?" he asked the pere-

grine as if for corroboration. "Not really sewing, more like
grafting." And as he moved along beside Grita he explained
that you cut the broken end of the feather at a slant, cut the
feather you are going to repair with it at the same slant,
measuring it off so that it comes exactly to the length it
should. "Then you take the fine needle, dip it in vinegar . . ."

"Oh, no. I'm not going to believe that!" Grita protested.

". . . slide half of it into the midriff of the broken
feather. Slide the repair feather onto the half of the needle
that sticks out, and of course use the finest possible Oriental
gum dissolved in spirits to join the two surfaces where they
come in contact."

"And what does the hawk do all this time? That is, if
you're telling me a word of truth." She gave a little skip to
catch up with his longer stride.

"Oh, it takes two falconers. And they've got to be friends
of the falcon, both of them; a bird doesn't like to be handled
by a stranger."

Grita burst out into laughter. "You're getting to be like
Gideon. And I'll have to be on my guard, because I really
believed you at first."

Kaspar gulped. "But it's true," he protested feebly. This
wasn't a time when he wanted to arouse her doubts, for there
was more to this expedition than just pleasant companionship. His future, as he saw it, might be decided this afternoon; his future and to some extent the future of the Hoorn
household. "It's utterly true, every word. And imping is one
of the easiest tasks connected with falconry. There's all the
'hacking' and 'manning' and 'entering,' and the slightest
error in judgment will ruin the very best of birds. And no
bird is like any other, not even of the same breed and taken
from the same nest. And you have to know more about their
ailments and their cure than a chirurgeon does of humans.
All the time the falconer thinks he is teaching the falcon, but
it is really the falcon who is teaching him."

Grita was laughing no longer. With a new and unwonted

seriousness, her slanting Spanish eyes roved from Kaspar to the falcon. "I ought to be envious of you, my lady," she told the peregrine. "Any woman ought to be mad with jealousy. For where, in all this world, does a mere human female get a tithe of such care and thought and consideration?" A thought struck her and she smiled again. "What happens then to a falconer's wife, Kaspar? And his family? Or hasn't he time to have either?"

Kaspar laughed too, a little ruefully. "You sound like Mother, my mother I mean."

Suddenly with a loud and startling whirr, a partridge got up almost from underfoot. He cast off the falcon. Too late, the quarry had gone.

They paused on the edge of the northern meadow, but still clear of the forest, while the falcon circled up into the hazy blue of late afternoon. And like the falcon herself, they looked down upon the farm, the river, and mile on mile of the patroonship of Rensselaerswyck dreaming in the warm sleepy sunlight. A country rich and fair, and worthy of any man's heart and loyalty. Kaspar was in no haste to beat up game. It would be good discipline for the falcon to wait on, overhead, awhile.

"Isn't it beautiful up here?" Grita's tones were low and quiet as her eyes took in the scene spread out before them. "When Mother was alive I used to come up here all by my-self and sit down on that big stone there, and think. Mostly about myself it was. Trying to find out who I was, and what I was. It was like coming up into a tower, and seeing people and animals and boats so far away and below and little, that they became unreal, just toys. And as they became unreal I seemed to grow more real, myself. And that was important because I wanted to find out who this Grita Hoorn was. But," she shook her head almost with sadness, "I never found out, I still don't know." She looked up at him sud-denly. "Have you met the real Kaspar de Selle? Do you know anything about him?"

Kaspar answered her as seriously as she had asked. "I know him too well. I'd rather find out more about Grita Hoorn. Though I suspect that I know her better than she knows herself." He looked down at her. "Do you still want to be like Mathias and Nelle?"

"Oh, *yes!*" she whispered, her eyes big, dark and hoping.

He shook his head. "You cannot be, Grita. You can be only yourself. And that's far more important. What does it matter that you don't know whom to pattern yourself on, so long as you pattern yourself on good folk, the Hoorns. You are free, freer than I ever was, or any of us who knew their parents and grew up with them. Free to be whatever you choose to be, and that should be yourself, just yourself. Don't you see that is what is important? That it would be a mistake to waste your life turning yourself into a copy of someone else?"

"Don't you see?" He put his hand on her arm. "Nobody would want you to be different in any way from what you are. What would be the sense in your having blue eyes when your brown ones are so beautiful?" His hand tucked back a lock of hair that was loose from the frilled cap. "And your hair, Grita, it's beautiful too. Spanish or not."

Grita gave a little laugh and moved away. Abruptly she asked, "And what of Kaspar de Selle? Does he still intend to be a Gideon Dolph?—a man who comes and goes, who helps one friend with his harvest, as Gideon did us these last weeks, then another friend with his gristmill. But has no harvest of his own, no corn of his own to grind. Do you really, Kaspar, want to be a boslooper?—a man without a lodge? Oh, I know I'm interfering. I've even asked the director. But he— he put my questions courteously aside and said, 'Ask Kaspar!' So I'm asking you, Kaspar."

Kaspar's arms went out to her. And this time she didn't step back.

Then the falcon dived. Both saw, both started to run. The same quarry, it must have been, which, thinking danger over,

had come out from the underbrush to feed on the dry grapes
still hanging from the wild vines.

They saw the strike. The falcon and partridge were lost to
sight behind the broad and yellowing leaves. Fear was in
Kaspar's heart as he ran. After so much hawking over un-
obstructed water, the bird had grown careless, and a falcon's
long delicate wings and high speed unfitted her for a scramble
among obstructing trees and vines. She might so easily harm
herself.

His eyes on the spot where falcon and quarry had disappeared, he raced up. Still nothing to be seen except a slight
movement in the leaves. The faint tinkle of her bells came
to his ears as he struggled into the thick undergrowth. Grita
was close behind him.

Again that faint tinkle. He parted the leaves above his
head where the sound had come from. And there, there was
the falcon.

Then something dropped onto his upturned face. A spot
of blood. He knew, he already knew as he reached up,
snapped off the dead piece of branch and gently lifted down
the bird. Slender as an arrow and just as deadly, that branch
had been. There was no hope, but it had to be done. With a
tug, mercifully quick, he drew it from the falcon's feathered
breast.

Grita behind him, gave a little sob. "Oh, oh, Kaspar," she
whispered hoarsely.

For the last time he set the bird on his glove. For a moment her talons gripped, the bird bowed a little, bating, as
she did to show her pleasure. Then his other hand had to go
up to catch her as she fell.

He stood there, not thinking for a bit, the bird lying still
in his right hand. "I'm sorry, my lady. So sorry." He stroked
her soft feathered back, gently, with one finger. Her head
straightened and from her eyes came a last proud glance.

Then the head dropped. A last twitch of the talons and
tinkle of the bells. And the falcon would never fly again.

Isaak would be disappointed. But somehow the last rite could be shared with no one but Grita. With his knife Kaspar dug a small hole in the turf, right beneath the vines, where, in the years to come, partridges would scutter in safety over the falcon's head. Grita's brown hands touched his as together they smoothed the earth over the dead bird.

"You didn't want to keep the bells and jesses?" she asked. "Next year you might catch another hawk and train her."

"The bells aren't mine; they belong to her." He said it gruffly, but Grita would understand. Would understand, too, that he was no longer a falconer.

And there was something else that Grita should understand but that he must find words for. "I'm not going to be a boslooper. I'm going to stay on and work your father's farm so that he can be free for the thing he wants to do."

"Oh, Kaspar, are you sure, are you sure?" She was back in his arms again, and the tears were drying on her cheeks.

"Quite sure. You do want me to stay, don't you, darling?"

Her voice came from somewhere under his chin. "More than anything in the world. If . . . if that's what you want."

"More than anything in the world." He echoed her phrase. He felt in his pocket and something shining and round and golden lay in his palm for her to see.

"Oh, Kaspar, it's the Kiliaen guilder," she whispered.

"It's all I have left to give you, Grita. Do you mind? But someday the silversmith in the Manhatens can make it into a gold ring. Would you like that, Grita?"

He could feel her head move against his chest. Firmly it moved up and down, in affirmation.